W9-DEU-010

DIRTY POOL

Also by Steve Brewer

Shaky Ground
Witchy Woman
Baby Face
Lonely Street

DIRTY POOL

Steve Brewer

ST. MARTIN'S PRESS
NEW YORK

ACKNOWLEDGMENTS

Thanks, as always, to Frank "Mr. Encouragement" Zoretich. I couldn't do it without you. Thanks, also, to my editor, Kelley Ragland, for going to bat for me, and to my agent, Rich Henshaw. And, finally, thanks to the many mystery authors and readers who make it a joy to do what I do.

DIRTY POOL

ONE

*F*riends come and go, but enemies are forever.

I knew I'd found such an enemy the first time I ever set eyes on William J. Pool. I hated on sight everything about him, from his LBJ curled-brim Stetson to his pointy snakeskin boots. He wore a pencil-thin mustache and a store-bought tan and Western-cut suits that should've had a slot in the back to accommodate his shark fin.

Pool's the type of Texan who gives the Lone Star State a bad name. I've met perfectly nice folks who happen to be from Texas, but they're outnumbered by scheming, blustering rednecks like Pool. They say everything's bigger in Texas, but, near as I can tell, that only applies to their mouths.

I was born in distant Mississippi, so this prejudice isn't inbred. I grew up equating Texas with cowboys and oil wells and John Wayne going down fighting in *The Alamo*.

But people in the states bordering Texas hold fiercely to a profound hatred for anything Texan. They're quick to tell you Texans suffer from a superiority complex. Texans are the rich country cousins who brag about picking up the check.

When oil was booming, Texans tried to buy up everything in my adopted state of New Mexico, from Santa Fe shops to the ski slopes. It's a wonder they didn't find a way to buy our postcard blue skies. The only thing worse than a loud Texan is one who's got the money to back up his boasting.

As part of the backlash here, some cars sprouted bumper stickers that said, "If God wanted Texans to ski, he would've given them mountains." The Texans responded with bumper stickers of their own: "If God wanted New Mexicans to ski, he would've given them MONEY."

It was during those boom days when I first met William J. Pool, and he did nothing to refute the stereotype. He strutted into Albuquerque—my town—throwing around his money and his experience and his big-shot private-eye surveillance toys. He made me look like a fool in a couple of cases where I could've been a hero. And he walked off with the retainers, too.

So let's say I was a little suspicious when Pool called me out of the blue and offered me a job.

I was having a nice, quiet Tuesday. It was late March in Albuquerque and the wind was blowing, which isn't as redundant as it sounds. Sometimes, March'll fool you here in the high desert. You'll have days when the sun shines and the trees are budding and a few robins are searching for early bird specials. Then you'll have other days—or, sometimes, the same damn day—when the wind howls and the temperature plunges and sleet beats hell out of the daffodils. Tuesday was one of the latter, and it seemed a good day to catch up on my paperwork. Not that I had much paperwork to catch up on, but that's what I call it when I stay indoors and goof off.

I was at my desk—rather than lying on the sofa watching Oprah or something—when the phone rang.

"Bubba Mabry Investigations," I answered. "Bubba speaking."

"Howdy there, Bubba. This is William J. Pool from Dallas."

"Pool?"

"Yessir. Answering your own phone today, hm? Your secretary out to lunch?"

I've never had a secretary in my life.

"She's running errands. What do you want, Pool?"

"Right to the point, just like always. I like that in a businessman."

The only thing Pool would like in a businessman is his hand in the businessman's pocket, but I didn't say so. I'd hear him out for a minute. If I didn't like what he had to say, I could find some true enjoyment in hanging up on him.

"I have a client who needs someone of your abilities," he said, "if your caseload would allow you to squeeze in a quick night's work."

My "caseload" was missing in action, and Pool probably suspected as much. It's feast or famine in the private-eye game. Pool had been at the feasting table as long as I'd known him. I, on the other hand, was pretty tired of going hungry.

"I might be able to take on another case," I bluffed. "Depends on what it is."

"A simple delivery. I'd do it myself, but I'm afraid I'm too easy to spot."

I was thinking: Maybe if you didn't dress like J. R. Ewing . . .

"Could you meet my client and me at the Hilton?"

"When?"

"The delivery is to be made tomorrow night, but the sooner, the better. We need time to plan."

"Plan a simple delivery?"

"Well, it's a little more complicated than that. Why don't we meet face-to-face and talk it over?"

"All right. I can be there in half an hour."

I cradled the phone before he could say anything more. It wasn't quite as pleasing as I'd hoped.

3

I went to the bathroom to spruce up, running a comb through my unruly hair and tucking my shirttail in properly. Then I remembered I was dealing with Pool, and wondered why the heck I bothered.

I headed out the door, shrugging into my new winter coat, a hip-length khaki number with a zillion pockets that my wife, Felicia Quattlebaum, had bought at some department store sale. I prefer my old beat-up denim jacket and I thought the new coat made me look like a terrorist, but I kept those objections to myself. It's my goal in life to keep Felicia happy.

The Hilton stands tall at the snarled interchange of Interstate 40 and Interstate 25, the crossroads that's largely responsible for Albuquerque's boom during the past thirty years. The "Big I," as the interchange is called, was blocked by construction crews and slow traffic, so I exited the freeway and drove west on Menaul, the six-lane thoroughfare that separates the Hilton from the acres of asphalt that surround the Duke City Truck Plaza, famous with truckers nationwide.

New Mexico caters to motorists. Truck stops and motels and tourist traps are as much a part of the landscape as red mesas and open prairies. You still find freeway exits in the middle of nowhere labeled only ROADSIDE BUSINESS. Felicia and I joke that Roadside Business is the most popular town name in the state.

Along its major thoroughfares, Albuquerque resembles one big freeway exit, with all the fast-food franchises and gas stations and clip joints and "junque" shops scrunched into block after block of signs and asphalt and noise. You end up with some strange juxtapositions. One block on Central Avenue boasts a shop that sells "smoking accessories" next to a shoe store called Happy Feet. We've got a burger joint beside a Western-theme gas station called the Bar-F. And, the Hilton's across the street from the truck plaza.

The Hilton tower, like most buildings in the city, is done up in stucco the color of mud. Inside, it's all cool tile and white arches, aimed at making you think of a Spanish mission

4

rather than how much the rooms cost. Pool waited for me in the lobby, sitting on a wooden bench with his hat in his lap.

He hadn't changed a bit, except for a little graying at the temples, and I didn't even trust that. Probably had his hairdresser add the gray so he'd look even more distinguished.

His face was broad and tan and handsome with just the right amount of Marlboro Man crinkling around the eyes. He wore a black suit that probably cost more than my annual taxable income and he had his legs crossed so I couldn't help but see his business logo—a magnifying glass—stitched onto the shaft of his custom-made boots.

"Bubba Mabry," he called, as if glad to see me. "Long time, no see."

Not long enough, I thought, but I said something neighborly and accepted a bone-crushing handshake. Pool had to overdo that, just like everything else.

"Where's your client?"

"Upstairs in his suite. He wants to talk up there."

Suite? That sounded promising. Anybody who could afford Pool and a suite at the Hilton could undoubtedly afford me, too.

We rode up in the elevator. Pool stood only a few inches taller than my six feet, but he still managed to tower over me. He asked how I was doing and I allowed that I was fine. The resulting silence required me to ask how he was, even though I didn't mean it.

"I been busier than a one-legged man in an ass-kicking contest," he drawled. "Just like always. I hear you got married."

I wondered where he might've heard that, but I admitted it was true, and I told him in the briefest possible terms about my six-month-old marriage to Felicia.

"Marriage is good for a man," he said. "I know. I've tried it three or four times myself."

"I'm hoping once will do it for me."

"That's what they all think going in. Well, it looks like it's agreeing with you. You've put on some weight."

I frowned down at my belly and tugged up the waistband of my jeans. Then the elevator door slid open on the fourteenth floor, and I turned my mind back to business.

I followed Pool down a carpeted corridor and watched him knock on the door. The door flung open with a whoosh, and a man who could've been Pool's balder brother stared out at us.

"Dick Johnson, meet Bubba Mabry," Pool said proudly, as if I were a prize steer.

"Come on in," Johnson said. "I just ordered up some coffee."

I followed Pool inside and let a low whistle escape at the size of the suite.

"Nice spread, eh?" Johnson said. "Should be, for what it costs."

I stepped past Pool to the windows and the vista of the western half of the city.

"Heckuva view."

"It is, ain't it?" Johnson said. "The skyline ain't much, but I like looking out at them volcanoes on the horizon."

"Nature's own skyline."

"I reckon that's the truth," Johnson said. "Come on over here and take a load off. We need to palaver."

Palaver? Bad enough Pool talked like Gabby Hayes; now I had to contend with two of them.

"Pool here tells me you know Albuquerque inside out," Johnson said as he sank into an armchair. He crossed his legs, exposing fancy cowboy boots. I was wearing my usual yellowed sneakers and felt like tucking my feet under my chair, but they wouldn't fit.

Johnson's jacket was hanging over the back of his chair, and he wore dark double-knit pants and a light-blue Western shirt with a silver bolo tie cinched up tight. Texas business attire. His high forehead reflected the overhead lights. Farther back, long strands had been carefully combed across to cover

6

some of his baldness. Like Pool, he wore a mustache, but his was broad and waxed smooth.

"I suppose Pool has told you all about me."

"Not a word."

"I thought it would be better to tell it all in person," Pool intoned. "No sense plowing the same furrow twice."

Johnson nodded, looking thoughtful.

"Well, sir," he said, turning back to me, "I build things. That's what I do. That's what I'm all about."

"What kind of things?"

"Commercial real estate. Strip malls mostly. I've thrown up more storefronts in this country than you can shake a stick at."

Yuck. Strip malls are what's wrong with Albuquerque and most sprawling Sun Belt cities. But Johnson said it with pride.

"I've made myself a right handy fortune," he continued. "But none of it means a thing unless I've got my boy to pass it on to."

"Your son?"

"Yessir, that's what this is all about. That's why we called you."

"What happened to him?"

"Well, I don't rightly know that, do I? I knew where he was, I wouldn't need not one, but two private eyes sucking off my bank accounts' tit. I'd go get him myself."

Pool interrupted again, as if he wanted to stop Johnson from going off on some tangent, such as how much private investigators cost.

"Dick's son, goes by the name of Richie, is somewhere in Albuquerque, but we haven't been able to locate him. Yet."

"He's hiding?"

"Not exactly." Johnson took up the narrative again. "He ran off a couple of months ago and got mixed up with some bad fellas. You know anything about skinheads?"

Enough that I knew I didn't want anything to do with them, but what I said was, "Some. They're racists, right? Always beating the shit outta people?"

"Richie's fallen in with some of those boys, and it worries me. I don't know where he'd get any kind of racism. That ain't the way he was raised. And Richie's no fighter. The boy's got a bad heart. He was born with it. Not his fault. But it's kept him sort of set apart all his life. He couldn't play football, couldn't dance, couldn't do all the things a boy oughta be able to do."

"How old is Richie?"

"Nineteen, but he's younger than that in the head, you know? He's never been able to do anything on his own, so he never grew up right. It's partly my fault. I've been too protective. And his mother, who passed away two years ago, Lord, she was a mother hen, always clucking over him, making sure he didn't do anything strenuous."

"So," I ventured, "you want Richie to come back home."

"That's the way it started out," Pool said, "but it's gotten more complicated."

"You keep saying that. Complicated how?"

Pool and Johnson exchanged a conspiratorial look. I didn't like that at all.

"Well," Pool said, "we have to be sure none of this leaves this room. We can trust you?"

"If you don't think you can, what am I doing here?"

Pool shrugged. "Got me there, Bubba. It's like this: Yesterday, Dick here got a phone call in Fort Worth. A ransom demand."

"Richie's been kidnapped?"

"Well, we don't rightly know. That's what the caller said, but it may be a scam."

"Like how?"

"These skinheads fellas, they might think they can squeeze Dick for some of his hard-earned money. I figure they're behind the phone call."

"But you don't know?"

"Hard to know something like that. But Dick doesn't want

8

to take any chances, and I have to agree with him."

"You call the FBI?"

Johnson sat forward suddenly.

"Nah, see, we don't want the law involved."

"Kidnapping's a federal offense. That's the FBI's territory."

"Hell, I know that. But what if it's not a kidnapping? What if it's a fake? I don't want Richie mixed up with the law again."

"He's had legal problems before?"

"A few." Johnson sat back and cast around the room as if looking for another subject. "I've always bailed him out in the past. In Texas, I know where to grease the wheels, know what I mean?"

I nodded.

"But here in Albuquerque, I don't know who to trust. I just want to take Richie home."

"How much did the kidnapper want?"

"Two hundred thousand."

It suddenly felt very warm in the room. I was still wearing my new coat and started wrestling my way out of it while I tried to think of something reasonable to say.

Then someone knocked on the door. Johnson leapt up and answered it, as if expecting it to be Richie, but it was room service bringing the coffee. We sat silently while the waiter arranged the pot and cups on the low coffee table. Johnson slipped the guy a ten, and the grateful waiter departed, softly closing the door behind him.

Pool sat forward and poured the coffee.

"We'd already tracked Richie to Albuquerque," he said. "One of my operatives, Mike Sterling, you know him? No? Well, Mike slipped up on these skinheads, looking for Richie, and got the tar whipped out of him for his trouble. Put him in the hospital."

I must've winced.

"But we don't want you to get mixed up with them," Pool

said quickly. "All we need is someone to deliver the ransom money."

"And that would be me?"

"Sure. Like I said, Richie seems to know I'm onto him out here. If I make the drop, they might figure it for a trap. But they don't know you."

I looked them both over. I wasn't crazy about being Pool's bagman.

"All I'd have to do is make the drop?"

"That's right. Tomorrow night."

"They didn't ask Mr. Johnson here to do it himself?"

"No. In fact, they specified that he not be the one. I'm not sure why, but they want a neutral party. I wouldn't let him go anyway. Too dangerous."

Johnson snorted.

"You think they'd try to snatch him, too?" I asked.

"No, it's not that," Pool said. "But from all accounts, these skinheads, they're rough old boys."

"I'm not afraid of those punks," I said, my voice cracking only slightly.

" 'Course you're not," Pool said, and I didn't like the way he was grinning. "You're a professional, right? Besides, it's just a delivery. Quick in, quick out. We'll put a note in the brief-case telling the kidnappers how to reach Dick here at the hotel, then we'll handle whatever happens next."

Knowing Pool, I figured there was a lot they weren't telling me. Especially about the risk. But I had one more question, the one that mattered most.

"How much?"

Johnson smiled slyly. I tried not to scowl at him.

"How does a thousand dollars sound?"

"For carrying around two hundred thousand dollars and possibly getting my ass shot off?"

The grin slipped off Johnson's face.

"Seemed fair to me."

I took a deep breath and let it out slowly.

"All right," I said. "I'm in."

So that's how I found myself carrying a briefcase full of money to mysterious kidnappers on Wednesday night. The instructions were simple: Drive to a phone booth outside a Lotaburger south of Zuni Boulevard in a mixed zone of garages, cheap storefronts, and warehouses circled with high fences. Leave the briefcase in the booth, get back in the truck, and drive away.

It sounded easy enough, but the neighborhood, if you could call it that, was spooky as hell and darker than the mouth of a cannon. At midnight, the Lotaburger was closed, and the nearby buildings looked abandoned. Each corner had a streetlight, but half were broken, including the one nearest the phone booth. I wouldn't have noticed the booth at all, except I was looking for it.

I turned my big Dodge Ram into the Lotaburger parking lot and wheeled it around until its headlights shone on the phone booth. Empty.

I took a deep breath. No time like the present. I doused the headlights—why make myself a target?—and eased out of the truck with the briefcase dangling from my left hand. The air was cold and my breath misted in front of my face before it was whisked away on the breeze.

I had my trusty Smith & Wesson .38 in my belt under my new jacket and I rested my right hand on its butt, ready if howling skinheads suddenly appeared from the shadows.

I approached the drop-off spot thinking, *When was the last time I saw an honest-to-God phone booth?* This one had cracked glass all around, but at least it was a true booth, not one of those unsheltered phone-on-a-stick things Ma Bell has erected all around the city. At least a person could get some privacy, something I guess is no longer valued in a world where people go around with cellular phones pasted to their ears, yakking their heads off for anyone to hear.

I yanked open the door and was hit in the face with the stench of old urine and ancient vomit. Whew. Maybe that's why the phone company has replaced all the booths. I hated to set Dick Johnson's tooled leather briefcase down in a sticky mess, but I guessed he'd probably never see it again anyway. Let the kidnappers figure out how to clean it up.

After I closed the door, I hurried back to the truck, trying to pick kidnappers out of the darkness. I didn't see a thing. No guns. No cars. No people.

But it sure as hell *felt* like I was being watched.

TWO

I watched my mirrors all the way home, long after it became apparent that no one followed, that the drop had gone off without a hitch.

My instructions were to go home and phone Dick Johnson. I could've called him from my new cellular phone, which Felicia recently persuaded me to buy. I keep it in my truck, as instructed, so she can always find me. At least that's the idea. It's still too new to me. Half the time, I forget to turn it on, so it's as useless as the other crap in my glove compartment. Besides, being within easy reach of Felicia feels a little too much like being on a leash. Man's got to put his foot down occasionally, even if it's only a matter of pushing the "Off" button.

Over the past few months, Felicia and I have made a cozy nest out of the little brick cottage she picked out near the University of New Mexico. I have my own office with its own entrance and its separate phone line, and Felicia's decorated the rest of the house nicely. Don't get me wrong. Felicia's no

Martha Stewart. Much of the time, all her matching furniture is buried under piles of old newspapers and overflowing ashtrays and hastily scratched notes to herself. I try to do my share, but I'm cursed with the bachelor mentality about house cleaning: If you can't see it, it ain't dirty. It's a wonder we haven't been overrun by dust bunnies. Clean or not, the place feels like home, and there's nowhere I'd rather be after a spooky night of ransom delivery.

The lights were on and Felicia was still awake and that made me happy. At least, until I got inside.

"Where the heck have you been?"

Felicia's not one to mince words.

"Working."

"At this time of night? I haven't seen you all day."

This isn't unusual in our household. Felicia is a star reporter for the *Albuquerque Gazette.* The *Gazette*'s a morning newspaper, so she often works deep into the night, wrapping up last-minute details on her front-page scoops. Private eyes aren't known for having regular office hours, either. Some days, we only see each other when one or the other of us is asleep.

"You worked late," I said. "I didn't leave here until nearly eleven."

Felicia ran a hand through her tangled brown hair, then fished in the pocket of her oversized Hawaiian shirt for a cigarette.

"It's been a long, long day. Not only did I have two stories to do, but I've got that intern following me around. She's driving me nuts."

Probably because she keeps her bosses perpetually pissed off, Felicia had drawn the short straw when it came to mentoring some college journalism student. She'd told me about it a few days earlier, but I hadn't given it another thought.

"She's a pain, huh?"

"Miss Meg Albright from the Medill School of Journalism at Northwestern University? What makes you think that?"

Sarcasm is one of my honey's strong suits.

"You said she was driving you nuts. What, she's an idiot?"

"Oh, no, Miss Albright seems very intelligent. Full of enthusiasm. Perky as she can be."

Uh-oh. Perky's about the last thing Felicia can bear.

"Likes to talk, does she?"

"My ears are tired."

"Very eager to learn?"

"Eager, anyway. These Medilldoes think they know it all already. But she's definitely excited to be working at a newspaper. I swear, it's like taking a toddler to the circus."

"She start calling you 'Mom' yet?"

"She does, I'll break her nose."

I risked giving Felicia a hug and a peck on the mouth. She didn't break my nose, but she didn't exactly seemed swept away, either. She took another drag off her cigarette before starting a new round of questioning.

"Got a case?"

"Just a one-night thing. I need to make a phone call."

"At this time of night?"

"The client's waiting to hear how it went."

"How what went?"

See, this is a persistent problem. My cases are confidential. That's why they call me a "private" investigator. But Felicia's a born newshound and she always wants to know every detail. If I try to evade her questions, she just gets more dogged. Of course, most of my investigations don't fall into the category of what she considers newsworthy. Missing persons, cheating spouses, and insurance scams rarely make the front page. A kidnapping, though, might get Felicia a little too interested.

"I'll tell you about it later," I said. "I really need to call my client right now."

I moved toward my office, but Felicia stepped sideways to cut me off.

"Come on, Bubba. What's going on?"

"I had to make a delivery for a guy from Texas."

I took another step. She cut me off again.

"In the middle of the night? What were you delivering?"

"Nothing much. Some money."

Another step. Again, she moved sideways to block me. Felicia would make a good basketball player.

"Money? For what?"

"I really need the phone now. This guy's waiting."

She snaked out a hand and grabbed me by the shirtfront.

"'Fess up, Bubba. What's the money for?"

I sighed heavily.

"Ransom."

Her eyes went wide behind her square glasses.

"A kidnapping?"

"The client thinks the whole thing might be a hoax."

"He's willing to cough up a wad of money for a hoax? How much?"

"Two hundred grand."

"Get outta here. For a hoax?"

"He's loaded. I get the feeling he won't even feel a pinch. He says he wants to get his son back in one piece, no matter how much it costs."

"This smells like news."

I flinched. "I've got to keep it confidential."

She frowned, searching me with her eyes, not liking what she found.

"So," she said finally, "did you see the kidnapper pick up the money?"

"No. I was supposed to just drop it off, then come back here and phone in. I need to call now."

"You just left two hundred thousand dollars somewhere? How could you do that?"

"Those were my instructions."

"What if somebody else finds it?"

"I don't know. I worried about that all day. But I think the kidnapper was watching the drop. I could sense it."

Felicia stubbed out her smoke, shaking her head.

"I can't believe the things you get mixed up with."

"Hey, I'm making a thousand dollars."

"Doesn't sound like enough for the risks you take."

I had no answer for that. She eyed me some more, then said, "Don't you have a phone call to make?"

"Why didn't I think of that?"

She stepped out of the way so I could finally get to my office phone.

"Want a sandwich?" she called behind me.

"No, thanks. But a bourbon might settle my nerves."

"Coming right up."

I closed the door behind me. As if it mattered. Before I could finish dialing the phone, Felicia arrived with my drink. She didn't seem inclined to leave. She leaned in the doorway, her head tilted to the side, watching me as the phone rang in my ear.

"Yeah?"

"Mr. Johnson?"

"Bubba. Is that you?"

"Yessir. Calling as instructed."

"What took you so long?"

I glanced over toward Felicia, then weighed my words carefully.

"I got hung up for a few minutes. But it all went fine."

"Hell, I figured that, or you wouldn't be calling at all."

I mulled that for a second. He probably was right. I reminded myself that I'd been the sacrificial lamb in this deal.

"I need you to get down here right away."

"To the hotel?"

"Isn't that where you called me? Yes, to the hotel. There's been a development."

"What happened?"

"Just get down here. Meet me and Pool at my suite."

Pool. Probably trying to find some way to screw me out of my thousand dollars.

I was dog-tired, and I didn't feel like getting back in the

truck and driving over to the Hilton. I certainly didn't feel like wrangling with Pool and Johnson again. I told myself to demand my check and hang up.

"Yessir, I'll be right there."

"Good."

Johnson hung up without saying good-bye.

Then I turned to explain myself to Felicia.

THREE

The Hilton lobby was empty except for a sleepy-looking bell-hop. I gave him a nod as I passed, but I didn't slow. Straight into the elevator, which whisked me up to Johnson's floor. Pool answered my knock.

"Evenin', Bubba." Pool looked solemn. What was going on here?

"Have you heard from Richie?"

"Not a word. But there's something you ought to see."

I entered the suite, leaving Pool to shut the door behind me. Dick Johnson sprawled in the same armchair where I'd last seen him. A phone sat on the coffee table, and Johnson glared at it as if he could make it ring through telepathy. His high forehead was shiny with perspiration, and he wore a white bathrobe over orange silk pajamas. He was barefoot, and could've used a pedicure. He scarcely looked up when I sat down across from him.

I was uncertain whether to say anything. I sat there like a stump, waiting for Pool. The slick private eye crossed to a desk where a TV-VCR combination sat waiting.

"Watch this," he commanded. Johnson continued to stare at the phone. I guessed he'd already seen whatever Pool had while I was driving over.

Pool hit a button and the tape inside clicked and whirred. An image flashed on the screen, dark and fuzzy, and it took me a second to recognize the parking lot outside the Lota-burger. My big red truck rumbled into view—though it looked gray in the image—and lurched to a stop near the phone booth.

"What the hell?" I demanded. "You followed me?"

"Sure," Pool said. "I used a new night-vision lens I got for my video camera. Needs hardly any light at all."

Great, more high-tech toys. All of us in this business have delusions of grandeur, I suppose. I secretly want to be hard-boiled, like the private eyes I read about in the paperbacks. Pool wants to be James Bond.

"Why the tail? You think I was gonna skip with that money?"

A grin tugged at the corner of his mouth.

"That never even occurred to us, Bubba. We told you we trusted you."

"Then what's this all about?"

"Just watch."

A fuzzy blob I recognized as myself crawled out of the pickup truck on the screen and hauled out the briefcase full of money. My head whipped around while I searched the dark parking lot. I looked sneaky.

The camera zoomed in closer, close enough that we could see my hand go to my belt inside my jacket.

"Looks like you were packing," Pool said, amused.

"Damned right. I didn't know what I'd find there."

"Man's gotta right to be cautious," he said.

Johnson now looked at the TV screen, too.

"You didn't take long to put that money where it be-longed," he said.

"No reason to stick around. I felt sure somebody was watching me, and now I know it was Pool."

"Not just me," Pool said. "Keep looking."

We watched me climb back into the truck. The taillights flashed; then the truck slewed around and I roared away.

"You know," I said, "keeping an eye on me wasn't part of the deal. What if they'd spotted you?"

"They weren't gonna spot me. I was cautious, too."

"Still. I could've been shot."

"No. He only wanted the money."

"You got that on video, too."

"Yep. It takes him a few minutes to come outta hiding."

Johnson grumbled. "Hit the damn fast-forward button, Pool. You know what's coming."

Pool did as he was told, and wavy white lines crawled across the empty parking lot on the screen. He let off the button half a minute later, saying, "Here he comes."

Another fuzzy figure appeared around the corner of the burger joint and hustled across the parking lot toward the phone booth. The camera zoomed in again as the man reached the booth. Pool knew his camera work, I had to give him that. As the man turned away from the booth, briefcase in hand, the camera framed his face, clear as could be. He was a frail-looking young man, wearing dark clothing that contrasted with his clean-shaven lightbulb of a head. He glanced around the parking lot, and Pool hit the "pause" button. The image went still, with the man staring right into the hidden lens. It was so sharp, it could've been a mug shot.

"That," Pool said, "is Richie Johnson."

"It is?"

"Yep. This proves what Dick and I suspected. Richie staged his own kidnapping. He even made the pickup himself. I wouldn't be surprised if nobody else was involved."

"Why would he do that?"

"That's the sixty-four dollar question," Johnson said. "If Richie needed money, why didn't he just come to me? Instead, he's scamming me out of two hundred thousand dollars. I can't believe it."

"Proof's in the pictures, as I always say," Pool said smugly. He hit "stop" and the screen went dark.

"Wait a minute," I said. "What happened next? Did you nab him?"

Pool cleared his throat. He looked a little sheepish, which is a neat trick for a wolf.

"Not exactly," he said. "I thought I'd follow him, find out where he was taking the money, see if anybody else was involved."

"And?"

"Well, I hate to admit this, but I lost him."

Johnson grunted, as if he still couldn't believe that part. It was all I could do to keep from laughing out loud.

"You lost him?"

"He was on foot," Pool said with a shrug. "I put down my camera and cranked up this rented Cadillac I was driving and swung around behind that burger place, but Richie was going over a board fence out back. By the time I got out of the car and chased after him, he was pulling away in an old yellow Volkswagen."

Johnson shook his head.

"Richie shouldn't be running and climbing over fences," he said. "He's gonna give himself heart failure."

"Is that all you've got to say?" I couldn't keep the astonishment out of my voice. "What about the money?"

Johnson gave me a sour look.

"I told you before, the money don't mean ratshit to me. I need to get my son back before he damages his health permanently."

"Yeah, but—"

"Don't 'but' me, boy."

I bristled at that, but said nothing. If he was stupid enough to kiss a small fortune good-bye because his son wanted to play games, fine with me. I needed to stay on Johnson's good side until I got my thousand bucks.

"The question now is," Johnson said, "what are we gonna do next?"

"It's like I told you, Dick," Pool said as he joined us at the circle of armchairs. "Me and my people, we'll track him down. It's just gonna take a little time."

"Time?" Johnson blurted. "You've had time, Pool. You've been looking for my boy for three weeks, and this"—he threw a hand toward the TV—"is as close as you've come. And then you let him get away with that money."

"I tried to catch up to him, Dick—"

"With that much money, the boy could go anywhere, do anything. He could be buying himself an airline ticket to Tahiti or someplace right now, and you wouldn't know a damned thing about it."

"I don't think they have any flights this time of night," Pool said.

"That's beside the point, Pool, and you know it. Your problem is, you don't know your way around this town. If you had some clue to the layout, you might've been able to head Richie off."

"He had it planned pretty well—"

" 'Course, he did! He's my son, ain't he? Certainly didn't get his brains from his poor mother. She couldn't follow a recipe, much less plan anything. But Richie's sharp. Boy goes around with a weak heart, always on the outs with everybody, he's got to figure ways to outfox people."

Pool nodded, watching Johnson out of the corner of his eye.

"Well, he certainly outfoxed me tonight," he said, and I could see it for the peace offering it was. Pool might be a proud, vain man, but he could play to the client's ego. Scheming shit.

Johnson paid no attention. He stared at the ceiling, as if he could see an idea up there.

"What you need, Pool, is a local boy, somebody like

Bubba here, who knows his way around."

"I had such a man, Dick," Pool said. "And your son's friends put him in the hospital."

"He's out of the hospital now, ain't he?"

"Yeah, but he's still got a broken ankle. He's in one of those walking casts."

"And that disqualifies him from helping?"

"Well, he won't be jumping over any fences, chasing after Richie."

I didn't like where this was heading. When Johnson turned to me, I liked it even less.

"What about you, Bubba? You could hire on with Pool here until this is over."

I was shaking my head before he even finished speaking.

"Afraid that's not possible. I work alone."

"Oh, you'll hire on for an easy delivery for a quick grand, but when it gets to be nut-cutting time, you're not interested."

I swallowed before I answered.

"It's not that I'm not interested," I said. "I just don't work with Pool."

Pool's eyebrows shot up and his jaw clenched, but he said nothing. Guess he could remember as well as I did how he'd screwed me in the past.

Johnson looked from me to Pool and recognition dawned and he smiled.

"You boys got some kinda history, don't you?"

"You might say that." I didn't want to volunteer any details, and Pool didn't seem ready to speak up, either.

"You don't like each other, but you're making nice for my benefit," Johnson said, and his face took on a glow. That made me nervous. Johnson was an old hand at manipulating people. You don't go around the country, throwing up ugly-ass strip malls, without knowing how to play zoning commissioners and union reps and anybody else who gets in your way.

Johnson sat up in his chair and rubbed his hands on his thighs.

"I tell you what, Bubba. Why don't you take on this case, finding Richie, and you can leave old Pool here in the dust."

"Now wait a minute, Dick," Pool said, "we've got a contract."

"Hell, I know that, and I've got lawyers who could tear it up and feed it to you if I gave 'em the word."

"We don't need lawyers," Pool said quietly. "We need to find Richie."

"That's what I'm gettin' at. I tell you what we'll do. I'll hire Bubba here, and I'll keep you on, too. We'll make it a competition."

Pool leaned forward in his chair, rested his elbows on his knees.

"That's not necessary, Dick. I tell you, I can find your son. Give me a couple of days."

"Naw, I'm tired of waitin' and worryin'. Let's make it a race. Bubba, I'll pay you your regular retainer while you're huntin' Richie. Whoever finds him first gets a big ole prize."

That got me leaning forward as well. It's a wonder somebody didn't fall out of his chair.

"A prize?"

"Whatever's left of that two hundred thousand dollars."

Silence sat heavily while Pool and I swallowed that. Pool was the first to speak up.

"Winner take all?"

"I'll pay you both for your time," Johnson said. "That's only fair. But only one of you walks away with the big payoff, and that's whoever finds Richie first. What do you say, Bubba? Are you in?"

"In?" My voice came out a croak, and it took three tries to clear my throat. "Yeah, I'm in. How could I not be?"

Johnson clapped his big hands together and sat back.

"All right, then. We've got ourselves a horse race. I want Richie back, unharmed, and you fellas do whatever it takes to make that happen. The winner gets the big payday."

Pool shook his head, frowning.

"This is extremely unorthodox, Dick," he said. "I don't think—"

"You've got three days."

Then I was on my feet, shaking Dick Johnson's hand and telling him I'd do my best.

"Keep me posted," he said. "Call here any time. I got a feeling I'm not going to sleep much until I get Richie home."

"Yessir."

I headed for the door, passing close to Pool. I slipped him a wink.

"May the best man win," I said, and then I was out the door, giddy over the notion of making a fortune on one case. And, even more, tickled to death that I might finally get the best of William J. Pool.

FOUR

*T*hursday morning, I snapped awake to Felicia banging around in the kitchen. The sink in there is stainless steel, and my sweetie has the habit of launching nonbreakable items— forks, spatulas, the random pot—at the sink from wherever she happens to be standing when she's finished with them. The neighbors probably think one of us plays the cymbals.

Waking to Felicia at home raised a question: Do I tell her about the competition with Pool and the chance to make two hundred thousand dollars? Or, do I keep it to myself, working whatever hours it takes, then surprise her with the winnings?

I lay under the covers, weighing the alternatives. If I told her about it, she'd be tempted to report the kidnapping hoax to *Gazette* readers, even though it might jeopardize the big payday. If I didn't tell her, then I'd be trying to keep a secret from a woman who's a walking polygraph machine.

The question answered itself. Felicia burst into the bedroom in her fluffy pink bathrobe, headed for the closet. I snapped my eyes shut, but it was too late.

"You're not fooling anybody," she said. "You're awake."

I blinked a few times for effect.

"Barely."

"What happened last night?"

"Last night?"

"With your client. Did they catch the kidnappers?"

"Uh, no. Turns out it was indeed a hoax. Pool videotaped the victim himself making off with the money."

"That's ballsy. So what happens now?"

I sat up in bed and told her about the race against Pool. She picked out clothes from the closet and threw them on while I talked. I was distracted by the sight of her in her underwear as she shucked on a slip and a dress. Married six months, and I'm still a lust-filled tiger every time I spy Felicia in her dainties.

I saved the best part for last.

"And," I concluded, "whoever finds Richie gets to keep the ransom."

That got her attention. "The whole thing?"

"Whatever Richie hasn't spent or given away."

"Then what are you doing in bed?"

"Good question."

I jumped up and pulled on my ratty flannel bathrobe. She said to my back as I went into the bathroom: "There's coffee. Grab some on your way out the door."

I turned back and did a Groucho with my eyebrows.

"Eager for me to get started, huh?"

She frowned at me.

"Just don't screw it up, Bubba."

I cleared my throat and ducked my head.

"Right."

Then I hurried toward the shower.

By the time I emerged, shaved and showered and scented, Felicia had left for her office. Guess she didn't want to distract me further.

My first stop was the cop shop downtown, where I got

buzzed up to the fourth floor and the office of Lt. Steve Romero. Romero runs Homicide, though his bosses might dispute that, and he's as sharp a cop as you'd ever want to meet. Since my encounters with him often include a corpse nearby, he's sharper than I like much of the time. But he's a straight shooter and a good-enough friend that he was my best man when Felicia and I got hitched.

I figured Romero could put me onto somebody in the Albuquerque Police Department who had information on the skinheads. Cops don't usually like to share such intelligence, particularly with a private eye, but I hoped Romero could put the arm on somebody for me.

He was at his desk, concealed by stacks of folders and reports. Albuquerque's not exactly the Murder Capital of the World, but we get enough dead drug dealers and slain spouses to keep him hopping. The pile of papers represented Romero's workload, which meant he didn't have time to be messing around with me. He emphasized that point, saying by way of greeting, "What do *you* want?"

"Now that's a fine how-de-doo," I replied, as I took a seat across from him. "Is that the way your mama raised you to speak to others?"

Romero lifted a heavy eyebrow at me.

"Let's leave my mother out of this," he said. "Have you ever voluntarily showed up at my office when you didn't want something?"

I pondered that a moment. I felt sure I'd stopped by just to say hello, but I couldn't recollect when.

"Maybe you're right."

Romero rocked back in his chair, and his slit of a mouth tightened into an almost grin. Romero's a big, square guy, wide of head and body, with thick hands that look like they could squeeze air out of a bowling ball. He ran one of them back over his short black hair.

"Look, Bubba, I'd love to sit around here and jaw with you. But see all this work I've got to do? We've had three stiffs already this week and it's only Thursday. What does that tell you?"

"We're going for a new record?"

"Very funny. What it should tell you is that I've got Captain LeRoy Schulte breathing down my neck to get 'em solved."

"He's not tall enough to breathe down your neck. Maybe up your neck."

Romero glanced around the room to see if anyone was listening. The three other cops in the Homicide squadroom looked busy with their typewriters and telephones.

"Don't make jokes about him here, Bubba. He has ears everywhere."

"Must be hell when he takes a shower."

Romero nodded impatiently.

"Always the wiseass. You've got a million of 'em. Now what the hell do you *want?*"

"Since you put it that way, I've got a case and I need some help."

Romero rolled his eyes.

"And you think I can just drop everything and help you make a buck? Maybe you haven't heard, but I've got a job. The taxpayers expect me to do it."

"I'm a taxpayer."

Romero glowered, probably calculating how much in taxes I actually fork over in a given year. I wouldn't be surprised if my IRS forms sat somewhere among all that paper on his desk. Romero seems all-seeing, all-knowing. I, on the other hand, am lucky I can find my way out of bed in the morning.

"Look," I said, "this'll only take a second. All I need is a reference."

"You finally gonna get a real job?"

"Not that kind of reference. I want you to refer me to somebody in the department who can give me some information."

"So it's not enough you're in here bugging me. You want me to sic you on somebody else."

"You could say you're helping out a tax-paying citizen."

Romero sighed.

"What kind of information you looking for?"

"Anything on skinheads."

"Why the hell would you be messing around with them?"

"I'm not. Not exactly. It's a long story—"

"They always are, aren't they?"

"C'mon, Steve, I just need to talk to somebody who can tell me about those shitheads. And then I'll be on my way."

"What are you up to?"

"I told you, it's a case. I can't talk about it."

"But you can come in here and bug me with questions about it. Just like always."

"Are you gonna help me or not?"

Romero took a long time to answer, long enough that I was sure I would be getting a "no." I squirmed in my chair.

"All right, Bubba. I'll give you a name. But only because it'll mean more trouble for you than it's worth."

"What's that supposed to mean?"

Romero's eyes got a happy gleam in them. I was sure I wasn't going to like this.

"There's a guy in the Gang Unit, a sergeant named Horton Houghton."

"Who?"

"Houghton. He could give you the history of any gang in town: the Eighteenth Streeters, the Crips, the Bloods, the Marielitos."

"No, thanks. I've got my hands full with skinheads."

"You got that right, Bubba. Let me tell you something: You go messing with those skinheads, and the next time I see you may be when they're zipping up the body bag."

"Is that what you meant by 'more trouble than it's worth'?"

"No," he said, and he truly grinned this time. Uh-oh. "I was talking about Houghton."

"He doesn't like private eyes?"

"He doesn't like anybody. I imagine he'll like you least of all."

I stood up, ready to leave.

"I can't imagine he'd be any grumpier than you."

"You don't know Houghton. Next to him, I'm the Pillsbury Doughboy."

Romero gave me directions to Houghton's office downstairs and said he'd call ahead to warn that I was on my way. Maybe he'd put in a good word for me. Yeah, right. And maybe William J. Pool and I could become blood brothers.

The Gang Unit occupied a warren of cubicles on the third floor and the occupants looked no less harried than Romero's comrades in Homicide. Albuquerque, like most cities of half a million people, has a whole slew of gangs gunning for each other with Uzis and Saturday night specials. I've always thought they should just let them shoot it out and thin some of the criminals from the gene pool. But here in the Wild West, the occasional innocent bystander catches a bullet and that keeps the citizenry in an uproar.

Corkboards along the walls bore the usual wanted posters and all-points bulletins above a display case full of weaponry labeled: CONFISCATED FROM GANG MEMBERS. Wicked-looking automatic pistols lay next to knives and brass knuckles and zip guns. Looking at them gave me a chill. I wondered what weapons skinheads favored.

"You need something?"

The voice came from behind me, and I turned to find a stocky cop with a blond crewcut giving me the steely squint.

"I'm looking for Sergeant Houghton."

He squinted harder. His face might fold in on itself.

"Why?"

Time to drop names.

"Lieutenant Steve Romero in Homicide sent me to see him."

"You involved with a homicide?"

"Not yet."

It took him a second to sort that out.

"Funny. Houghton's over there, through that door."

"Thanks."

I tried to sidle past him, but he snagged me by the arm.

"Word of warning. Don't be a smartass with Houghton. He's not a nice guy like me."

If this cop qualified as a nice guy, Houghton must be Dracula.

"Thanks for the advice."

I tapped on Houghton's door and turned the knob when a grunt sounded from inside.

Houghton stood up as I entered. It took awhile. He stood well over six and a half feet tall and probably weighed more than three hundred pounds. And not an ounce of fat on him. He had arms like telephone poles and a chest that was as thick as it was wide. His skin was a shiny ebony, and his hair was shaved on the sides and flat on the top, so it looked like he had an anvil sitting on the broad shoulders of his dark blue uniform.

His face was creased in what seemed to be a permanent scowl, but he went downright baleful when he got a look at me. I seem to have that effect on people.

"Um. Lieutenant Romero called ahead for me?"

Houghton huffed, and it seemed I felt his cigarette breath on my skin, even though I stood six feet away.

"The lieutenant said I could help you out. If I feel like it."

"Good thing I caught you in a good mood then."

Houghton's expression didn't change. Maybe it never did. Maybe his face only shifted through graduated levels of pissed-off.

"What. Do. You. Want."

"Right down to business, huh? Okay, then. I can respect that. Mind if I sit down?"

What is it about menace that makes me babble? Houghton glared, and I decided standing would be fine.

"I was hoping you could tell me a little about the skinhead groups in Albuquerque," I blathered. "I've got a case with some skinhead overtones, you might say, and I know nothing about them. Who they are or where they hang out or what they're all about . . ."

That scowl caused me to run out of steam.

"You finished?" he asked in such a way that I knew I was.

"Sure. Sorry to run on. I know you're busy—"

"That's right. I don't have time for this shit, but the lieutenant said talk to you. And me, I'm just a lowly sergeant, right? So I guess I'll talk."

"That would be great. I just—"

"I said *I'll* talk. You listen. You know how to do that?"

"Yes. I mean, yes, sir."

"Good. Now here's the first thing I'm gonna tell you about the skinheads."

I tried to look eager to receive the information.

"Stay the fuck away from them."

"Sure. That's certainly what I had in mind—"

"Thought you were gonna listen."

"Oh. Right. Sorry."

"Damn, you're a sorry sonofabitch, aren't you? You've been sorry ever since you got here."

"I'm just trying to be cooperative."

"Then stop apologizing and shut your piehole."

"Why are you being such a hardass? What did I do to you?"

Houghton leaned across his desk, shifting his weight to his ham-sized fists.

"You're wasting my time, that's what. Every politician in this city is after my ass to arrest those skinheads. And now I've got some jerkoff in here asking questions."

I resented that, but all I said was, "Why are the politicos so interested?"

He let the silence build awhile. I think I gulped.

"Do you read the newspaper?" he asked.

Do I ever. If I don't have some ready comment on Felicia's byline stories when she gets home each day, I can count on the cold shoulder. But I didn't know what he was getting at, and I wasn't about to mention Felicia.

"Sure."

"Then you might recall that several people got the shit stomped out of them downtown on New Year's Eve."

"Put 'em in the hospital, right?"

"That's right, Sherlock. Your friends the skinheads were responsible for that."

"They're not my friends."

"Damned right, they're not. You better remember that if you run across 'em."

We were getting nowhere fast.

"Look. I've got a client, his kid got mixed up with some of these skinheads. I'm not trying to cross them. I'm just trying to track down the kid."

"What's the kid's name?"

I hesitated. Dick Johnson said he didn't want the cops involved. But it wouldn't pay to argue with this behemoth, especially if I expected him to give up the information I needed.

"Richie Johnson."

Houghton looked thoughtful, then shook his head.

"That's a new one on me," he said. "He can't have been around too long."

"I think he's new to town."

Houghton picked up a pencil and wrote down Richie's name, which made me fidget.

"If he's a new recruit," he rumbled, "he's likely fallen in with Mayhem and that bunch. I've got APBs out on them right now."

"Mayhem?"

"That's what he calls himself. He's the leader of the main skinhead club in town. His real name's Percy Kilpatrick. He's a fuckin' Brit. That's where all this shit started, over in England, in the eighties. Ain't that where all the trends start? Fuckin' Brits."

"They're not all bad. What about the Beatles?"

He ignored me. "Mayhem is into the full menu of hatred—racism, anti-Semitism, Nazi salutes. You'd think Brits wouldn't be so crazy about Nazis, considering the Blitz. But Mayhem and the rest of these losers weren't even born then."

Daring to venture another question, I asked, "Are they mostly British?"

"Naw. Just Mayhem. The rest are local boys, trying to be tough, trying to piss off their parents. To them, shaving their heads and wearing combat boots is a fashion statement."

"Should make 'em easy to spot."

"You'd think so, but most of these losers only come out at night. They sometimes hang out at this nightclub downtown, Pandemonium. It's in that old brewery down by the railroad tracks. You know it?"

I shook my head.

"You stay away from there. Guy like you wouldn't last long if he stands up to the Oi Boys."

"Oy? Isn't that Jewish?"

Houghton shook his head in disgust.

"It's Oi, spelled 'O-I.' It's a kind of music these badasses enjoy. White supremacy lyrics set to heavy metal music. Real shit. Give me Luther Vandross anytime."

"That's what they listen to at this club, Pandemonium?"

"That and some other shit, all cranked so loud who can tell what it is."

"Drugs?"

Houghton frowned at me.

"They're not into drugs. These boys are just into partying, drinking a lot of beer. Then, when they've got a good head of steam, they find some poor sonofabitch and stomp hell out of him."

"They all live in the same part of town?"

"Some in the student ghetto. Others in the war zone. Couple of 'em live up in the Northeast Heights with their white-bread parents, who probably think Junior's going through a 'phase.' "

Houghton's glare had softened a little at the sound of his own voice.

"I think that's what we've got with Richie," I said. "A phase. His father just wants him to come home and then they'll sort it out."

"You don't get these kids back," he said. "Once they get a taste of hatred, true hatred, they're gone for good."

"I've got to try."

Houghton reached into his shirt pocket and fondled a pack of cigarettes hiding there. He glanced at the wall clock, then back at me. The scowl returned.

"Try all you want," he said, "but don't get in my way. I'm gonna nail these little pricks to the wall, once I catch up to 'em. I need to bust 'em before they get any worse. They've been busy lately, some stuff we've kept out of the newspapers. They painted swastikas on Temple B'nai Israel. They beat up some other people, too, including a private detective."

He arched his eyebrows, and I said, "I heard about that."

"Yeah? Guess you weren't paying very good attention if you still want to mess with Mayhem and the Oi Boys."

I thanked Houghton for his time, being as polite as possible, and hurried out of the cop shop. No wonder the APD has so many public relations problems. The whole place reeked of discourtesy.

I couldn't blame Houghton for feeling the way he did about the skinheads. He'd probably spent his whole life standing up to people who wanted to judge him strictly on the color of his skin. That might account for his sour outlook on the world. Might also be the reason he ended up a cop. Then a bunch of punks go around town, spewing venom and listening to this Oi music, saying they're superior strictly because of the genetic accident that makes them Caucasian. Losers come in all colors, and the worst kind are those who try to compensate with bigotry.

I think of myself as a recovering redneck. It's tough to overcome the prejudices that surround you when you're growing up. My formative years were spent in Mississippi during desegregation and I've seen just how ugly people can be. Luckily, I wasn't reared that way; Mama taught it was un-Christian to hate. I try to be colorblind. I think people are the same, whatever their skin tone, and you don't hate them until they've earned it. But once they have, I'm as capable of hating as the next guy. Look at the way I felt about William J. Pool.

FIVE

*A*fter what Houghton told me, I didn't expect to find skinheads roaming around in broad daylight, but I went cruising anyway.

The student ghetto, as it's so charmingly called, is a wide-ranging neighborhood south of the University of New Mexico that caters to the student rental population. UNM covers acre upon green acre north of Central Avenue, old Route 66. On the south side, there's the usual jumble you find near any college: coffee houses, fast-food joints, Laundromats, tattoo parlors, copy shops, bars, and convenience stores, all aimed at siphoning money off the thirty thousand people who call UNM home for at least part of the day. South of the commercial strip, the ghetto starts up in earnest. Its elm-shaded streets—all named after universities—are lined with a mix of immaculate family homes, rundown rental properties, and mammoth apartment complexes squeezed onto tiny lots.

You find all kinds in the ghetto. There's one house that's

covered with graffiti because the lady who lives there thought the street artists could work out their inspirations that way without getting arrested. Besides, she told the newspaper, it's cheaper than repainting. The neighbors hate it. There's a couple who runs a "free porch," where folks put their castaway clothes and other junk so the homeless can stop and shop. The neighbors hate that, too. And, there's a sprinkling of crack houses and dope dens that cater to students. The neighbors really hate that.

Don't get me wrong. For all its internal bickering, the student ghetto is the most tolerant neighborhood in the city. If you're going to live around college students—who are intent on trying anything new, especially if there's a chance it'll piss off their parents—you might as well go into it with an attitude of acceptance.

I knew a guy who lived over there, on Wellesley between Coal and Lead, the busy thoroughfares everybody calls "the one-ways." One day, I'm over visiting him, and we find a dozen tie-dyed Deadheads camped on his lawn in a circle, passing around a hash pipe and listening to a boom box. Me, I would've gone ballistic and lectured the stoners on the laws against trespassing. My friend? He studied them for a few seconds, then shouted, "You guys aren't planning to spend the night there, are you?"

One of the more alert members of the ragtag party yelled back, "No, man, we're just resting here for a while. Then we're walking back to our van."

"Okay, that's cool."

See? A tolerant neighborhood. Still, I'd bet the most open-minded liberal would get a little edgy if Mayhem and the Oi Boys moved in next door. And, he'd probably be afraid to object, too. Skinheads wear those heavy combat boots for a reason.

There weren't many pedestrians in the ghetto on this day— the biting March wind saw to that—and I was about to give it up when I spotted exactly what I'd been looking for. On Bryn Mawr, his chest thrust out and his head glinting in the sun, strutted a skinhead. I whipped the Ram over to the curb and jumped out into the snatching wind.

"Excuse me?" I called after him.

He kept walking, so I trotted along to cut him off.

"Excuse me? Got a minute?"

He pulled up short when I stepped in front of him, which in itself was an act of courage, considering how he looked. He wore an unzipped bomber jacket dotted with patches, tight jeans cuffed over shiny boots and narrow suspenders over a black T-shirt. A silver stud glimmered in one nostril. A swastika tattoo decorated the side of his neck, and the backs of his hands were covered with black tribal tattoos.

I know a guy, Harley Jim, who does tattoos. He told me once he refuses to imprint them on hands, heads, and necks. He only inks them in places that can be covered by clothing, in case the recipient one day looks for a job. Whoever tattooed this skinhead apparently didn't have the same high professional standards.

"What do you want?" the skinhead snarled, and I noted that this had become the theme for my day.

"I'm a private investigator. Mind if I ask you a few questions?"

"No time."

The skinhead kept walking. I fell in beside him. His bald head was pink from the cold wind. I can't understand why somebody would intentionally shave off his hair; it seems like such a precious commodity now that mine is falling out. Michael Jordan looks cool without hair. Everyone else in the world ought to think twice.

Up close, I could see he wasn't much over five feet tall. It was hard to tell how he was built under the bulky jacket, but I figured such a little guy couldn't pose much of a threat. The tattoos and the pierced nose worried me, though. Somebody who's that much into pain could be hard to stop in a fistfight.

"Won't take a second," I said brightly. "You know a guy named Richie Johnson?"

The skinhead hesitated just enough to show me he indeed knew Richie, then said, "Never heard of him."

"What about a guy who calls himself Mayhem? You one of the Oi Boys?"

The skinhead pulled up short and turned to glare at me. It would've bothered me more if he hadn't been such a sawed-off little number. All he was getting was a good view up my nostrils. Still, I kept my distance. I needed a few feet between us in case he came at me. Room to throw a punch. Or, more likely, a head start.

"I told you, mate," he growled, "I got no time to talk to you."

The use of the word "mate" answered my question. Only Brits talk that way, so this kid clearly picked up the use of the term from Mayhem or someone like him. Out West, you're more likely to be called "pardner" or "dude."

"That's not very friendly," I said. "I just want a little information."

He glared.

"I'd pay for it."

A smile tugged at the corners of his mouth. Now I was getting somewhere. Offer a little money. That always does the trick.

"You think I'd rat out Mayhem for a buck?" he asked. "I'd fucking well be crazy."

"So be crazy. The way this wind is blowing, we're all a little crazy today."

"Fuck off."

He turned and strode away, never looking back. Damn.

I shambled back to the Ram, muttering. The only good side I could see to the conversation was that I was sure Pool wouldn't have fared any better. In his Stetson and his shiny suits, Pool wouldn't exactly fit in down in the ghetto.

I climbed into the truck, relieved to get out of the sharp-edged wind, and my new cellular phone tweedled at me. I fished it out of the glove compartment, unfolded it, and pushed the button that made it answer.

"Hello?"

"I'll be damned. You actually remembered to turn on your phone."

Felicia. The sound of her voice made me check myself in the rearview mirror. My thinning brown hair had been blown every which way by the wind. I looked like an angry porcupine.

"I thought you might need to reach me," I said as I brushed my hair back with stiff fingers. "What's up?"

"I just got the strangest phone call here at the office," she said. "Guy named Ralph Upshaw. You ever heard of him?"

"No."

"Well, he's heard of you. He's got a message for you from your father."

I felt suddenly dizzy, as if someone had whapped me upside the head. I hadn't heard from my father in more than twenty-five years.

"That's not possible."

"Big surprise, huh?" Felicia said brightly.

"Yeah."

"Hold on a second." She covered the receiver, but I could hear her woofing at someone nearby.

My father was named Wilton Mabry, just like me. And, like me, he went by a nickname rather than being called Wilton all his life. My old man was known across the country as "Dub." Last time I saw him, he was climbing aboard his shiny Peterbilt truck, preparing for another long haul across the nation. He never returned. And I never heard from him again.

"Sorry, sugar," Felicia said, when she came back on the line, "my intern had a question."

"She's still there?"

"You don't know the half of it. Anyhow, this guy Ralph, sounded like a real goober, said you should call him. I've got the number."

"I don't want to call him."

"Sure, you do, Bubba. Don't you want to hear from your father? What's it been, thirty years?"

"Nearly. I was nine last time I saw him."

"See? You should call. What would it hurt?"

How to answer that? All the years of hurt, the wondering and the waiting for Dub's return. There was no way to express it.

"I'm not calling him."

"You should check it out," she said. "Maybe you could see him, see what you'll look like in your old age."

"I take after my mother's side of the family."

"How do you know? It's been a long time."

"Besides, I don't want to know whether the rest of my hair is going to fall out, or whether I'm going to get an even bigger gut. Sometimes, ignorance is better."

"It's bliss, from what I hear," she said. "But I think you should call anyway."

She rattled off the phone number, and I automatically wrote it down on the pad I keep on the dashboard.

"I don't know, Felicia."

"Just call Ralph. Then you can decide."

I told her I'd do it, and she said, "Gotta run," and hung up.

I stared at the phone in my hand. No choice now. She'd expect a full report. Shit. I didn't want to call Ralph. I didn't want a message from my father. I didn't want to resurrect a past I'd managed to bury so successfully.

It began at the end of the 1960s. We lived in a white clapboard house in the piney woods outside of Nazareth, Mississippi. It was a fine life for a kid. Creeks and forests to explore, a short

44

ride to school on a yellow bus, a happy home life. My dad was gone much of the time, hauling vegetables and furniture and frozen fish across the nation, but Mama ran things at home just fine. We always had plenty to eat, clothes that were clean if not new, a dilapidated Ford that would get us into town for the occasional stop at Rube's Ice Cream Parlour. I was an only child, my mama's blessing from the Lord, and if I wasn't spoiled rotten it was only because of the strictness of my Bible-heavy upbringing.

All that changed, though, when Mama met Jesus. I mean, Mama already had a personal relationship with Our Lord and Savior. But one night, while she sat up late, sipping tea at the kitchen table, Jesus walked right in. Mama, being a Southern lady, swallowed her fright and surprise, and offered the Good Lord some peach cobbler she'd baked fresh that day. Jesus took a liking to her cooking, and started appearing in the kitchen in the wee hours several nights a week.

I knew nothing of these visitations at first. I was snug in my bed when they occurred. But Mama soon let the whole world know. She mentioned her experiences to the local newspaper editor, who could smell a buck when one wafted his way. Pretty soon, network news shows and the wire services and big papers from back East all sent reporters to search out our humble home in the woods.

To say we became the town curiosity is putting it mildly. Some dried-up old crones believed it all right, and began delivering groceries and gifts to the house for Jesus's consumption. Others hooted and jeered when they saw us driving into town. And the whole thing blew up in Mama's face when the sheriff discovered a long-haired hippie living in a wigwam in the woods not far from our home. The drug-addled revolutionary, something of an oddity around those parts, even in the late 1960s, was arrested for trespassing and fraud and impersonating the Son of God. These were serious crimes in Mississippi, but Jesus was released on his own recognizance and promptly vanished.

Mama couldn't just let it go. She insisted the hippie had indeed been Jesus Christ, and we became the town laughing-stock.

On the road through most of the hubbub, Dub got home to find himself and his wife the subject of wide-ranging ridicule. He tried to stick it out, laughing it off or defending Mama's right to believe anything she wanted. But it became too much after a while. Dub climbed into his Peterbilt and disappeared.

I never forgave him. Bad enough that he was gone when Mama needed all the help she could get, but he abandoned me as well. Pretty soon, I was running the household, looking after Mama, who was too busy fretting over the Messiah's return to take care of the washing or the shopping.

And that was the story of my life until I graduated from Nazareth High School ("Home of the Fightin' Apostles") and fled to the welcoming arms of the U.S. Air Force. In my own way, I was as guilty as Dub. Given the first opportunity, I skipped town. But I couldn't take it anymore. I wanted to go far away, someplace where they didn't know my past or my family. The air force obliged by sending me to Kirtland Air Force Base in Albuquerque, New Mexico. And I've been here ever since.

I keep in touch with Mama, sending her birthday cards, even calling her on occasion, which is better than Dub ever did. But our telephone conversations never last long before she's beating the Jesus drum again, and I find an excuse to hang up.

Now this. A telephone number that threatened to open the door to Dub. That's one door that needed to remain closed, maybe secured with a big honking padlock. What if it really was Dub? What would I say? How would I keep from coldcocking the son of a bitch?

It took three tries to dial the number.

"Hello?"

"Ralph Upshaw?"

"Speakin'."

"My name is Bubba Mabry. You called?"

"Ah, Bubba. Hello, son. How are you doing?"

I'm thinking: *Don't call me "son."* But what I said was, "Fine. You got a message for me?"

"Well, sir, I'm an old friend of your daddy's, and I'm worried about him. I thought I'd look you up and see if you could help."

"Help with what?"

"Why, your daddy, of course. He's got some kind of health problem."

I remember the unfiltered Camels that Dub used to eat like popcorn.

"Cancer?" I asked somberly.

"Hell, I don't think so. Maybe. It's not that kind of health problem. I'm talking about his mental health."

That would be fitting, somehow, after the way he abandoned my wacky mama.

"I don't know anything about it," I said. "I haven't talked to the man since I was nine years old."

"Yeah, I understood there was some kind of rift. Dub never went into the particulars. But he knew you lived here in Albuquerque, and—"

"How'd he know that?"

"Well, son, I don't rightly know. Maybe he talked to your mother. She's back in Mississippi, right?"

"Yeah, but—"

"Anyhow, as I was saying, he told me you lived here and I thought I better call you and sorta alert you to the situation. Dub's been actin' strange. He sorta drifts away, you know? Me and some of the other truckers were thinkin' he oughta be checked out before he spends any more time behind the wheel of a big rig."

That made sense. Enough of those truck drivers are addled

as it is. It's scary as hell to drive on the interstate, knowing that eighty thousand pounds of steel is rocketing along behind you, steered by somebody who hasn't slept in four days.

"I don't see how it's my problem," I said.

"If that's the way you feel, there's nothin' I can say to change your mind. But I thought you might want to take a look at him. He's right here in town."

"He is?"

"Yeah. He's stayin' at the Terminal Inn, over by the truck terminal? By the Big I, where the freeways meet?"

"I know where it is."

"Well, sir, he's in room 120. I thought you'd at least want to say howdy."

"It's been a long time."

Ralph Upshaw let the silence do the talking for him.

"Okay, Ralph, maybe I'll stop by there. I appreciate the call."

"My pleasure. Sure hope you can see your way clear to helpin' him out. He's quite a feisty old man."

"Is he now?"

"Sure. We all love Dub. He's a character."

"I wouldn't know."

I dialed Felicia's number at the office. She couldn't talk long, but she insisted I go see my old man. If he's got a mental condition, Alzheimer's disease or something, maybe we could help him, she said. Either way, bring him home for dinner, she ordered.

"What if I kill him? Do you want me to bring home the body?"

"You're not going to kill him," she said. "Mind your manners. He's an old man."

"That's not my fault."

"Bubba—" Felicia has a stern way of saying my name that causes me to instantly obey. This was one of those times.

"Okay, okay. I'll go see him. But I'd like to point out that

William J. Pool is probably finding that Johnson kid while I'm messing around with this."

"Maybe this is more important."

"I doubt it."

SIX

*T*he Terminal Inn earned its name: It looks like the end of the line, the last stop you'll ever make. It's a flat-roofed, one-story Roach Motel of a place that caters to truckers and the hookers who service them. Lots of motels have sprouted up around the giant truck plaza and they're the usual mélange of Spanish mission and aluminum contemporary and even one yellow Alpine-looking eyesore. But none could match the Terminal Inn's paint-peeling, roof-dipping, prefab decrepitude.

I swung around the truck stop's ocean of asphalt. It was afloat with Macks and Kenworths and Peterbilts and Freightliners. Somewhere out there was parked Dub's livelihood, his ticket out of my life.

By the time I arrived at the motel, I'd worked myself into an emotional froth, thinking about Dub and how he'd deserted Mama and me. How dare the bastard show up now, when *he* needs somebody! I needed him all those years, and I got zip.

It's hard for a boy to grow up without a father. Certain skills are passed on from man to man. Fishing. Spitting between one's teeth. Cursing. Knowing the difference between confidence and arrogance, between honor and foolhardiness. I had to learn those lessons the same way I'd learned about sex—on the street corners of Nazareth, Mississippi. And the information often was just as unreliable.

I don't mean to sound maudlin, but you lose something else, too, when a parent runs away. You lose self-esteem, the notion that you're loved. Mama did what she could, but I didn't feel complete until Felicia Quattlebaum bustled into my life and conceded that she loved me, no matter how much of a goof I can be.

I harbored a lot of ill will toward Dub all those years, and I'm not sure I knew how much it had festered until I pulled into the potholed parking lot of the Terminal Inn. My teeth were clenched so tightly my jaws ached. My hands gripped the steering wheel like it was a lifeline. I was afraid to look in the mirror, but I could feel the cramp of a scowl on my face, squinched so tight I saw spots before my eyes. Hardly the expression one wants to carry to a reunion with long-lost relations, but I seemed incapable of changing it.

I stalked to the door of room 120, and gave it a good pounding.

The door swung open and I looked into my father's brown eyes for the first time in twenty-eight years. It was like being punched in the gut.

I recognized him immediately, though the years hadn't been kind to him and my perspective had changed considerably. For one thing, I was about four inches taller than him now, so I was looking down into his hound-dog eyes. For another, all those years in a truck seat had changed his shape. Dub always had been a tough, wiry guy. Now he had a buzzard neck, and gravity had moved much of him to the waist and hip areas. He resembled a withered pear. He wore a long-sleeve plaid shirt and threadbare jeans and round-toed work-boots that looked as if he'd had them since I was a boy.

"What do you want?" he demanded when I just stood

there like an oaf, and I thought, *Here we go with that question again.* But how to answer it? I want revenge? I want all those years back? I want to get one good look at you, then get the hell out of here? None of those seemed to work, since he clearly didn't recognize me.

"You, uh, you're Wilton Mabry Sr.?" I managed.

"Everybody calls me Dub." The reply was automatic. There was still no recognition in his eyes as he squinted up at me from under a once-yellow gimme cap that said CAT on the front of it.

"My name's Wilton Mabry, too," I said. "But everybody calls me Bubba."

He blinked at me a couple of times. Slowly.

"Bubba Mabry?" he said finally, rolling the words on his tongue as if he could taste them. "Then you must be my son."

"I'm afraid that's right."

His face creased into a grin, displaying tobacco-stained teeth.

"Well, hell," he said. "What do you know about that?"

He didn't seem to know how to take it. I knew exactly how he felt.

"Unless you've come here to punch my lights out," he ventured, "I reckon you should come on in."

Funny he should mention a punch. But Felicia was right. He was a senior citizen. I'd been reared to respect my elders. All I could do was nod somberly and enter.

Empty Budweiser cans crowded the top of the dresser, and dirty shirts and underwear were strewn about the floor. The room had that old man smell of hair oil and mentholatum and papery skin. A talk show flashed on the TV screen, but the sound was off. Bleached-blonde women silently screamed at each over some familial wrong. It occurred to me that my long-lost father and I were perfect candidates for Oprah.

"Sit down," he offered, and I took the one armchair. Dub perched on the end of the unmade bed, directly across from me and maybe four feet away.

Silence weighed on us for a minute or two. I didn't know where to begin, and Dub seemed satisfied to just stare at me. Getting studied made me sit up straighter.

"Well, sir," he said finally, "it's been a long time."

He looked down at the floor when he said it. It knocked some of the bluster right out of me.

"Yes, it has," I said quietly. "Twenty-eight years."

"So that makes you what? About forty-five?"

"What? No. I'm thirty-seven."

"That's right. We had you when I was twenty years old. And I'm fifty-five now."

I blinked rapidly. I'm no math whiz, but anybody could tell that didn't add up. He was twenty-seven when I was born, which would make him, oh, sixty-four. I cocked an eyebrow to question his addition, but he just stared at me with blank eyes. Uh-oh.

"I was nine when you left," I said. "I'm thirty-seven now. That makes twenty-eight years."

Christ, I didn't come here to lecture the old fool on mathematics. I felt my patience ebbing away, and changed the subject.

"You're living here now?"

He looked around the room as if he'd never seen it before.

"No, I live on the road. Always have. Even when I still had you and your mama back in Mississippi."

"Where's your truck?"

"Over at the terminal. I was feeling poorly yesterday, so I parked it and rented this room."

One look at the room told me he'd been there longer than a day. I'd lived in cheap motels for years. I knew what they looked like after someone's been staying there a while. Not homey, exactly, but used.

"I got a call from a friend of yours," I said. "Ralph Upshaw?"

"I don't know any Ralph Upshaw." Belligerence crept into his tone. He didn't like my questioning his math, and he didn't like these other questions either.

"He said he knows you."

"Hell, boy, I know who I know and who I don't. I been on the road for sixty years. I know everybody, and there's no driver named Ralph Upshaw."

Well, now. He certainly hadn't been "on the road" for sixty years, no matter what age he might be claiming. And I hadn't said anything about Ralph Upshaw being a truck driver, so he'd jumped to that conclusion on his own. Was he hiding something? Or, as Ralph had said, was he losing his marbles?

"Anyhow," I said, trying for forebearance, "this Ralph—whoever he is—said you were having some health problems."

"I'm fit as a fiddle."

He fished a plug of Day's Work tobacco from his pocket and wagged it at me.

"Ever since I gave up cigarettes in 1972 and took up this shit here, I've been healthy as a horse."

He produced a penknife from his pocket, which I eyed carefully. He opened it and cut a corner off the plug. He stuffed the tobacco in his mouth, and chewed thoughtfully. It looked like he was working a cud.

"Yum," he said through a mouthful of spit. "Hand me that can over there, wouldya?"

He pointed at a Campbell's soup can, an old-fashioned one like Andy Warhol painted, that was sitting beside my chair. I lifted it and it sloshed, and I didn't dare look inside before I handed it over. He drew up a big wad of brown juice and spat it into the can.

He looked me over, as if he'd just remembered I was sitting there across from him, and said, "So you're how my son turned out."

At least that much of his mental faculties seemed to be functioning. He remembered my introduction, and it had been a long ten minutes ago.

"Yessir."

"So what do you do with yourself? You a farmer?"

I look less like a farmer than anyone I can imagine. I glanced down at my clothes. The usual stuff. A polo shirt, jeans, sneakers. A city boy all the way. I blamed the new coat Felicia bought me. They call them barn coats for a reason.

"No, I'm a private investigator."

"A what?"

"A detective. I track down things for people."

He squinted at me, tightening the network of wrinkles around his eyes. I could imagine him peering through a windshield, scrunching his eyes against the sunshine and the monotony of the road. He spat into the can before asking his next question.

"Is that what people would call an 'honorable profession'?"

I took a deep breath before I said, "It's not driving a truck, but it's a living."

He pressed his lips together and studied about it. Then something dawned in his face.

"You got any kids of your own?"

"No." The answer came too quickly and with an edge of what sounded like panic. I wondered about that. "I just got married about six months ago."

"Is that a fact? How's married life?"

"Fine, so far."

"It's early yet."

"I think this is one of those marriages that will last forever," I said pointedly, but he didn't rise to the bait.

"How long you been here in Albuquerque?"

"Eighteen years," I said. "It's home to me now."

"Must be nice to have someplace to call home," he said wistfully, and I felt anger roil up within me again. He'd had a perfectly fine home until he let Jesus run him off.

"I've been living out of my truck so long, everyplace seems pretty much the same to me," he said. "I always liked Albuquerque, though. I love that Mexican food, those hot peppers, but it gives me gas like the Hindenburg."

I winced at this little revelation, but he just spat into his can again.

"You have to think about these things when you're drivin' a truck," he advised. "Particularly in cold weather. Don't want to roll the windows down unless you just have to."

I scrambled for another topic.

"Look," I blurted, "this Ralph who called me, told me where you were, said you were having mental problems."

"Mental? There's nothing wrong with my mind. I told you, I'm pretty spry for a man who's nearly eighty years old."

"So you're not having any trouble remembering things?"

He spat a long stream into the can.

"Try me."

"Well, for instance, you know your Social Security number?"

"Never could remember that. Try something else."

"What's your middle name?"

"Aw, now, that's a trick question. Ain't got no middle name. Everybody calls me Dub 'cause Wilton begins with a 'W,' you know."

I tried to come up with something else.

"You remember my mama's name?"

His eyes misted up, but he didn't blink. He stared at me like I was a bad memory.

"Her name's Eloise, and she's about the sweetest woman who ever lived."

He looked as if he meant it. The tears in his eyes made something snap inside of me, and I felt my resentment and rage trickle away.

We both displayed an inordinate interest in the ratty carpet for a time before I resumed my interrogation.

"You been having any problems out on the road?"

Dub looked up sharply.

"Is that what this Ralph Upshaw-I-never-heard-of told you?"

"No. He said he was worried—"

"I'll have you know I have a perfect safety record."

"Really?"

"Well, not exactly perfect, but nothing that's ever been my fault. No 'driver error' here, nosirree. But there are Acts of God. Weather, shit like that. You drive hundreds of thousands of miles every year, the odds are against you."

Somehow, I'd impugned his honor. Question his sanity, apparently that's okay. Question his driving record, and he's ready to duke it out.

"You said earlier you'd stopped in here because you were feeling ill. Remember that?"

"I tell you, I'm right as rain. I don't want anyone—even you—coming around here and suggestin' I'm not fit to drive my truck. I won't stand for it."

His eyes blazed, and some primal memory stirred inside me. Dub scolding me when I was a tad, trying to contain his anger over something I'd broken or spilled. He'd changed in many ways—and so had I—but those brown eyes were just as I remembered.

"I wouldn't dream of telling you to stay off the road."

Dub harrumphed and spat, his point made.

"I just got this phone call," I said, "and the guy sounded worried."

"I never heard of no Ralph Upshaw."

"So you said."

"Don't matter anyhow," he said. "However it happened, I'm glad you showed up. I'd wondered how you turned out."

I sat up straighter, trying to look as if I'd turned out all right, and smiled.

"Dub, what would you say to coming home with me for supper?"

His face split into a grin, and a little tobacco juice leaked out the corner of his mouth.

"That's right neighborly, Bubba. Sure the little woman won't mind?"

"It was her idea."

"Ain't that sweet?"

"Get your coat and we'll go. But let me give you a word of advice: Don't call Felicia 'the little woman.' Not if you want to keep your teeth."

He cackled. "She's tough, huh?"

"Tougher than me, that's for sure."

SEVEN

Mighty fine truck you got here."

Dub patted the Ram's dusty dash, then brushed his hand clean on the knee of his jeans. I spend a lot of time inside the cab of my big red truck, working, and the interior tends to look like Dub's motel room.

"Thanks," I said. "It's a little flashy for surveillance work, but I like it. It was a gift from a client."

"That a fact?" Dub looked all around the truck again, sizing it up. "Helluva gift. This private investigator business might be all right after all."

I gave him a brief version of how the late publisher of the *Gazette* had left me the shiny truck in her will.

"You must've done all right by her," Dub said when I was done.

"Well, I didn't exactly solve the case," I muttered. "In fact, all I brought her was bad news. But she appreciated it anyway."

"Must've been one helluva woman."

"She was."

We stopped at a red light at Menaul and University, right next to the huge truck stop, and a big rig pulled alongside us, its engines rumbling. The truck had mud flaps that said JESUS CARRIES MY LOAD. Dub rolled down his window to wave at the driver high above us, but the driver didn't see him.

"Guess he don't recognize me 'cause I ain't in my rig," Dub said cheerily. "It's funny. I know all these old boys, but we recognize each other more by our CB handles or the color of our cabs than by faces."

I wondered about a lifestyle of constant motion. Truckers are modern gypsies, speaking their own language and having their own secrets. My life was constant sitting still, watching and waiting. But both Dub and I spent a lot of time in our trucks.

I followed University Boulevard's rolling hills south until I came to Central Avenue, my turf, and turned east to pass in front of UNM. Usually, you can count on lots of lovely coeds crossing the street or parading along near the university, a sight that can renew your faith in the beauty and innocence of humankind. But it was breezy and cold at dusk, and the few pedestrians we saw were bundled up and hurrying to get indoors. Dub didn't have much to say for himself, just riding quietly in the passenger seat, taking in the sights. Past UNM, I turned north into a residential area and wound through the back streets until I pulled up in front of the house I share with Felicia.

"This is it, huh?" Dub said as he studied the cottage through the windshield. "Real nice neighborhood. Quiet, I'll bet."

"Yep."

"Your house stucco?"

"No, that's brick." As any fool could tell from three blocks away.

"Good. I don't trust stucco. You only see that shit out

here in the desert. Back in the South, the damp will turn it into cottage cheese."

"It's real common here."

"You know what stucco is, don't you?"

I opened my mouth to explain about concrete mixtures and the chicken wire that holds it in place, but he wasn't looking for an answer.

"Stuck-o's what you get when you step in gummo."

His laugh reminded me of an ailing rooster. I smiled politely.

"That's Felicia's car," I said. "So she's home. Probably already cooking supper."

"A woman's place is in the kitchen," Dub declared.

"I'd keep that to myself, too, if I were you. Felicia's a newspaper reporter. She's only home now because you're coming for dinner."

"Sounds like you picked a winner there, son. She brings home the bacon and she can cook it, too."

I grimaced. If Dub spouted this old-man conservativism around Felicia, she might smack him with a skillet. Might be just what he needed to put his mind back on track. Maybe I'd even suggest it.

We let ourselves in the front door, and I resisted the urge to do my usual Desi Arnaz impersonation: "Hon-eee, I'm ho-ome." We trundled through the littered living room and straight back to the kitchen, where Felicia stood over the stove, a wooden spoon in one hand and a cigarette in the other.

She turned from the stove when she heard us tromp into the room, and she gave Dub the once-over. He'd slipped on an old denim vest lined with soiled shearling before we left the motel, and it did nothing to improve his appearance. A good two inches of plaid belly peeked out between the bottom of the vest and the dipping waistline of his jeans.

"You must be Bubba's dad. I see the resemblance."

I didn't see it at all.

"Call me Dub," he said, extending a hand. "Everybody does."

"Okay, Dub. I'm pleased to meet you."

"You're just pretty as you can be, ain't you?"

I squinted at Felicia, awaiting some outburst, but she giggled and—omigod—blushed before turning back to the stove.

"I see where Bubba gets his southern charm," she said.

I wanted to scream. Felicia was supposed to be immune to flattery, for cripe's sake. It's part of her newshound nature that she questions everything she hears, up to and including compliments. Somebody tries to polish her apple, she suspects a worm.

I closed in on her, leaned over to give her a hello kiss.

"You don't have to be nice unless you just want to," I muttered.

"Don't be silly, Bubba. He seems sweet."

Wait until she gets a load of him spewing tobacco phlegm into a soup can.

Dub kept his distance, standing across the kitchen, his hands behind his back, rocking from heel to toe and humming absently.

"How's it going?" Felicia whispered.

"I don't know. And that's the truth."

"You can't tell?"

"Never been in a situation like this before."

"Can't be any weirder than my parents," she whispered, which wasn't even true. Felicia's parents are fine people, upstanding citizens, and they live far away in Indiana, which is about the best thing a newlywed can hope for.

I turned from her, back to the old man who was never my "old man" the way other kids talked about their dads.

"Dub," I said, feeling awkward; I couldn't bring myself to call him by any of those endearments—Dad, Daddy, Father, Papa—"could I offer you something to drink?"

"Beer!"

He shouted the word, a childish contentiousness in his

voice, and I looked at him sharply, trying to discern whether his brain had slipped a cog again. He didn't *look* any different, but the tone of voice and the way he stared into space past me gave me the creeps. I sure hoped there was some beer in the fridge.

One last bottle of Heineken sat on the shelf, its green glass glinting.

"Oops, last one," I said cheerfully, and handed him the bottle.

"This is Kraut beer!"

"It's Dutch."

"Same thing! Don't you have any American beer?"

"No, that's the last one."

Dub grumbled, but he used the opener I handed him and popped the top. He took a slug, which made his eyes water.

"Kraut beer."

"Dutch."

"Not bad, though. I'll have to say a prayer tonight, and ask God to forgive me for drinking it."

This was the second time Dub had mentioned God, and it would be fine by me if it was the last. I didn't need two parents lost to the Jesus juggernaut.

"Dub," Felicia called from the stove, where she'd returned to tending her steaming pots. "Do you like pesto?"

"Presto?"

"Pesto. On pasta."

Dub blinked at me.

"What the hell is she talking about?"

"Pesto sauce," I offered.

"Never heard of it."

"You'll like it," she said. "It's garlicky."

Jeez, don't get him started on the internal combustion thing again.

"Does it go good with this Kraut beer?"

Felicia giggled. "You bet."

Well, wasn't this just the picture of domestic bliss? Slap a mole on my cheek and call me John-Boy. Good night, Grandpa! Try not to belch that Kraut beer too much! Good night, Felicia Ann! Try not to be taken in by aging country boys! Good night Bubba-Boy! Try to sleep tonight, knowing your long-lost father has returned and is making goo-goo eyes at your wife. Good night, suckers all!

The meal was splendid, of course. Felicia can really cook when she sets her mind to it, which happens as often as a lunar eclipse. We had the pasta with pesto, some crusty sourdough she'd picked up at Fred's Bread and Bagel especially for the occasion, a salad that Dub didn't touch, and iced tea. Felicia was flushed with her triumph, Dub was complimentary and kind, and I felt like I'd eaten a hot cannonball.

Dub talked throughout the meal, and seemed to be back on track. He spent most of his attention on Felicia, who ate it up faster than the buttered bullshit that it was. It occurred to me that this was the way Dub had spent his life, stopping the truck long enough to have a hot meal served up to him. No wonder he was a hit with Felicia. He'd spent thirty years practicing on truck stop waitresses. This thought didn't improve my digestion.

Then we were finished and plates were cleared and it was time to move to the living room for after-dinner chat and Rolaids.

"You sure you don't have another one of them Kraut beers in here?" Dub asked, peering around the corner into the kitchen, where Felicia and I were stacking the dirty plates.

"No, that was the last one," I said. "How about another glass of tea?"

"Bubba, take him to the store so he can buy some beer."

"What?"

"Run him over to the 7-Eleven. They have American beer there."

Felicia grinned slyly at Dub, who hooted. I didn't like this one bit.

Don't get me wrong. I didn't mind driving the old coot

over to the 7-Eleven so he could further putrefy his liver, even if it was after nine o'clock. It was the way Felicia and Dub were cozying up that irked me. I didn't want her to get too attached to him. This was one stray that was going back to the pound, just as soon as I could figure out a polite way to send him.

Despite what Ralph Upshaw had said, Dub didn't seem any wackier than any other geezer. A little problem with numbers, not much in the way of social skills, but no hard evidence of Alzheimer's or insanity. Hell, what did I know? Maybe he'd always been this way.

So I figured, I'd drive him to the convenience store, let him get some beer, take him back to the Terminal Inn. Then we could go our separate ways.

It's funny how wrong I can be sometimes.

EIGHT

See, Dub," I said, after we were in the truck, "I really don't have a lot of time to get reacquainted right now. I'm in the middle of a big case."

"That so? What are you doing?"

I didn't want to explain the whole thing to him, so I said, "I'm in a race of sorts against another private eye. Whoever wins gets a big payoff."

"Strange way to do business."

"It's different, that's for sure."

"But I guess I've seen similar things in the trucking industry. Companies are always after the drivers who'll deliver their loads fastest, even if it means they're popping wide-awake pills the whole time and putting folks in danger."

A steady diet of uppers over the years might explain what was wrong with Dub's brain. Assuming something was wrong. I kept telling myself he seemed fine and it was none of my business anyway.

The 7-Eleven nearest my house sits on Central Avenue

between a couple of the low-rent motels that shine their ancient neon on old Route 66. Whenever my new life starts getting to me and I need a reminder of the weirdness and danger of the red-light district they call the Cruise, I just pop over to the convenience store. Let a few winos hit on me for money. Maybe get propositioned by a hooker. Step over the occasional pool of blood in the parking lot. Pretty quick, I'm ready to go back to my white-bread lifestyle with Felicia.

Since I'm a private eye, a lot my business hinges on the no-tell motels. I make a point of keeping in touch with some of my old buddies on the Cruise in hopes it'll generate some casework. It's a good excuse to drop in at Frank's Tavern and knock back a few beers.

The city's after the old motels again. Periodic crusades aim at eliminating prostitution and drug dealing from the old firetraps that once were the city's lifeblood, back when motorists in the great westward migration chugged right through the middle of town instead of zipping by on the freeways. The latest crusade, mounted by the mayor and the City Council, targets the motel owners. They've been warned that if they're caught hosting hookers and dopers, the city will go to court to shut the motels down as public nuisances. And then the hookers and dopers will have nowhere to live, and they'll try to move into the nicer neighborhoods. That'll start some other kind of crusade.

Taking the owners to court will never work anyway. A judge won't shut down a place of business just because the owner unwittingly rented rooms to the wrong clientele. And you can bet your ass the owner will say it happened unwittingly; even if the junkie who rented the room had a syringe hanging out of his arm when he picked up his key. All this strategy will accomplish is putting more money in the pockets of lawyers.

And if they did succeed in getting rid of the colorful old motels? What would they put in their place? More strip malls?

Dub tried to get me to reveal more details of my case as

we pulled into the 7-Eleven's well-lighted parking lot, but I put him off, telling him it was confidential. I didn't want the old cuss knowing too much about my life and my business. I didn't want him to get any ideas about staying in Albuquerque and helping me out. I had all I could handle, trying to defeat William J. Pool, and I didn't need Dub bird-dogging me.

I parked right in front of the store's door, the safest bet in this neighborhood, and told Dub I'd wait for him in the truck.

"Okey-dokey, cowpokey."

He swung down from the Ram and sauntered inside. The clerks are required to greet everyone who enters, part of the company's plan for reducing robberies. Their theory is that a robber will be put off if that little bit of human contact is made right away. I don't know much about psychology, but I doubt a forced "hello" is going to dissuade anybody who's desperate enough to hit a convenience store.

I saw the lonely clerk behind the counter greet Dub, and my old man waved in reply and marched straight back to the cooler where they keep the beer.

I recognized the clerk. I mean, I didn't know him personally, but he'd waited on me in the past. Like a lot of the motel owners, he was from India. He had dark skin and straight black hair and wily eyes, and the standard 7-Eleven red jersey did nothing to make him look less foreign. Seemed to me I remembered the clerk's name badge read "Madesh" or something like that. Could've been "Radish" for all I knew.

I watched through the store's glass front while Dub hefted a twelve-pack of Bud from the cooler and walked toward the counter with it. Madesh, or whatever his name was, stepped up to the register, ready to ring up the sale, but Dub sailed right past him.

I saw Madesh's white teeth flash as he shouted after Dub, but Dub kept walking. He reached the door before Madesh shouted again, but then he turned and I inhaled deeply to sigh in relief that the old man had caught himself and would now pay for his purchase.

Instead, Dub reached up under his vest to the back of his belt and pulled out a long-barreled chrome revolver. What the hell?

Madesh might be new to the United States, but he knew a Colt when he saw one. His eyes were Ping-Pong balls in his dark face and he threw himself to the floor behind the counter so quickly it looked as if he'd disappeared.

Dub pushed his way out the door, laughing his ass off.

I'd frozen in surprise, but the thaw came quickly, and I launched myself out of the truck.

"You see the way that sucker hit the dirt?" Dub called, guffawing.

He was tucking the pistol back into his belt, which I took as a good sign, and I hurried into the store past him.

"Are you all right?" I called to the clerk. He still hadn't reappeared above the countertop, and it occurred to me he might rise with a shotgun in his hands. But he answered from his post on the floor.

"Is he gone? The robber?"

"Yeah, yeah. Get up from there."

I've never been so embarrassed in my life, and I've had lots of practice.

The clerk clambered to his feet and I saw his name tag said "Vedesh," so I'd been close. He looked around cautiously, saw Dub climbing into my truck, and turned back to me, alarmed.

"It's okay. That old man's crazy, but he won't shoot any-body."

Vedesh's words tumbled forth like spilled marbles.

"The old man, he came into the store and he got his beer and he did not give me the money. I shouted for him, 'Meester, you must pay.' Then he turned and pulled out the biggest pistol I have ever seen. 'I am not paying for anything,' he said. And I am not one to argue such a point—"

69

"Calm down, will you? I saw the whole thing. He's crazy, I tell you. But I didn't know he had a gun on him. I'll pay for the beer."

"I am calling the police now."

"No, no, don't do that. I'll make it right."

"This old man, he cannot point guns at people—"

"I know. I'll take care of it. Look, here's ten bucks for the beer. That oughta cover it, right?"

"It is not just the beer. He gave me an awful fright, awful. I cannot just let you walk away from this—"

"Okay, I get it. Look, here's a twenty for you. Pain and suffering and all that. Let's forget the whole thing."

He looked down at the twenty in his hand and back up at me, and his eyes went sly. I know that expression. I've seen it often enough on the motel owners' faces, usually when I'm trying to pump them for information.

"That's all I've got on me."

I spread my wallet so he could see the empty inside.

"That'll have to do, okay?" I was pleading now, but what difference did it make at this point? Better to beg a little than to bail Dub out of the slammer. "We're square?"

"I recognize you, do I not?"

I could see where this was going. I'd feed this guy twenties for the rest of my life. Or find a different convenience store for my late-night munchies.

"I'm a regular customer. I'll keep bringing my business here."

"But not the old man; you will not bring him here again?"

"You can count on it."

The clerk nodded and stuffed my money in his pocket. I noticed the ten for the beer went in there with the twenty.

"I'm sorry. Really. Just forget the whole thing."

"It will be hard not to remember that big gun."

"I can see that. But don't call the cops, okay? I'll get him settled down and take the gun away from him. Deal?"

He nodded some more, and I got out of there, my face burning.

Dub sat in the passenger seat, slugging down a Bud.

"What the hell do you think you're doing?" It was the calmest reaction I could muster.

"Drinking a good American beer. What's it look like?"

"You just committed armed robbery!"

"What? What are you talking about, boy?"

"The beer. The gun."

"What gun?"

I opened my mouth to argue further, but his brown eyes were empty.

I cranked up the Ram and left before the clerk got ideas about writing down the license plate number. I needed to talk to Felicia. I needed help sorting this out. I needed this crazy old man in my life like I needed a bleeding ulcer. Another incident like this, and I'd have both.

NINE

Felicia had finished in the kitchen by the time we got home. She was curled up on the sofa, a *New Yorker* magazine in her lap and a Virginia Slims polluting the air around her head. She looked a little surprised that I'd returned with Dub in tow. I hadn't told her I'd planned to deposit him back at the Terminal Inn, but she usually knows what I'm thinking.

"Hi, Dub," she called, looking right past me. "I see you got some American beer."

"That's right, honey-pie. Nothing beats a Bud."

To illustrate, he turned up a can and chugged its contents. I'm thinking, *Don't call my wife "honey-pie," you lizard.*

"What's the matter with you?" Felicia said to me. "You look like you've seen a ghost."

"I saw something all right." I jerked my head toward Dub, but Felicia just looked puzzled and Dub didn't seem to notice a thing.

"I need to see you in the kitchen for a second," I said to Felicia. I went that direction without waiting to see whether she followed, but I heard her behind me, telling Dub to make himself at home. My teeth ground together so hard, I thought they'd turn to powder.

"Okay, what happened?" she said as she followed me around the corner. "Did you two have words?"

How to explain it? I could see Felicia was ready to blame me for whatever had gone wrong. I grasped her elbow and steered her farther into the kitchen, out of Dub's earshot.

"He tried to knock over the 7-Eleven."

"What?"

"He walked out of the store without paying. When the clerk called him on it, he pulled this big hogleg out from underneath his vest and aimed it at him."

"You're kidding, right?"

"Do I look like I'm kidding?"

"No, but sometimes it's hard to tell with you."

This I know to be true. My face often lets me down when I try to be funny. It's been hangdog too long to learn new tricks.

"It's no joke. I about wet my pants when I saw that gun."

She giggled at that. I still wasn't trying to be funny.

"There's something wrong with his brain," I said. "He doesn't remember doing it."

"Really?"

"He just stared at me. He said, 'What gun?' "

She glanced back over her shoulder to make sure Dub hadn't wandered into the kitchen behind her.

"Is he still armed?"

"Yes. And I'm not too crazy about that either."

"Well, go in there and make him hand it over."

"The gun?"

"Yes, the gun. We can't have him going around pointing pistols at people."

"Um. I'm not so sure that's a good idea."

"Oh, go on. It's not like he'd shoot his own son."

"Tell that to Marvin Gaye."

She arched an eyebrow at me.

"Look, our father-son relationship isn't that tight. Until today, he probably hadn't given me a thought in twenty-eight years."

"Oh, never mind. I'll go get it from him."

She turned to go back to the living room, but I snagged her arm again and wheeled her around.

"Don't do that. I don't want him shooting you."

"He won't shoot me. He likes me."

True, he seemed to have taken to Felicia a lot more than to me. But he was a veteran flirt, that much was clear. And Felicia didn't haul around the familial baggage that I couldn't disguise.

"I'll do it," I said. "Just give me some time. Maybe we should offer to let him sleep here, and I'll get the gun away from him after he's out cold."

Felicia nodded approvingly, and we marched back into the living room to carry out our new plan.

Dub didn't seem to have missed us. He was sucking on another Bud and flipping through the *New Yorker,* snorting at the cartoons. Two empty beer cans sat on the coffee table. The man could definitely put them away. *Maybe that's what's wrong with his brain,* I thought, *maybe it's pickled.*

Dub grabbed up one of the empties and spat tobacco juice into the little hole. Ugh. I'd hate to pick up the wrong can by mistake. Felicia seemed undisturbed by the sight of spit.

"Dub," she said brightly, "we were just talking about whether we could get you to spend the night here with us. That way, we could have breakfast together in the morning."

Damn, she's good. I forget sometimes that much of Felicia's professional life is built around back-slapping and glad-handing and outright deception. Dub tried to hem and haw, saying his stuff was back at his motel room and making other excuses, but he didn't stand a chance in the face of Felicia's persuasiveness.

"That's mighty sweet of you, girl," he said finally. "Guess

I could stand a little more home cooking. Don't want to get spoiled, though. I have to hit the road tomorrow."

He drained another can of beer—half the twelve-pack on the table seemed to be empty—and got unsteadily to his feet.

There's an old sofa bed in my office where I spend a lot of time stretched out, staring at the ceiling and waiting for the phone to ring. We unfolded it and Felicia found fresh linens for it.

"Just treat this room as if it were your own," Felicia said, and I felt my jaw clench again.

My office is my private sanctuary, and I hated to sacrifice it to Dub, even for one night. I made a show of locking the filing cabinet before we surrendered the room to him. I didn't want him prowling through my case files, trying to see whether I actually make a living as a private eye. Guess I didn't want him to know the truth, which is that Felicia is the breadwinner in this family. If it depended on my income, we'd be breadless.

We moved to the living room, where we whispered while we waited for Dub to fall asleep.

"There's a doctor I know who specializes in Alzheimer's," Felicia said. "I wrote about him once for the paper. Maybe he could take a look at Dub."

"Aw, I don't know, hon. It would probably take a week or more, just to get him an appointment."

I certainly didn't want Dub hanging around my life that long. I know it sounds selfish, but I had this big case to pursue. Having Dub show up had muddied the waters something fierce, and keeping him around longer would make it worse. Besides, I still wasn't sure how I felt about reestablishing contact with my dad. I'd gotten accustomed to having no family at all. Mama's so far away—both physically and figuratively—and I've lost track of all my country cousins and crazy aunts and whittling uncles back in the land of Faulkner and Elvis. Now here was Dub, barging into my life and requiring—as kinfolk usually do—help.

"You underestimate the power of the press," Felicia said.

"That was a pretty wonderful story I wrote about Dr. Graves. I think he can squeeze in a quick appointment for Dub."

"Dr. Graves?"

"Yeah? You know him?"

"No, but I think that's a pretty awful name for a sawbones."

"It could be worse. There's a dentist in town named Paine."

"Get out."

"Really. You want me to call Dr. Graves?"

"It's nearly ten o'clock."

"I'm sure I can get his home number."

"I doubt it. Doctors guard their home phone numbers like they're government secrets."

She smiled as she rose to her feet.

"See? You're underestimating me again."

I stayed on the sofa while Felicia used the phone in the kitchen to badger her way through God knows how many flacks and secretaries. I drank one of Dub's warming beers. I should've put the others in the fridge, but I didn't want to go in there while my sweetie was browbeating Graves's underlings. It takes the mystery out of the marriage to see her like that. I wasn't sure I wanted Dub's beer in my refrigerator anyway. He'd already taken over my office and my wife. A man has to draw the line somewhere.

Felicia breezed back into the room half an hour later, just as I tuned to some tits-and-ass TV program disguised as a fashion show. I quickly snapped off the set with the remote.

"Well?"

"Dub has an appointment with Dr. Graves at eleven o'clock tomorrow morning."

I was stunned. She's a wonder. If I had half as much determination and grit as Felicia, I could be the world's best private eye, more famous than, say, William J. Pool.

"But you'll be at work then," I moaned.

"So? You can take him."

"You know I hate doctor's offices."

Felicia gave me her stern look.

"Bubba, this is no time to be a baby. Your father needs you."

"I wish you'd stop calling him that."

"Your father? But he is, Bubba. Anyone could tell that, just by looking at the two of you. Why are you having so much trouble coming to grips with it?"

I shook my head.

"Lot of history there."

"I know that, but he's still your father. And he clearly needs help. It's your responsibility to help him."

"Oh, yeah? Where was he when I needed help? He got along fine without me all those years. I don't see why I have to drop everything to help him out now."

"I'm not asking you to drop everything. It's just a doctor's appointment."

"I know, but—"

"You think he'd go if you didn't take him?"

"No, but—"

"Then you have no choice, do you?"

"You could do it. He likes you."

"I can't, Bubba. I've got Meg Albatross hanging around my neck. I've got to take her to City Hall tomorrow and show her how to look up public records."

"Maybe we should get *her* to take Dub to the doctor."

Felicia smiled. "He'd probably like that."

"Okay, I'll take him," I said, "but I don't have to be happy about it."

"No, you don't. But it might be easier if you tried."

"I hate it when you make so much sense."

She came close and kissed me on the forehead.

"I know. Now why don't you sneak into your *father's* room and see if you can get that gun?"

"Think he's asleep?"

"Sounds like it."

I'd been so deep into my own misery, I hadn't been listening. Sure enough, I could hear Dub snoring away in my office. Either that, or he was using a buzz saw on my desk.

"Okay. You wait here."

I crossed the room and slipped open the office door. In the light that spilled through the door, I could see Dub flat on his back, his mouth open wide as a water basin, the snores emanating from deep within him. He had the blanket up to his chest, but I could see the straps of his old-fashioned T-shirt hanging loose around his bony shoulders. It was the first time I'd seen him without a cap, and he was nearly completely bald on top. The hair around his ears skewed in every direction. It seemed unpleasantly familiar, a little too much like what I see in the mirror every morning.

I tiptoed into the room, looking for the pistol, but Dub had made it easy. His clothes were piled in my chair, and the shiny revolver was on top of them. I picked it up like it was something hot and sneaked out again.

I showed the gun to Felicia. "Believe me now?"

"I always believed you. That story was too crazy to have been invented."

"Here. Take it."

Felicia put her hands behind her back like I was handing her a rattlesnake.

"I don't want it."

"You might need it. I've got to go out, and I'm not happy about leaving you here with Dub. If he gets up and starts roaming around, acting crazy, you might have to shoot him."

"I'm not gonna shoot him. Put that thing away."

I shrugged and walked the revolver into the kitchen, Felicia trailing behind me. I hid it away in a high cabinet, one Dub couldn't even reach unless he stood on a chair. It's the cabinet where we keep the electric wok and the Salad Shooter and the other crap we never actually use. Seemed a good place for a pistol.

"What did you mean, you're going out? It's bedtime."

"Only for us old fogies," I said. "This time of night, things are just getting hopping in the heavy-metal nightclub scene."

"You're going to a nightclub?"

Felicia knows I'd just as soon poke out my eyes as spend any time in a smoky, noisy dance bar. I don't dance, and I don't want to learn. I certainly don't want to do any slam-dancing, or whatever violent body-crashing they do at the heavy metal joints these days.

"I have to," I said. "It's the only lead I have on Richie Johnson."

I told her what Sgt. Horton Houghton had said about the late-night club called Pandemonium, and how the skinheads sometimes hung out there.

"Sounds dangerous," she said.

"Yeah, but it's all I've got to go on. I'll take my gun."

"It's illegal to carry firearms into bars in New Mexico."

"Yeah? It's illegal to stick up convenience stores, too, but we've already done that tonight. I thought I'd try something different."

Felicia shook her head, questioning my good judgment.

"Okay, Bubba, but you be careful. I'm going to bed."

"I'll be careful. You lock the bedroom door. I don't want Dub barging in, gun or no gun."

TEN

never would've found Pandemonium except for all the cars parked outside along First Street. The exterior of the old brewery was dark and filthy and blank, with no sign to indicate there might be a bar inside. That, I supposed, was part of the allure. People love feeling they're in on a secret.

I wandered the dark street for a few minutes, trying to figure how to enter the building, before I drifted around to the south end and saw a door. It was a loading dock, or had been at one time, and I imagined this was where the trucks were loaded with barrels back when the brewery was something other than a dusty concrete relic. A handful of people stood at the base of the steps that led up to the dock, smoking cigarettes, trying to look cool, which was tough in the dark.

A little light spilled from the dock every time a thick steel door opened up there, and I decided that must be the place. I bounded up the steps onto the loading dock, only to be greeted by a giant who was nearly as big as Sgt. Horton Houghton and twice as ugly. Despite the breath-fogging cold, the man wore a leather vest that left his beefy arms uncovered so we could all see the lovely tattoos of fire-breathing dragons and tribal zig-zags that covered them. He wore a walrus mustache, but his hair was clipped to within a half-inch of his scalp. Filthy jeans and boots completed his uniform, and he had an odor that suggested he didn't change often.

"Uh, hi. Pandemonium?"

He glared down at me, looking a little cross-eyed because his bulbous nose twisted to the side and it was hard for him to see around it.

Let me guess. He's going to say, "What do you want?"

Instead, he said nothing. He looked away, as if I didn't merit his attention.

"Does that mean I can go in?"

He turned back to me, and seemed mildly surprised that I still stood there.

"Never seen you before," he said, in a voice only slightly deeper than an oil well.

"I'm new."

He grunted, looked away again, scanning the lurkers down below for any sign of trouble. I could imagine this giant bouncer leaping down onto people from his post atop the loading dock. You wouldn't want to be on the receiving end of that.

"So is there a cover charge?"

I'd stopped by an automatic teller machine on my way to the nightclub, since Dub's fiasco at the 7-Eleven had taken all my cash. I expected to pay the usual five bucks to get in and maybe buy a couple of drinks while I got a feel for the place and asked around about Richie Johnson.

The giant looked me up and down a couple of times, taking in my sneakers, my jeans, the lines on my forehead.

"For you?"

"Yeah, for me. Who else?"

"For you," he said, "the cover is twenty bucks."

"What?"

"You heard me."

He turned away again, giving me time for that to soak in. Two kids who couldn't possibly have been twenty-one came tripping up the steps toward us. They were the kind of street urchins you see loitering along Central Avenue—pierced eyebrows, black fingernail polish, ratty clothes, and fluorescent hair. Geek chic. Punk fashion was invented so ugly kids could be popular, too.

The titanic bouncer waved them right in, not even flinching against the wave of noise that thundered out the door before it clanged shut again.

"Wait a minute," I said, and I couldn't keep the indignation out of my voice. "They go in free, but it costs me twenty bucks?"

The bouncer glanced my way and grunted, "They're regulars."

"How do you know?"

He looked me over again, snorted and grinned.

"I recognized them, Pops."

Pops? I'm not even forty years old, you freaking tub of lard. Frustrated, I dug out my wallet.

"Okay, here's a twenty. Can I go in now?"

He smiled, showing teeth that might've been brushed sometime during the Nixon administration.

"Did I say twenty? I meant thirty."

"Thirty bucks?! Just to get in?"

"Hey, you want to play with the kids," he rumbled, "it's gonna cost you."

"I'm just looking for somebody. I won't even be in there long."

"Thirty bucks."

"Jesus Christ, what a racket."

"You tryin' for forty?"

"No, no. Here, shit, take the thirty. Just let me inside."

He folded the money and stuffed it in his pocket. Then he grasped the heavy door and swung it open wide.

"Welcome to Pandemonium, Pops."

The wall of sound nearly rocked me off my feet. Granted, I know next to zip about the latest tunes, but I didn't see how this noise could qualify as music. It sounded as if someone was killing an electric guitar with a chain saw in the middle of a buffalo stampede.

My eyes had squinched shut at the explosion of noise, and I could barely pry them open enough to march inside past the Man Mountain, who grinned at me with his disgusting teeth. The thought that I amused him straightened my spine a little. But once the door slammed behind me, I stuck my fingers in my ears.

The door was at the top of a ramp, which I guessed was how they once rolled the beer barrels up to the loading dock. Along the left wall ran the expected bar, though this one had none of the hospitality of the elbow-rubbed mahogany I prefer. It was constructed of sharp-edged stainless steel and the front was covered only by a screen of chain-link fencing. At the far end of the huge room was a stage where spike-haired noise-makers were doing damage to perfectly good guitars and drums. Black speakers were stacked to the thirty-foot-high ceiling on either side of the stage.

Apparently, the speakers used all the building's electricity, because there was very little light in the place. A couple of factory-style lamps hung on chains above the bar, so the bartenders wouldn't mistake window cleaner for vodka. Red and blue spotlights illuminated the gyrating performers on the stage. Otherwise, the place was dark, except for a couple of ceiling spotlights that shot shafts through the dimness. The spotlights wandered the crowd jerkily, adding craziness to the chaos.

The dance floor was what I think they call a mosh pit. Nobody seemed to be dancing together, the old-fashioned way. Down in the darkness, people slammed into each other as they whirled. A fistfight seemed to be going full-bore to my right, but the spotlight operators were ignoring it, so it was hard to tell.

The "dancers" wore black clothes mostly, the ones who hadn't peeled off their shirts, and this just added to the sense of violent confusion. It was hard to tell where one person started and another left off. Except in the places where the spotlights struck, the whole dance floor seemed a tangled mess of disembodied heads and hands.

I didn't want to go down the ramp into that madness. It would be like plummeting into hell. But Richie Johnson wasn't going to come find me. I took a tentative step or two before someone crashed into me.

I threw my hands up to protect myself before I realized it was a girl. Her hair was dyed jet black and spiked out in all directions. Silver pierced her nose and her eyebrows and her black-inked lips. She surprised me by smiling about our collision.

"Isn't this great!" she shrieked over the noise. At least, I think that's what she said. Who could tell, really? She might've said, "Isn't this fate!" or "I have a snake!" I nodded at her and edged away. Someone bumped her from behind and she pressed up against my chest, close enough that I wondered whether it was accidental. She threw her head back and laughed maniacally, and I backed up some more, not wanting to tip over. Whoever fell to the ground in this joint was dead meat.

I moved into the thrashing crowd and tried to sidle around toward the bar. To survive this night, I needed booze in me.

Even at the edges, the crowd was a writhing mass, and nobody moved out of my way. Usually, you move too close to somebody, get in their bubble, and they'll relinquish passage. If they don't notice you, you can clear your throat or say, "Excuse me," and they'll give way. But this crowd seemed mesmerized by the band and they certainly couldn't hear me, so I resorted to something a little more personal.

If you make a fist with your hand, but leave your thumb

sticking out stiffly, it makes a pretty good tool. I punched the nearest guy in the ribs with my thumb, seeing if I could get a reaction, but he didn't even look at me. He just took a step back, his eyes fixed on the stage. I managed to take a step forward before the next bouncing dancer was in my way, so I gave her the thumb, too, and she yelped and hopped backward. Another step. I moved along the edge of the room by this method, goosing my way through the crowd until I reached the near end of the bar.

Some out-of-control mosher crashed into my back and I nearly fell before I caught myself on the steel bartop. I'm sure I made it clang, but I could hear nothing but the roar of the music.

Gripping the edge of the bar tightly, I scooted sideways as if pulling myself along a rope. About halfway down the thirty-foot-long bar, I managed to make eye contact with a bartender with a shaved head and a goatee. I held up a finger in the international sign for "I need a drink."

He looked at me quizzically, probably wondering how this old fart made it past the doorman. I shouted, "Bourbon!" at the top of my lungs, but he couldn't hear me. He turned toward the wall of bottles behind him and pointed at a quart of scotch, raising his eyebrows in question. I shook my head and pointed farther down the selection. He moved along, pointing and questioning, until we settled on a bottle of Jim Beam. He poured me a stiff one and held up four fingers. I gave him a five, wondering if they only hired deaf people to work here. Might as well. They'd be deaf before long anyway.

The bourbon went down smooth and quick, and it seemed to help a little. My nerves were badly shaken by the noise and the darkness and the flailing crowd. While I poured down the anesthetic, I scanned the crowd, trying to spot anyone who looked like Richie Johnson.

They *all* looked like him. Lots of shaved heads. Glittering nose rings and tattoos and black leather clothing apparently were de rigueur for both genders. It was hard to tell the girls from the boys.

Jeez, I don't get this fashion statement. I mean, I know they're young and rebellious and style crazy. But why would anyone want to look like some sort of mutant Nazi? And what's with all the piercings and tattoos? Is that supposed to show everyone that they're tough, that they're impervious to pain? I'd be more impressed if I could see somebody who looked impervious to fads. I sometimes imagine this whole generation in their old age, with their grandkids gathered round their knees, and the toddlers saying, "Tell us again about the time you got the tattoo, Granny."

I went through my rebellious period, too. I desperately wanted to be a hippie, which was difficult in a place like Nazareth, Mississippi. Longhairs often were taken out behind the football stadium and beaten senseless. And that was by their peers. You can imagine how the older generation of rednecks reacted. They sat around, just like I'm doing now, saying, "What's with these kids today? You can't tell the boys from the girls!"

I guess each generation has to go to further extremes to upset their jaded parents. Bring home a little pot these days, and Boomer Dad probably will help you smoke it. Grow your hair long, and he'll tell you his was longer back in the sixties. But shave your head and get your tongue pierced and, ooh, look at Dad now! He's having a coronary!

Youthful rebellion never worked for me. I had no parents to rebel against. Dub was long gone by the time I'd reached my teens, and Mama was so pitiful and removed, she barely noticed what I was wearing or how grungy my friends were. With nobody paying attention, rebellion sort of lost its appeal. I couldn't become a Jesus freak, because Mama already had that market cornered. And I couldn't run away, because then I would've been just like my worthless old man. Instead, I drank beer and hung around the pool hall and pretty much acted like a respectable—if shaggy—citizen until I took off for the air force. And then the drill sergeants took over, and rebellion was pretty much out of the question. You don't rebel in the military unless you really enjoy push-ups.

The bartender and I went through another round of hand signals that resulted in bourbon. I downed it quickly. I didn't expect to ever hear again, but at least with a snootful of booze I wouldn't mind so much.

Then the band stopped so abruptly that it's a wonder everyone in the place didn't get whiplash. I looked to the stage, but the band members weren't bowing or waiting for applause. They dropped their instruments to the floor and walked off, as if they couldn't care less whether anyone had enjoyed the performance. Just as well, I suppose, because several beer bottles shattered onto the stage as they departed.

The sudden absence of noise made my ears pop, as if I were adjusting to a change in altitude. Then I could make out that the crowd was roaring and applauding, most appreciative of the decibels that had assaulted them.

I needed to get moving now. The bar had been my life raft in the tossing sea of moshers, but now was my chance, while the crowd wasn't bouncing around like people being electrocuted, to search for Richie Johnson.

The club had no furniture, no tables and chairs for sitting and chatting and enjoying your drink. This was a place for dancing. Furniture would become missiles and weapons with this bunch. Without anywhere to sit, the dancers crowded the bar, shaking perspiration from their faces. Yuck. I moved toward the center of the room, away from the safety of the bar, rather than take a sweat shower.

And then I saw Richie Johnson. Simple as that. He and several other skinheads were clustered at the far side of the stage, slugging beers and cooling off. Even in this zoo of a crowd, they were easy to spot by their regimentation. The same boots, the same suspenders, their jeans cuffed just so. Their pale heads glowed. Some of them had removed their bomber jackets on the steamy dance floor and their bare arms were mottled with tattoos. The whole glowering crew was given plenty of room by the milling throng.

I knew Richie, and he knew me. Or, at least, he knew I was there for him. Our eyes met across the crowded room, and recognition slapped him in the face. I looked so out of place here, he must've guessed his father had sent me. He said something to the other skinheads, who turned to look my way. I didn't really want their full attention, but I had no choice. I couldn't let him get away. I waved, smiling. He shot me the finger and disappeared around the corner of the stage.

I followed, giving the other skinheads such a wide berth that Richie had plenty of time to split out a door that was behind the stage. I saw the door closing behind him, and took off running, weaving through the moshers like a halfback, trying to catch up and score.

I hesitated a second at the door. What if Richie stood on the other side of it, waiting to brain me?

The door swung inward, so I grasped the knob and pulled it toward me, staying back as far as my arm could reach. It was dark out there, though not much different from the interior of the bar, and I saw no one. I stepped out into the cold, and realized I was in an alley that separated the north end of the old brewery from the next building over. The buildings were tall and the alley was narrow. At one end, the railroad tracks were hard by the building, and an Amtrak overnighter was parked there, its silver sides gleaming in the moonlight.

The other end of the alley emptied onto First Street. The alley was empty, and I figured Richie had sprinted for the street, probably had his little Volkswagen parked out there somewhere.

I was turning to chase after him when the door to Pandemonium creaked open behind me.

ELEVEN

I knew what I would find before I turned around. Six skinheads stalked out the door toward me, shadowy figures except for their heads, which glinted in the light from the alley's one weak streetlight. They spread out, blocking the alley and closing in on me. The alley was open behind me, and I had a clear shot at reaching First Street. But one look at these young toughs told me I'd never make it. I'm not a fast runner. Even with those big freaking boots on, the skinheads could catch me from behind. And that would be bad, very bad.

I backpedaled a step or two, trying to keep out of lunging distance, and searched for something to distract them.

"Hi, fellas."

Oh, that was good, Bubba. That'll have them quivering in their boots. Why not offer to show them your recipe collection?

"I'm, uh, looking for a friend of yours. Richie Johnson? I think he just left, but I don't see him anywhere now."

My voice sounded funny in my own ears, sounded as if I

was talking underwater. The high decibel level inside the club had damaged my hearing, I was sure of it.

The skinheads tended to be of a uniform size, a few inches shorter than me and a good deal more muscular. The smallest was the one who'd stiffed me the day before in the student ghetto; I recognized the swastika on his neck. The tallest, who stood at the center of the pack, was uglier than a sack of assholes.

His head was shaved, of course, showing a twisted scar that ran from his naked brow up to the crown of his head. The scar was shaped like a question mark. It gave the impression of a cartoon figure, one who was wondering about something. He had wide cheekbones and a thick neck and rubbery lips that were clamped around a thin cigar.

He dressed the same as the others—open bomber jacket, cuffed jeans, boots, suspenders—but his clothes seemed to have a little more wear and tear, as if he was a veteran at doing whatever skinheads do. I had a feeling I was about to find out what they did, and I didn't like that at all.

"What do you want wit' Richie, Pops?"

Had Felicia embroidered "Pops" on my jacket when I wasn't looking?

The skinhead spoke with a British accent, which tipped me off to something Horton Houghton had told me.

"You must be Mayhem."

That caught him off guard. He paused a second, then turned to the others. "This bloke thinks 'e's smart, 'e does." Then he snatched the cigar from his lips and pointed its slimy end at me. "S'that right, mate? You're smart?"

I tried grinning at him, but it didn't take. "Oh, yeah, I'm a crackerjack."

" 'Ow do you know me?"

"You're famous, right?"

He sneered, exposing that form of dental construction that's peculiar to the British. He looked like he could eat pumpkin through a picket fence.

" 'Ear that, boys? I'm famous."

I put my hands on my hips, trying to keep cool. My hands wanted to dance around, and I thought it would be better if they stayed planted somewhere. Unfortunately, there was no way to nail my mouth shut.

"Oh, yeah," I said, "you're quite popular down at the police station. They've been looking all over for you."

That brought the scowl back to his face.

"You a bloody copper?"

Took me a second to sort that out. Where I'm from, a "copper" is a penny.

"No, I'm private. Name's Bubba Mabry. Richie's father hired me to find him."

Mayhem puffed out his chest some more.

"You're doin' a bang-up job so far."

"I could've chased him, I guess. But then I would've missed this opportunity for a pleasant visit with you boys."

Why can't I ever shut up?

"I'll show you fookin' pleasant."

He flung his cigar to the ground. Sparks swarmed the butt when it hit the asphalt.

"Now, now, Mr. Mayhem, no need to get bent outta shape. This can all be friendly."

He took a menacing step toward me, followed by the rest of the gang. I stepped backward, and thought maybe we could tango this way all the way to First Street. Maybe there would be a cop out there. And maybe I'd start shooting party streamers out my ears and farting "Hail to the Queen."

"Look, Mr. Mayhem. Could I call you May?"

He frowned at me, as if nobody had ever mocked him before.

"You do, and it'll be the last bloody thing you ever say."

I took another step backward. They followed. Any second he'd give the signal and they'd rush me in a storm of fists and boots.

"I don't want any trouble with you," I said. "I'm just trying to find Richie. Do you know where he lives?"

"I'm not tellin' you a bloody thing."

"I'll pay."

Mayhem's face twisted into even more of a scowl, though I hadn't thought that possible. He looked like his face might crack.

"You think we would 'and over our mate for money?"

It had seemed worth a try.

They advanced another step, and I backed up two. None of them seemed to be armed, but they had the advantage of numbers and apparently that had always worked for them before.

"Look, forget I asked," I said. "I'll be going now."

"I don't think so, mate."

He came at me purposefully, closing the little distance I'd maintained. The others were right at his heels, obedient pups that they were. My time had run out.

I reached inside my jacket and whipped out my Smith & Wesson .38, which had been waiting for just such an opportunity.

The skinheads braked quickly.

"Now, see," I said, "I didn't want things to go this way. But you're being rude, and I don't take kindly to that."

Most of the skinheads edged backward, as if a few feet would make a difference to a gun. But Mayhem stood his ground, his eyes shifting from me to my pistol and back again.

"I'll shove that pistol up your arse."

"No, I don't think so. Pulling the trigger is such an easy thing. I could click it six times before you took two steps."

"You fookin' pussy. Put down that gun and try to push me around."

I shook my head.

"Nope. You missed your chance to be polite. Now we'll talk on my terms."

I felt like Gary Cooper. Point the gun at them, make them talk, lord it over them a little.

"I'm not tellin' you a fookin' thing."

"Wrong answer. Where's Richie Johnson?"

"Fook you."

I let the gun barrel stray from him for a second, letting it wander the others in the gang to see if any of them were more intimidated. But they seemed more scared of Mayhem than of anything I might do to them, bullets included.

I pointed the gun at Mayhem and said, "Last chance."

He spat at the asphalt at his feet. He was careful to miss his boots.

We had a standoff. Mayhem wasn't coming any closer, but he gave no ground either. The others, despite their initial fear, seemed ready to follow him right down my gun barrel. And I didn't want to shoot anybody, no matter how much they might deserve it.

"Okay," I said finally. "We're not getting anywhere here. I'm just gonna back up now, go back to my truck. Anybody tries to follow me out of this alley gets ventilated. Clear?"

"You fookin' sod."

I never have understood that term. I mean, I suppose it has something to do with sodomy, but anytime I hear somebody say "sod," I think of green turf. We use a lot of sod in Albuquerque. It's the only way to approximate a lawn in the desert.

I kept backing up, ignoring the grumbles Mayhem sent my way. I made it to the mouth of the alley and began to turn away, but he had one more volley to deliver.

"This isn't finished, you bastard! We'll track you down and do you damage!"

TWELVE

I awoke Friday morning to the aroma of sizzling bacon. What is it about the scent of searing pig meat that makes salivary glands work overtime? I thought I'd drown before I could get untangled from the bedcovers.

I pulled on my robe and padded into the bathroom to brush my teeth and wet down my thinning hair. The bloodhound eyes staring back from the mirror made me think of Dub, and I wondered whether he was up and around yet, and whether he'd missed his pistol.

I hurried into the kitchen to find Dub sitting at the table, grinning like a possum as Felicia set a heaping, steaming plate in front of him. Bacon and eggs, biscuits and gravy. Damn. My old man gets the royal treatment. Most days, I'm lucky if Felicia takes time to scrape some toast. She never eats breakfast herself, greeting each day with only coffee and cigarettes.

I told Felicia good morning, and looked past her shoulder to see whether any food remained in the skillets. Some. Not as much as she'd served Dub, but it would certainly do.

"You sure were late last night," she said. "I didn't even hear you come in."

"Yeah. Well." I shot a glance Dub's way to show her I didn't want to discuss in front of him. "Breakfast, huh?"

Felicia was still in her fluffy robe and she had the warm glow of the overheated chef. She wiped her forehead with the back of her hand and pushed up her glasses.

"Just a little something I whipped up," she said. "Want some?"

"You bet."

I poured myself a cup of coffee and sat at the table while Felicia dished it up. Mm-hmm.

"Good morning, Dub," I offered. "How are you today?"

Dub swallowed mightily and said, "Fine, thanks to this pretty lady's cooking."

I grimaced.

"Did you bring in the paper yet, hon?" I called to Felicia.

"No, I've been busy slaving over this hot stove."

Oops.

"I'll get it."

I leaped up from the table and hotfooted it to the front door to fetch in the *Gazette*.

The sun was shining brightly, and the wind was still asleep, and it looked as if it could be one of those early spring days tourists mention in postcards to tweak the folks back home. The sidewalk was cold on my bare feet, though, and I was moving too quickly to fully enjoy the weather. I snatched up the newspaper and turned to go back inside. Then I saw something that would've made me fall off my shoes, if I'd been wearing any.

Someone had sprayed graffiti all over my house. And they hadn't even been creative about it. It was the same symbol over and over, high and low: a white circle slashed by a capital *A*.

"Shit."

I took a few steps across my winter-crunchy lawn and

looked around the side of the house. The graffiti went all the way down that direction, too. Whoever did this must've used three cans of spray paint.

What did I mean, whoever? I had a pretty good idea who, and it scared the hell out of me.

I hurried back inside, the newspaper under my arm, my bathrobe flapping around my knees. I skidded to a stop in the kitchen, where Felicia had joined Dub at the table and they were laughing about something. Probably something I'd done.

"What took you so long?" Felicia said to me. "The delivery boy throw it in the bushes again?"

I hate to bring bad news to Felicia. She doesn't always respond well in the face of stress. Whoever's standing closest may get both barrels of her frustration. It's usually me, but I'm learning to live with it.

I cleared my throat and said, "I've got some bad news."

"Yeah?" She still was smiling over whatever Dub had been saying, and it appeared she didn't take me seriously.

"Somebody sprayed paint all over the house."

"What?"

"Outside. Graffiti everywhere."

The smile vanished. Felicia turned red in the face and leaped up from the table. "Let me see."

She hurried past me toward the front door. I cast a longing look at my cooling breakfast, then followed her. Dub seemed perfectly happy sitting at the table, blinking at our consternation.

I joined Felicia in the front yard, where she stood with her fists on her hips, glaring at the house. The sidewalk was still cold. I hopped from one bare foot to the other.

"I can't believe this shit," my sweetie said, and I nodded in agreement, even though the evidence was right there before our eyes. "What have you done now, Bubba?"

"I got crossways with some skinheads last night," I muttered.

"I figured that much," she said. "That's why they tagged

our house with this."

I looked at the circled *A* symbols some more, wondering what she meant.

"That *A* stands for *Anarchy*. But you knew that, right?"

"Oh. Sure."

She squinted over at me, and I tried to look composed.

"What did you do last night? Give them our address?"

"No, but the leader of the pack, this guy they call Mayhem, said they'd track me down. Guess they did."

"Guess so." She looked plenty put out with me, but she turned her attention back to the graffiti before I could start making excuses. "That's brick. We'll never get that paint off there."

"That bad, huh?"

"Maybe. They've got those high-powered sprayers you can hire. That might take it off. But they cost a bundle."

"Maybe I can make Dick Johnson pay for it."

She gave me the eye again, as if questioning whether I've ever been able to make a client do anything. She had a point there.

Dub came trundling out the front door, going at his teeth with a toothpick, looking contented. I remembered my breakfast as if it were a long-lost friend.

He turned to see what we were staring at and pronounced his opinion: "Dang, that's a mess."

Thank you, Dub.

He looked up at me from beneath the bill of his cap.

"Looks like you pissed somebody off."

"Nicely put. Some bad boys are trying to send me a message."

"What'd you do? Tell 'em where you live?"

How come everyone assumes I'm an idiot? Whatever happened to innocent until proven stupid?

"No, I didn't tell them anything. They figured it out on their own. Of course, I'm in the phone book, so it couldn't have been too tough. Now they know where to find me when

97

they're ready to kick my ass."

Felicia stalked back into the house, shaking her head and muttering under her breath.

Dub went over to the nearest wall, reached up, and poked at the paint with his thumbnail.

"Yup, it's already dried. You got a big clean-up job to do."

The man had an innate grasp of the obvious.

"Come on, let's go inside. My feet are freezing."

I located Felicia in the bedroom, where she was throwing on clothes.

"I've got to get to work," she snapped. "I'll leave it up to you to hire somebody to remove that paint."

"Can we afford that right now?"

"No. But we can't just leave it. Every jerk in town will be over here adding his own tag. That's the way graffiti works. You give in a little, and they're swarming around your house like bees."

I'd thought of something else while I was looking for Felicia, and I decided to broach it now. She was already upset. What could a little more hurt?

"Maybe you'd better find another place to stay until this blows over."

"What?"

"The skinheads know where we live now. I wouldn't want something to happen to you while I'm off looking for Richie Johnson."

"I'm not going anywhere."

"But, hon, wouldn't it be a good idea if—"

"I'm not moving out! These bastards don't scare me."

"They sure as shit scare me. You should've seen them—"

"I don't care. I'm not going anywhere. They show up here while I'm around and I'll blow them off the lawn with Dub's pistol."

I put my finger to my lips and looked over my shoulder to make sure Dub hadn't sneaked up behind me.

"Don't mention that gun, okay? He doesn't seem to have missed it."

Felicia rolled her eyes and stepped into her flats.

"I don't have time for this. I've got a million things to do today."

"Me, too. I've got to call Dick Johnson and—"

"You've got one thing that absolutely must be done," she interrupted. "You've got to take your father to the doctor."

"But—"

"You want to run off and chase after your big case. And you can. But getting Dub to his appointment is the first order of business."

"But—"

"No more, Bubba. Just take care of it. I'm late for work. The doctor's name and address is on a piece of paper on the kitchen counter. Take care of it."

"Yes, dear."

She gave me a sour look, then snatched up her purse and her car keys and jangled toward the door. She waved good-bye as she passed Dub, who was sitting on the sofa with his boots up on the coffee table, watching *Good Morning, America* at top volume. Felicia turned to me for a parting shot.

"Call me once you're done with Dr. Graves. I'll want a full report."

I nodded rather than risk saying something and getting my head snapped off again.

She slammed the door behind her.

Dub looked up at me, grinning. "That girl's a firecracker, ain't she?"

"Oh, yeah. And I'm a match."

He sniggered at that, then fell silent again, entranced by the flickering TV screen. I shuffled off to the bedroom to dress, my breakfast now forgotten.

It had seemed like such a nice day, too.

THIRTEEN

What is it about doctors' offices that always make you feel worse? If you're already sick, they just confirm it. If you're not sick, they'll find something wrong with you. If they can't find anything wrong, they'll poke and prod and stick you with needles until you feel like hell anyway. No matter what they find, it's a sure bet they'll order you to give up some bad habit that makes life worth living. Even if, like me, you're only escorting a sick person to the doctor, you could still pick up a germ from the coughing, sneezing invalids in the waiting room. All this, and it's expensive, too.

Dr. Graves's office was nicer than most, owing to his brain specialty, but the mauve waiting room was full of ancient people, most chaperoned by worried-looking adult offspring. The whole room fairly reeked of decay and Depends and impending death, despite the bouncy Muzak.

Dub hadn't shaved or put on fresh clothes, and he looked like a wino as he joshed with the old-timers and yakked with anybody who'd listen. I kept my nose buried in a tattered copy of *House & Garden,* hoping to find a Handy Tip for removing paint from brick.

Even though I only half listened, I could hear Dub carrying on with his wild stories about life on the road and doctors he'd known and women he'd loved. He either had lived the richest life since Lawrence of Arabia or he was a stupendous liar or there was something wrong with his brain. I hoped the doctor could sort it out. I sure as hell couldn't.

When the nurse at the check-in window called out "Wilton Mabry," Dub and I both jumped.

"You want me to go with you?" I offered, though the words practically choked me.

"Naw. Hell, boy, I think I know how to stick out my tongue and say, 'Aah.' Besides, they might make me take my clothes off. Haw-haw."

I hid behind the magazine.

He was gone a long time, and I tortured myself imagining the paces Dr. Graves was putting him through: blood pressure cuffs and drawn blood and ice-cold stethoscopes.

Finally, the door opened and the doctor stuck his head out. He was a match for every doctor in every movie you've ever seen. White lab coat with a stethoscope hanging around his neck. Chest pocket full of pens and strange instruments. Thin gray hair cut short. Rimless eyeglasses.

"Mr. Mabry?"

Even though I was looking right at him, and he was looking right at me, I still jumped when he called my name.

"Yes?"

"May I see you for a minute?"

"Uh, sure." I threw the magazine aside and it slipped off the tabletop and I squatted to retrieve it, then had to hitch at my jeans to keep from giving everyone a nice view of my butt cleavage. I hurried through the door behind the doctor, who hadn't hung around to watch.

He was halfway down a narrow corridor lined with closed doors by the time I caught up.

"Let's talk in my office," he said, and I followed him into his private chambers, which were just as sterile and orderly as the rest of the place.

He sat behind an oak desk that bore a little sign that said JASPER GRAVES, M.D. I sat in a narrow chair opposite and clasped my hands between my knees.

"I've examined your father," he said without preamble, "and I must say he's in pretty good shape for someone's who's eaten in truck stops his entire life. Physically, he's about where he should be for a man his age. Though he could do with a little exercise, as could we all."

He twinkled at me. I sucked in my stomach and sat up straight.

"But, of course, it wasn't his body you came to see me about," he said. "It was his brain. And there, I'm afraid, we've got a problem."

I nodded uncomfortably. Just as I'd suspected.

"Your wife—a lovely woman, by the way—told me on the phone last night about the incident at the convenience store. But your father seems to have no memory of it."

Whatever glow might have arisen within me at the compliment to Felicia was immediately snuffed out by the memory of the 7-Eleven holdup.

"And," he said, "I've found other signs today that something's not quite right in there."

"Such as?"

"Well, for instance, he doesn't seem to know anything about you and your life."

"We'd been separated from the time I was nine years old until yesterday."

"Ah, that would explain it. But he couldn't seem to make that clear for me. Also, he has real trouble with numbers and dates of any kind. I gave him a few standard tests, little question-and-answer things, and he either couldn't or wouldn't keep up."

"Wouldn't?"

Dr. Graves gave me a smile so polite it wouldn't dream of actually showing any teeth.

"Forgive me for saying so, but your father seems to have something of a cantankerous streak."

I nodded briskly.

"I see it in a lot of my patients with Alzheimer's, and it often gets worse. They get so confused that they're actually cruel to people whom they love deeply."

"I haven't seen him be cruel, exactly," I interrupted. "Though he did scare the pee out of that convenience store clerk."

Graves nodded and smiled some more, waiting for me to stop talking so he could continue. Doctors.

"What I'd like to do, Mr. Mabry, is run some more tests on your father, including a CAT scan. Do you know what that is?"

"Sort of. You look inside his head with it, right?"

"Yes. It would give us a better idea what we're facing here."

"It would tell us if he's crazy?"

Graves frowned, then pulled his pleasant, I'm-not-a-doctor-but-I-play-one-on-TV expression back together.

"You're suggesting that your father suffers from psychosis of some kind?"

"He acts nuts, if that's what you mean."

I've seen a lot of craziness in my life, starting with Mama and running right through half the people I've met. You live on the Cruise very long and you see every kind of insanity marching past.

Graves sighed. Apparently, terms like "crazy" and "nuts" didn't fit his clinical manner.

"I don't think we're talking about a psychiatric illness here, Mr. Mabry. But your father may have some sort of organic brain problem, such as Alzheimer's disease, that would cause his odd behavior. That's why it would be a good idea to take a 'look inside his head.' "

I nodded quietly, mulling over what he was telling me. I wasn't sure what to do with this new information, but one thing came to mind and naturally I blurted it out.

"These tests, they're expensive, right?"

Graves nodded somberly.

"Yes, I'm afraid they are. And your father has no insurance."

A muscle twitched in my jaw. I couldn't afford the tests, not unless I won the big Richie Johnson jackpot. Hell, I couldn't even afford to buy Dub insurance, not for the premiums they'd charge for a man his age, one with a preexisting condition. I couldn't afford my own health insurance, except that I'm covered through Felicia's benefits at the *Gazette.*

"Your father seems a little confused about his age, but he showed me his driver's license and he's not quite old enough to qualify for Medicare," the doctor said. "I'm afraid you're caught betwixt and between."

I thought it over for a minute, but I couldn't see any simple solution.

"I need to talk this over with my wife."

Referring to Felicia as my wife gives me an emotional thump. It's still so new. We've been through a lot together, both before we got married and since, but nothing like this business with Dub.

"I understand," he said. "In the meantime, you should keep a close eye on your father. He could be a danger to himself or others, as that business at the convenience store shows."

"You mean, I shouldn't leave him alone at all?"

Graves shrugged slightly.

"He might be fine, but I'd stick right beside him if I were you."

I nodded, already trying to figure how I could baby-sit Dub and hunt for Richie Johnson, too. Dr. Graves stared at me.

"Oh, so we're all done here for today?"

"I've done all I can do until we're ready for those tests."

I eagerly got to my feet. I wanted to get the heck out of there.

"Thanks, Doctor." I reached across the desk to shake his cool hand. "I appreciate you squeezing us in this way."

"It's the least I could do. Your wife once wrote a very nice article about my work with Alzheimer's."

I was backing toward the door, but he added, "We laminated the article. It's hanging in the hall there, if you want to see it on your way out."

"Thanks again."

A heavyset nurse showed me to the examination room where Dub waited. He looked more rumpled than ever, sitting on a paper-covered table, playing with a couple of tongue depressors.

"Okay," I called to him, "it's time to go."

Dub stuffed the tongue depressors in his shirt pocket as if they were party favors, and followed me outside.

"That doctor seemed like a pretty nice feller," he said, as we reached the parking lot. "Said I was healthy as a horse. 'Course, I coulda told him that and saved us a lot of trouble."

You don't know the half of it. I thought. *The trouble's just beginning.*

As we climbed into the cab of the Ram, the air was split by a loud chirping. My cellular phone. I fumbled in the glove compartment and managed to answer by the third ring.

"Bubba?"

"Yeah?" I didn't recognize the voice, but the reception was fuzzy. The line clicked and roared.

"Dick Johnson here. How's it going?"

"Fine, Mr. Johnson," I lied. "Making progress."

"Good. Lord knows your buddy, Pool, doesn't seem to be making any headway. Come on over to the hotel and tell me all about it."

"Now?"

"Yes, now. You got something more important to do?"

"No, but I've got my father here with me—"

"Hell, bring him along. I don't care. I want some good news. Meet me and Pool at that restaurant off the lobby, the Ranchers Club. We'll have lunch."

Lunch at the Ranchers Club. Normally, I'd jump at the chance. The restaurant's a ritzy place with great food and decor like a hunting lodge. Just the sort of place where Dub could embarrass the hell out of me.

Johnson hung up, and it was clear I had no choice but to take Dub with me. *Maybe*, I thought as I cranked up the truck, *Johnson will see what I'm up against with Dub and give me a break. Lord knows I'm due.*

FOURTEEN

*A*lbuquerque's a casual town. There are probably only three or four restaurants in the whole city where you might catch funny looks if you show up in blue jeans. The Ranchers Club is one of them.

The blonde hostess tried not to look down her nose at Dub and me and the way we were dressed, but it was such a prominent nose that she really couldn't help herself.

The tables were ringed by guys in suits, local movers and shakers and connivers. Here and there, the occasional female sharpie was mixed in, but the Ranchers Club has a real man's feel to it. The house specialties are meats grilled over mesquite—heaven to most men—and the sedate restaurant is decorated with trophies of buffalo and pronghorn and deer. Even the chandeliers are made of antlers. Everything but a sign out front saying: VEGETARIANS BEWARE.

The hostess trooped Dub and me through the power lunchers. I tried to tiptoe so as not to get the muckety-mucks noticing my jeans and sneakers. Halfway across the room, I snatched Dub's cap off his head and handed it to him. His hair stood up on either side of his bald head like Bozo's.

He gawked like a kid at a carnival, and his brown eyes shone blankly. First, I take him to a doctor's office, where he'd gotten what he confessed had been his first examination in decades. Now, the Ranchers Club. That's me, all right. Showing the old man the sights. Next, I suppose we'd go down to Old Town and buy him some turquoise jewelry from a real live Indian.

Dick Johnson had reserved one of the private dining rooms that flank the Ranchers Club, which I at first took for a blessing. At least we wouldn't be out in the middle of the restaurant with the power brokers staring at Dub. But as it turned out, one wall of the little room was glass floor-to-ceiling, looking out into the main hall of the Hilton. Anyone walking by could look in and compare tousled Dub and me to the two mustachioed Texans who sat across the table from us in their expensive suits and bolo ties. It felt like feeding time at the zoo.

I shamefacedly introduced Dub to Pool and Johnson, who shook his hand and acted as if there was nothing wrong with bringing one's father along to a meeting with a client. Texans have manners, even if they forget them sometimes.

"Mighty fine to meet you both," Dub brayed.

He had a speck of brown tobacco at the corner of his mouth, and it was all I could do not to lick my thumb and clean him up like he was a four-year-old.

We didn't leap into business right away. Menus awaited, and free-range waiters flocked round the table. Dub, clearly assuming the Texans were paying, ordered the most expensive item on the menu, a sampler platter of grilled meats with vegetables on the side. He also wanted a beer. After casting a sidelong glance at Dub's tub of a stomach, I ordered a low-calorie chicken breast plate and a diet Coke.

Once the waiters had gone away and closed a sliding door behind them, Johnson said, "Now, then, I want to hear all about Richie. Who wants to go first?"

I wasn't too crazy about sharing my information while Pool listened. But Johnson wanted everything on the table, as it were, and Pool shot his cuffs and opened a folder beside his plate, ready to reveal his findings.

"Dick," he began, "we haven't found Richie yet, obviously, but we have been doing what we can to run him down. We can do amazing things with computers these days. We checked county clerk records on whether Richie had bought any property, including a car, and couldn't turn anything up. Now, we know he's driving a yellow Volkswagen because I saw it the night of the ransom pickup, but he doesn't have it registered under his own name."

I couldn't help but smile. Pool had just used a lot of words to describe Zero.

"We also checked phone company records, bank records, credit reports, the electric and gas companies, and the airlines."

Johnson interrupted. "And what did you find?"

"Nothing," Pool admitted. "The phone company and the utility companies won't cooperate in this state. But we did learn that Richie hasn't opened a bank account or gotten any charge cards since he came to Albuquerque. And he's not flying anywhere."

More zero. I was grinning ear to ear. At least I'd seen Richie Johnson, albeit briefly. Dick Johnson, meanwhile, was getting red in the face.

"Have you turned up anything except where Richie *ain't?*"

"Now, Dick, we're taking every possible step," Pool backpedaled. "These are just preliminaries. I've got people scouring the streets, trying to turn up any sign of these skinheads. Once we get ahold of one of them, I guarantee you I can make him reveal Richie's whereabouts."

"But you haven't found any of them yet."

"No, sir, but we're looking. In the meantime, it only made sense to check out all the databases to see if we could come up with anything."

The doors slid open and a cadre of white-shirted waiters marched in, bearing platters covered with silver serving domes. They set the platters in front of us, then gathered around the table so they could lift the covers all at once. I guess we were supposed to all go, "Ooh," or something because the waiters looked disappointed when we didn't.

"Thanks," Dick Johnson said flatly, and he waved them away.

Once the door was closed, Johnson turned to me.

"Bubba, it sounds like Pool has come up with a big ole goose egg. You do any better?"

Pool had his fork halfway to his mouth, and it froze there while he looked to me, his black eyebrows raised. I wished briefly that I had some notes to refer to, or something that looked official, but all I could do was wing it.

"I saw Richie last night," I said, taking a great deal of secret pleasure in watching Pool's mouth fall open. The bite of steak still hovered in the midair, waiting to land.

"You did?" Johnson exclaimed. "Where?"

"At a nightclub here in the city. He was there with a bunch of those skinheads."

"Did you talk to him?"

"I didn't get the chance. I stood out in the crowd, if you know what I mean, and he got a look at me and took off out a back door. Richie knows people are hunting for him. Guess we have Mr. Pool here to thank for that."

Johnson shot Pool a hateful look, which no amount of "Who, me?" posturing by Pool could deflect.

"Then what happened?"

"I lost him in the alley. I was going after him, but his skinhead buddies followed me out there. They wanted to give me a beating the way they did Pool's associate, Mike Sterling, but I pulled a pistol on them and they backed down."

Dub had been shoveling food into his face as if he were in a race, but he paused long enough to say, "Them boys put paint all over Bubba's house."

Thanks again, Dub.

"They what?"

I tried to sound blasé.

"They spray painted graffiti on my house during the night. Guess they hunted down my address. They weren't too happy about me making them back down."

I wondered whether now was the time to broach the idea of Johnson paying to have the paint removed, but he had other things on his mind.

"How did Richie look?"

How to describe it? He looked like all the other hairless, tattooed, pierced-face freaks at the nightclub.

"A little pale," I said finally, "but maybe he always looks that way. I only got a glimpse. But he seemed okay. Nothing wrong with his legs. He hauled ass out of there before I could catch up."

Dick Johnson ignored the food on his plate. I would've loved to dig into mine, but I wanted Johnson to think he had my undivided attention. Pool seemed to have lost his appetite, which tickled me. The only one still eating was Dub, who looked as if he'd been served his last meal.

"I'm worried sick," Johnson said. "Richie's not a strong person. If he got involved with drugs or something, his heart might give out."

"According to my information, they don't do drugs," I said. "They're all high on hate. Seem to drink a lot of beer, but that's about it."

I was overstating my limited knowledge of the skinheads, but maybe it would make Johnson feel better, and that had to be worth something.

Johnson shook his head, fretting over his son. I glanced at Dub to see if he was picking up any lessons on how a father should act, but he was patting his mashed potatoes with the back of a spoon, building little mountains, then leveling them off. I tore my gaze away from him, hoping the others hadn't noticed.

No such luck.

"So, Bubba," Pool said brightly, "is your father helping you find Richie?"

I stared into my food for a time, trying to decide which item would go best with Pool's suit if I hurled it at him.

"Dub popped up in my life yesterday. We'd been separated for a long time."

"That a fact?" Johnson sounded halfway interested, though he was looking at his food and finally giving some of it a try.

"Yeah, we had a reunion of sorts yesterday." The thought of the convenience store made me frown. "But I made it to the skinheads' nightclub after he went to sleep."

I wanted to keep their attention on my modest success, not on the fact that my old man was burping and grunting next to me.

Pool smiled wolfishly.

"Dub might come in handy," he said. "He could watch your back."

"I work alone, but I did have some business to conduct with him this morning. I appreciate you letting him come along for lunch, Mr. Johnson."

Johnson nodded, too busy ruminating to answer.

"Bubba here took me to the doctor," Dub announced, and I reached with my foot, trying to locate his toe so I could stomp it if he said the wrong thing. "All that poking and thumping around on me."

Dub shook his head.

"The doc said I was healthy as a June bride," he added.

Pool nodded encouragingly, and I could see in his eyes he was trying to make me look like a fool. Again.

"As soon as lunch is over," I cut in, "I'm taking Dub home and getting right back after Richie."

Johnson oinked his approval.

"I heard on the street that the cops are looking for the

skinheads," I said, not wanting Johnson to know I'd been to the police myself.

Johnson looked me over.

"That makes it all the more urgent that we get Richie away from them," he said.

"My thoughts exactly."

"I don't want Richie mixed up with the law," Johnson lectured. "He doesn't need that kinda excitement. I'm sure he's not taking his medication. It could go bad."

"I agree," Pool chimed in. "I'll do everything I can to find him in a hurry."

Johnson pointed at Pool with his fork.

"You're gonna have to do a damned sight better than you have so far," he said. "Bubba's been on this case twenty-four hours and he's already gotten closer to Richie than you have in three weeks."

I tried not to smirk.

"I want results, and I want them now."

Johnson used his napkin to wipe the perspiration off his bald dome.

"We're working on it, Dick," Pool said. "These things take time."

"We don't have time, goddammit! If Richie kept that ransom money for himself, he's a walkin' target. Somebody'll try to take it away from him, and that could be just the thing to give him a heart attack."

Pool and I nodded like a pair of those stuffed dogs people used to keep in their rear windshields. Dub chuckled under his breath, but didn't look up from his plate. Guess he found all this scolding funny as hell.

We ate in silence for a while, but then Johnson rushed us along.

"Don't feel you need to linger, boys. Ain't likely Richie's gonna come in here looking for us."

Dub cackled, but I could take a hint. I folded my napkin beside my plate and grasped Dub by the elbow.

"I ain't finished with my beer!"

"You've got some more at home," I said. "Let's get going."

I thanked Johnson for the meal and was nearly out the door before he said, "Call me soon, Bubba. And it better be good news."

"Yes, sir."

Dub started laughing again, and I shoved him out the door.

FIFTEEN

I had no choice. I had to get after Richie Johnson immediately, which meant taking Dub with me. I couldn't let him out of my sight until he got those medical tests, or until Felicia lost her enthusiasm for the whole "father" project, whichever came first. I wasn't happy about having him tag along, but I couldn't just wait around, doing nothing, until Felicia got home from work to baby-sit him. Every minute that passed might be the one that allowed William J. Pool to find Richie—and my bonus money—first.

Dub and I climbed up into the cab of the Ram, and I goosed it out of the Hilton's landscaped parking lot and into Albuquerque's mean streets.

Dub cut a chaw off his plug of chewing tobacco, watching out the truck windows as the scenery zipped past. Maybe he wanted to go home, or back to his truck, or wherever. Maybe, in a sense, I was holding him against his will, and he was too polite to say so.

"Dub, you feel like riding with me for a while?"

"I got nothin' better to do."

"You said something last night about hitting the road."

"I did. But I can tell you need me to stick around. You got a lot ridin' on this here case, don't you?"

"Yeah, but—"

"I like what that nice man, Mr. Pool, said about me watchin' your back. I think that's a good idea. These yahoos already figured out where you live. Probably just a matter of time before they make a run at you."

I appreciated this show of concern, but what he'd said first stuck in my craw.

"He's not a nice man."

"What?"

"Pool. He's not nice. Never make that mistake."

"The hell you say! He seemed a perfect gentleman."

I looked over, a scowl on my face, only to find Dub grinning at me like a well-fed mule.

"I take it," he said, "that you don't much like that cowboy."

"You could say that."

"How come?"

"It's ancient history."

"Hell, boy, so am I. What's between the two of you?"

I glanced over at him again, and he seemed truly interested. Rational and alert. Maybe a whale-sized portion of grilled meat was all he needed to pull himself together. I sighed. What could it hurt to tell him?

"It started about ten years ago," I said. "First time I ever met William J. Pool."

I looked over at him as I changed lanes on Lomas. He was watching me with his full attention, and a little grin tugged at the corners of his mouth.

"You sure you want to hear this?"

"Better than listening to the wind whistle through the windows."

He punctuated this statement by spitting a brown stream

out his half-open window. The window was showing traces of splatter, and I opted to keep my eyes on the road.

"I was working on a case. My client was a defense attorney named Virgil Gonzales, who was representing this guy Dunhill, who'd been accused of murder. Dunhill's girlfriend had vanished, and the cops thought he'd done it, but they were having trouble proving it because they couldn't find the body."

"He killed her?"

"I'm getting to that. Just hold on to your turnips."

Dub chuckled. He seemed to be enjoying my tale of woe.

"Gonzales didn't want to look like a jackass, so he had me trace Dunhill's movements in the days before the woman disappeared. I checked everything. I knew when he went to work and when he was sleeping. He went to a funeral for his aunt the day his girlfriend disappeared. Looked like she packed her stuff while he was at the funeral and took off later that day."

"So he didn't kill her?"

"It didn't look that way. The man had alibis up to his neck."

"What happened to her?"

"You want me to tell this or not?"

"Go right ahead, boy. I ain't stopping you."

"Okay, so Gonzales decides to go public with our findings, a couple of days before the trial is scheduled to begin. Try to get that good publicity going, right?"

Dub nodded right along, as if he had any idea what I was talking about.

"He calls a press conference down at the courthouse to make his announcement. And just as he was saying Dunhill had triple alibis going and was a truly innocent man, William J. Pool stands up at the back of the room."

"Pool was there?"

"Working for the dead girl's family. They wanted him to find her body and send Dunhill to the death chamber."

"Ouch."

"So Pool stands up, and he shouts over the heads of all

these reporters that he can prove my guy is guilty."

"Bet that got their cameras turned around."

"You said it. Pool announces that he's seeking an exhumation order for Dunhill's aunt. He thinks Dunhill buried the girl in his aunt's grave, maybe the night after the funeral happened. Get it?"

"Two-for-one sale at the graveyard."

"Right. So Gonzales is looking at me, like, How could you miss that? And the reporters are all looking at him. And I'm looking for an exit."

"How had Pool figured out she was in there?"

"Just a hunch. Then he got some guy to use a high-powered metal detector, and the guy turned up a bracelet or something that was under only three feet of dirt. That was enough for a judge to issue the exhumation order."

Dub nodded, working the tobacco in his cheek. I could see the white hairs among his whiskers glowing in the sunlight that streamed through the window.

"And they dug up two bodies," he said.

"That's right. And Dunhill got sentenced to the needle."

"What needle?"

"Fatal injection. That's what they do in this state."

"There's no electric chair?"

"No, just a doctor. Probably a lot like that Dr. Graves."

"I like the chair. It gives the whole thing a sense of spectacle."

He was staring out the windshield, his jaw slack. I reminded myself the man was crazy or senile or something. No matter, sometimes he said the strangest things.

"You've given this a lot of thought, have you?"

Dub snapped to a little, and grinned.

"I've given many things a lot of thought," he said. "I've spent a lot of years riding in a truck by myself."

"What do you think about Pool now?"

"Sounds to me like he skunked you, pure and simple. Can't blame a man for doing a good job."

I ground my teeth.

"But it was the *way* he did it. Pool knew about the metal detector crap days before he announced it at *our* press conference. He'd even been in meetings between the two legal teams. But he never said a word, not until he could make the most of it by grandstanding."

Dub's eyes twinkled.

"Ain't that the same thing you woulda done if you'd gotten the information first?"

"I never volunteer anything to the news media. That's why they call me a *private* eye."

"What about that wife of yours? Bet she's written about you a time or two."

"That's different."

"Not much."

"I never volunteer anything to her, either. She just gets a lot of opportunities to worm things out of me."

Dub hooted. "Bet she's good at it, too."

"Pretty damned good, yeah."

"Why didn't you get her to keep Pool out of the newspaper?"

"Don't work that way. Felicia would snap my head clean off if I tried to get her to stop somebody's story for my benefit. Besides, she didn't even live in Albuquerque then. That's not the point anyway. The point is that Pool cheated by announcing his solution the way he did. You can't trust him."

"Fella's got a way about him, though. He spends a lot of time thinking about making a reputation for himself, getting in the newspapers and all."

I thought Dub had sized that up fairly well. Maybe he had more on the ball than it seemed. Or maybe whatever was wrong with his brain faded in and out. His thought patterns might be like the CB radio in his truck—sometimes things get fuzzy in the mountains, but other times the distant signals are loud and clear.

"It's all part of Pool's act," I said, "just like all that high-tech computer stuff and the expensive equipment he flaunts. All the gizmos in the world won't beat good legwork. But they make a big impression if you're a publicity hound."

"Maybe he got rich off all this publicity. You see the diamond in his pinky ring?"

I let that lie there like the warm manure it was. Any man who'd wear a pinky ring is by nature a show-off and should be avoided. But gaudy jewelry would go over big among Dub's set down at the truck stop.

"And maybe the gizmos work, too," he said. "I seem to remember hearing something about a metal detector?"

I'd turned north off Lomas and was nearing the area around Sandia High School, looking for an address I'd written in my notepad that morning. The neighborhood was one built by a developer named Mossman, and the homes were uniformly ranch-style with pitched roofs and decorative brick veneer. The Heights, or the Blights, as we center-of-town snobs call them, consist of miles of subdivisions crowded against another. A fellow can get lost easily. It didn't help that Dub kept distracting me.

"That the only thing Pool ever do to wrong you?"

"No. There've been a couple of other times when he's meddled in my investigations. But they all turn out the same."

"Never gotten the better of him, huh?"

"No, but I'd like to this time. That ransom Johnson mentioned at lunch? Whoever finds Richie first gets to keep it."

"No shit?"

"None at all."

"No wonder Pool's so hot to trot."

"Yep. Put some money on the line and the sharks will bite every time."

"And you're trying to do the same?"

I hated how he kept pointing out the holes in my logic. I know they're there, damn it. Sometimes, my logic resembles Swiss cheese. I didn't need my "father" to help me keep tally.

"Look, son," he said, and he angled his knees around in

the seat to face me, "I know all about holding a grudge. I had this old boy from Texas who pestered me for years. Every time our paths crossed, he'd make fun of me in front of the other truckers. I outshined him a couple of times, beating deadlines for this company we both contracted with, so he had it in for me."

Here's some common ground, I thought. *The old man's actually trying to share.* That's what conversation's all about, isn't it? I tell you something and you say, "The same thing happened to me . . ." Back and forth, discovering how much of the human condition consists of apples and oranges.

"One night he went too far. We were in a bar in Abilene with a lot of other truckers, and he started mouthing off about how I was short and how did I reach the clutch and that sorta shit."

"You're not short."

"Compared to him I was. This sucker was taller than you, and went about three hundred pounds."

"Yikes."

"He kinda got up in my face—he was drunk, you know—and he's talking loud and holding me up to ridicule. I didn't even look at him. I was trying to be dignified about it. I just drained my beer, smacked my lips, then whammed him upside the head with the mug."

I laughed. I couldn't help myself.

"He go down?"

"Like he was shot."

"Didn't he try to get even later?"

"Naw, that seemed like enough for him. Once clobbered, twice shy."

I was chuckling as I made my turn onto Utah, the street I'd been hunting.

"We're almost there," I said.

"All right."

Dub hadn't asked where we were headed, which I found a little odd. He seemed happy to ride high in the tall truck and gab, no matter where we were going.

"I was gonna ask you about something, son."

"Yeah?"

"That gal of yours said you two wrote a book. Is that right?"

Dang. Felicia didn't have to mention that.

"I don't like to talk about it."

"Why not? Seems like something to be proud of. Every dumbass on the planet goes around saying how they're gonna write a book someday, and share all their wisdom with the rest of us knuckleheads. But you really did it."

"It didn't turn out so well."

"Why not?"

"Because nobody believed it."

"They didn't? Why?"

"I really don't want to talk about it."

"Aw, come on, son. You can tell me. I'm trying to catch up with your life here."

"All right, all right. The book says I was hired by Elvis Presley."

"You worked for Elvis? But that ain't possible. You were only about fourteen when he died."

"I was sixteen, but that's beside the point. This was later, after he died."

"You worked for Elvis Presley's ghost?"

"No, look, it was just this guy, you know, who looked like Elvis and he sounded like Elvis and doesn't the living Elvis keep popping up all over the place? You're always hearing how somebody spotted him in a Laundromat in Buttcrack, West Virginia, or someplace. It seemed possible, that's all I'm saying. But when we wrote the book, I guess we didn't make it clear enough that we didn't *really* think it was Elvis himself. People thought we were a couple of lunatics."

Dub guffawed and slapped his bony knee.

"That's a good one. You thought it was really him, didn't you?"

"Naw, I—"

"Sure, you did. You're your mama's son, after all. It's only natural that someone famous should drop into your life, too. Of course, Elvis doesn't exactly hold a candle to Jesus Christ himself . . ."

I whipped a quick left onto a side street, causing the Ram to lean and Dub to whack his head against the half-open window. I can't say I meant to do that, but I wasn't sorry when it happened. He'd better not mock Mama.

"We're there," I said brusquely. "Wait in the truck."

Then I was out the door and walking up to the front stoop of Mike Sterling's rundown home. Behind me, faintly, I heard Dub say, "Wish I'd brought a beer."

SIXTEEN

*I*t took Sterling a long time to answer the doorbell. I could see why once the door swung open. He had a walking cast on his left foot. It resembled an oversized boot and it was Windex blue. He stood awkwardly, leaning his weight on his good leg.

Sterling was a large man, looking me in the eye at six feet, bigger than me through the shoulders and chest. His brown hair was cut short and parted on the right side. He had a big square jaw and tiny ears and, most noticeable of all, a bright red, crescent-shaped scar healing at his left eyebrow. I could tell it had been a deep wound, to the bone.

Jesus Christ. If that's what the skinheads did to this tough-looking hombre, what would've happened to me if I hadn't pulled my pistol on them? A shiver ran through me, a physical reminder that I needed to be more careful.

"Mike Sterling?"

"That's me."

"My name's Bubba Mabry. I'm a PI."

"I've heard of you."

"Yeah?"

"Sure. You're the guy thought he met Elvis."

Reminded of my worst faults, twice in one day. I made a face. Sterling grinned at me.

"Anybody who's got that kind of clientele should come in and have a beer."

"I was hoping you'd see it that way."

Sterling hobbled to one side and I came through the doorway, casting a glance back at Dub as Sterling closed the door behind me. Dub was still in the truck, back straight, launching a huge loogie onto Sterling's lawn. Nice.

The front door opened directly into one big room that was divided into living room on the left and dining room on the right. The dining table sat on a tattered rag rug that looked like one Sterling might've inherited from a grandmother. The rest of the house had the chaotic look and dirty-socks smell of a bachelor pad.

"Pull up a chair. I'll get us a beer."

Sterling limped into the kitchen and fetched a couple of Buds out of the fridge. The sight of the beer made me feel strangely guilty for leaving Dub in the truck like an unruly dog.

"You seem to be getting around pretty good on that thing," I said.

Sterling slumped into a chair across from me and used his hands to drag his leg around to the front.

"It's getting easier. I lost a lot of strength when I was laid up in the hospital."

"How long were you in there?"

"Eight days. I would've gotten out sooner, but I got some kind of infection and they had to keep an eye on me."

I shook my head in sympathy.

"Pool told me what happened to you," I said. "Musta been rough."

"Those skinheads worked me over pretty good."

Sterling grinned. I couldn't tell whether he admired the

skinheads' handiwork or thought getting beat halfway to hell was simply one of life's amusing mishaps.

"You still working for Pool?"

"Hell, no. That bastard owes me money for that last job. And he's holding back the money that's supposed to match the health insurance. The hospital's sending bills in the mail every day because he won't pay the employer's share."

"That sounds like Pool."

Sterling took a slug of his beer. He shook a Marlboro out of a pack, lit it with a kitchen match, and huffed the smoke toward the ceiling.

"I don't blame Pool because those skinheads pounded me. Shit happens, as they say. But he's been a weasel about everything that's happened since. I'm pretty mad at him."

I mulled that over, thinking I could use this fresh grudge to my advantage.

"You been working for him long?"

"Naw, about a year. I've only been in Albuquerque a little longer than that. I grew up in Florida, but the private eye business is pretty competitive there. I inherited this house from an aunt I barely knew, and decided to try my hand out West."

"Guess it's not going so well so far."

"Why do you say that?"

"You got beat up and all."

Sterling grinned and gave me a shrug. "Comes with the territory."

Now it was my turn to shrug. I didn't know exactly where I was heading with this conversation, so I covered my indecision by glugging away at the beer.

"Why are you here, Mr. Mabry?"

"What's that?"

"I don't think you were sent over here as a representative of our respectable industry, just to see how I was getting along."

"No, but—"

"So what can I do for you?"

"I've been hired by Dick Johnson to find his kid. I was trying to get an idea of what I was up against and how I might locate those skinheads."

"I thought Pool still had that case."

"He does, sort of. Johnson hired both of us and we're in a kind of race."

"And you want me to help you whip Pool."

"If you can. I know about confidentiality and all that. I don't want you to do anything that makes you uncomfortable."

Sterling's wide face split into that grin again and smoke trailed out of his nose.

"I've been a private eye for nine years now, Mr. Mabry. I've used that same line a hundred times myself."

Forgot I was dealing with a pro here. I needed to cut the bullshit. I sat forward and looked Sterling in the eye so he could see I was leveling with him.

"Johnson got a message saying Richie was kidnapped. He hired me to deliver the ransom. Pool filmed the delivery and we saw Richie himself pick up the money. Then he vanished again. We've been looking for him ever since."

"And you and Pool are trying to see who'll find him first."

"Right. And whoever does gets to keep the ransom money."

Sterling took a healthy drink from his beer, stifled a burp, and said, "How much?"

I didn't want to tell him. It might encourage him to go after the reward himself. But look at him, all bunged up, his foot in a cast. How could he compete? Maybe he'd see it that way, too, and agree to help me. Especially if he was already mad at Pool.

"Two hundred grand. Winner gets to keep whatever's recovered."

Sterling loosed a low whistle.

"Damn, that's not a bad gig if you can get it."

"But it means running up against the skinheads."

Sterling's smile slid off his face, and he thought it over

while he stubbed out his cigarette in a tin ashtray.

"Don't know," he said finally. "Might not be worth it. You might end up spending all that money on wheelchairs and doctor bills."

"I'm willing to take that chance."

Sterling cocked an eyebrow at me, the one with the scar, and he winced at the tight skin there.

"I guess I would be, too," he said, "if I weren't already out of the game."

"Then you'll help me?"

"I don't know. If Pool gets that money, maybe he'll settle up our debts. I think he's on the brink of bankruptcy. People stop paying their bills on time, that's always a bad sign."

I nodded, letting him work it out for himself.

"But if I help you and you win, what do I get?"

I knew this was coming. I would not pledge Sterling a cut of the reward. I could see the guy was strapped, being out of work and fresh out of the hospital, but I didn't feel I could keep a promise of sharing the money with him.

"You get even with Pool," I said.

Sterling's face split into the big jock grin again, and suddenly it was as if birds were singing and flowers were blooming. He was going to help me. I was sure of it.

"You're counting on me being madder at Pool than I am greedy."

"Guess I am."

"Sounds like you must hold a grudge against him yourself."

"Several."

Still smiling, Sterling nodded along, considering everything.

"I tell you what," he said. "You bring me another beer out of the icebox and I'll tell you the whole thing."

"You got it."

I practically tripped over my own feet, hurrying to the refrigerator before Sterling could change his mind. He lit another cigarette while I was away and clouded the air with smoke. It smelled good to me. I haven't smoked in years, but I still crave one occasionally. I tried one of Felicia's a few months ago, but I felt silly smoking Virginia Slims. Just as well. I've got enough character flaws; I don't need another bad habit.

Once we were settled back at the table, Sterling wet his whistle and began.

"The skinheads were squatting in an old warehouse over in the war zone. It's at the southern end of Memphis Street. You know where that is?"

I nodded.

"Sure, you do! Memphis, that's where Elvis lives, right?"

Sterling had a nice laugh at that. I waited.

"Anyway," he said after he got control of himself, "this warehouse used to house something called Belshaw and Company. It's an old wooden building, practically a ruin. I got a tip the skinheads hung out there, making fires inside to keep warm so they can party without being disturbed."

"America's youth," I chimed.

"Right. So I'd heard about this warehouse and I crept up on the place around dusk, just trying to get a look around, see if I could find any sign that this was where Richie hung out."

"What happened?"

"I thought I was safe, see. They had a boom box in there and they were playing some kind of thump-thump music—"

"Oi."

"What?"

"That's what the music's called."

"Whatever. You want to hear this or not?"

I clamped my lips shut.

"I peeked in the window, trying to see if any of these yo-yos are Richie Johnson, and somebody tapped me on the shoulder."

"Uh-oh."

"Right. I turned around to see that ugly Brit they call Mayhem. You heard of him?"

"Charming boy."

"And that's the last thing I remember. I woke up in the hospital. If somebody hadn't seen me lying there on the sidewalk and dialed 911, I probably would've frozen to death that night."

"Damn."

"That's what you're up against. I got nothing else to offer except that warehouse and I doubt if they're still hanging around there."

"How come?"

"The cops were called. They're probably keeping an eye on that place."

"It's been a couple of weeks. They've probably gotten distracted by now."

"Maybe the skinheads will see it that way, too. I'd love for you to be able to catch them, especially at the place where I got the shit stomped out of me."

I slapped my hands on my knees and rose to leave.

"I'll check it out," I said. "I'd better be going now. Thanks for your help."

Sterling called my name just before I went out the door.

"Yeah?"

"Watch your ass."

"Don't worry. After seeing what those skinheads did to you, I'm gonna be tiptoeing."

"I wasn't talking about the skinheads. Watch Pool. He'll stab you in the back first chance he gets."

"Don't I know it. I wouldn't trust that snake for a second."

Sterling gave me a thumbs-up, and I left him there at the table with his beer.

SEVENTEEN

It took us nearly an hour to reach the warehouse after we left Mike Sterling's place. We got snarled in a traffic jam caused by a fender bender on Louisiana Boulevard near two of Albuquerque's big shopping malls. Then I tried to get on Interstate 40, but the ramp was blocked by a construction crew. So I continued south on Louisiana, only to find half its lanes closed by orange barrels. No workers around, no torn-up pavement, the lanes were simply blocked. So I got off Louisiana on Central, my old standby, and managed to go six or eight blocks before I ran into another construction zone.

This is a fine summation of Albuquerque, where the orange barrel is the municipal mascot and the city motto is "Seek Alternate Route." One problem with living in a Sun Belt boomtown is that the whole damn city is under construction. And, there's no coordination between the projects. Somebody in City Hall wants to lure the tourists here, then never let them leave. Just keep them driving around and around until they finally decide it would be easier to live here forever than to find their way home.

Every passing minute meant I was that much closer to rush hour, when everything would get more crowded. Plus, the western sky was growing sun-kissed orange, and I didn't want to check out the warehouse in the dark. My frustration grew as I sat behind the wheel, waiting for idiot motorists to make up their minds.

If Dub noticed my discomfort, he didn't comment on it. He seemed happy to sit in the passenger seat and stare at everything we passed. Maybe he was looking for something familiar in an alien landscape, trying to anchor himself.

The clapboard warehouse Sterling had identified was in a block of similar buildings, a block that made the zone around Richie's Lotaburger look like the country club neighborhood. Windworn fences topped with concertina wire circled concrete bunkers and moats of black asphalt. Windows were covered with wrought-iron bars that made sure the inmates inside were safe from the felons outside. Others were nailed shut behind sheets of graffiti-spattered plywood, the owners giving up on keeping up appearances.

Once, this must've been a bustling commercial area, with trucks pulling in and out of loading docks, shipments of goods going out across the nation, welding and hammering and crafting going on behind the doors. But now the place was a ghost town, emptied by gunfights and the bad boys who ran this part of the city.

Driving around Albuquerque, you can forget such dangerous pockets exist. You stay on the main streets, with their familiar wallpaper of fast-food joints and franchise stores, and you cruise past without recognizing that life just a few blocks away is like living in Colombia.

Albuquerque keeps growing in all directions, new buildings going up so fast that you can stand still and watch a Pizza Hut go up around you and be ready to eat by the time the construction crew finishes. But the growth leaves behind empty blocks like this one. It's easier to move to the frontier than to stand and fight.

The warehouse was near the end of the block, separated from its neighbors by fences and skinny alleys that ran between the buildings. It looked as if it had been abandoned a long time, and most of the windows were broken. It once had been dark brown, but the paint had peeled away over time to reveal weathered gray lumber underneath. Just enough of the paint remained for me to make out the sign, BELSHAW AND COMPANY.

The front of the building had a regular door on the left side and a large, roll-up garage door on the right. When I stopped the truck in the street out front, I could see another door opening into the alley that ran alongside the building. Easy access all around.

I parked near a stand of naked elms that reached out over the street from a strip of vacant land across Memphis from the warehouse. The street was wide here, built to accommodate eighteen-wheelers, and it would be easy enough to pull a quick U-turn if I needed to leave in a hurry.

"Dub?"

"Yeah, son?"

"I want to go have a look in that warehouse over there. Will you be all right here in the truck?"

"Sure. This truck's got a good heater. Better to sit here than to get out in the cold."

The wind had picked up again, as it often does in late afternoon, and I figured Dub was right about the chill outside. Litter and tumbleweeds skittered across the street in front of the truck.

"Okay," I said. "I'll leave the keys in the ignition. If you need to run the heater again, you know what to do."

"That's a big ten-four."

"And Dub?"

"Yeah?"

"Keep the door locked after I get out, okay? This is a pretty bad part of town."

"Looks like it."

"Best to be safe. Just sit inside here with the doors locked. If anybody bothers you or looks suspicious, hit the horn and I'll come running."

"All right."

He seemed terribly vacant again, as if he'd drifted too far afield while we rode in silence in the truck.

"You're gonna be okay?"

"I'm happy as a preacher with a congregation fulla women. It's nice to be the passenger, you know? Riding around, looking at things, without having to keep an eye on the road. I don't get to do that much."

"I didn't exactly bring you to the most scenic spot in town. But I need to check out this warehouse."

Dub nodded me off, then turned his attention back to the outdoors, watching a little black-and-white mutt chase after a paper cup that tumbled in the breeze. The dog disappeared around a corner, and Dub looked back at me with empty eyes.

"Okay, I'll be right back."

I stepped out of the truck into a gust of wind that snatched at my new jacket before I could get it zipped up. I slammed the truck door, made sure it was locked and gave Dub a hearty wave before I trekked across the potholed street in search of skinheads.

I wasn't feeling so hearty. For one thing, I felt awfully alone, even with Dub watching me from the truck. Mike Sterling offered ample evidence of what happens to the foolhardy. For another, I didn't have my gun with me.

I know this was stupid. But I didn't need it when I started the day, taking Dub to the doctor, and I didn't want it available in case Dub went nuts again and wanted to knock over, say, a bank. He didn't seem to have missed his own pistol, and I sure as hell didn't want him getting his hands on mine.

If I'd seen any sign of life in the old warehouse, I might've turned tail and gone home for my Smith & Wesson. Or, at least ditched Dub so he wouldn't witness me getting an ass-

134

whipping. But the place was so clearly devoid of life, I figured I could take a quick look around without being armed.

I hurried through the wind directly to the nearest window in the warehouse. One look inside, then run like hell if I see anybody. But there was no one. Even the shadowy corners offered no sign of movement, no sound but the wind howling through the broken glass.

The interior was a big open room, and there were only a few places behind crates and old machinery and other junk where someone might be hiding. Lot of litter in there, and the concrete floor was scorched in the center from past bonfires. Beer bottles glinted here and there among the trash on the floor. The interior walls were marked all over with black and red paints, sprayed on in Anarchy symbols and swastikas and other gibberish.

Jesus, what a mess. Imagine being the absentee landlord, coming into Albuquerque to inspect your properties, and finding a clubhouse for Hitler Youth.

Since the place was so clearly empty, I thought I'd venture inside, just long enough to look around, see if the skinheads had left any obvious clues lying among their rubbish. The front door of the warehouse was locked, and I didn't really want to climb in through a window. What if a wandering patrol car happened by? As if that could happen in this neighborhood. You call a cop in this part of town, you get an extra delay while he straps on his flak jacket.

I opted for the side door. I slipped down the alley about thirty feet to the door, tried the knob, and it swung right open.

The building had been used to store some kind of machinery, but the gadgets had been so stripped and scoured and damaged over the years that I couldn't tell now what kinds of machines they once had been. Woodworking machines, maybe, or the types of drills and saws used to create tools and parts. The few that remained stood around in the corners, looking out of place and uncomfortable. I skirted the wide room, peeking into corners and around empty crates, making sure I was alone.

Finding nobody, I turned to the junk I assumed the skinheads had left behind. An ungodly number of empty beer bottles formed shard-sharp piles around the empty room, and there was other trash—potato chip bags and cigarette butts and old lengths of rope and a couple of used condoms like the shed skins of slimy snakes. But nothing that would identify the skinheads or tell me more about them. No political tracts, no party invitations, no stray address book that might reveal Richie Johnson's whereabouts. The warehouse might as well have been a cave, and the trash the left-behind detritus of a vanished culture.

I kicked my way through the debris, watching intently for anything that might help me. Even over the noise I was making, I heard something skitter through the shadows and I wheeled around to look. The noise wasn't a human footfall. It was the click of claws on concrete, the slippery sound of something scurrying. I peered into the gathering darkness, expecting to see a rat, but got a glimpse of something else. It was a four-legged creature, all right, flitting out of sight behind some wooden crates, but it was no rat. It was larger and sleeker than a rat and it was the sickly grey color of something hairless. A cat, maybe, but without fur. Brrr.

The quick glimpse of the animal made me move my feet. I needed to finish in the warehouse and get the hell out of there before somebody saw me. And I needed to get back to Dub. God forbid that he wander off in this part of town. We'd never see him again, and whatever happened to him would be all my fault.

The warehouse had another door that I hadn't seen from the front. This one was cut into the back wall, and I thought I'd take a quick look around behind the building before heading back to the truck.

The door wasn't locked, but it stuck when I pushed on it and I gave it a harder shove. It banged open, revealing a narrow alley behind the building that was screened with a tall wooden fence topped with coils of razor wire. The dead-end alley was just wide enough for a car, and I was so happy to see the one parked there that I nearly whooped out loud. A sun-bleached yellow Volkswagen snuggled between the building and the fence like a caterpillar in a cocoon.

I checked the alley for any signs of life and found none. I approached the Volkswagen and looked inside. No one. And no sign of Dick Johnson's leather briefcase.

The doors were locked, but the VW was an older model with triangular vent windows up front, and it was a snap to pry one of them open and slide my arm inside. It took some feeling around to reach the lock, and I wasn't happy being stuck there, up to my elbow in somebody else's car. But I finally popped it open, and then I was inside.

Even with the door closed, the Volkswagen let in plenty of the whistling wind. I ignored the cold, letting the excitement get to me. If Richie left his car here, he must be somewhere nearby. Maybe I could just sit in my truck, watching the warehouse and waiting for him to show up. Waiting meant I'd be trapped in my truck with Dub the whole time, but it would be worth it if I landed the big payoff.

I searched through the trash accumulated on the floorboards until I found what I needed. A telephone bill envelope lay under some old newspapers. The stub that you send in with your payment was gone, but the rest of the bill had the information I sought. The name "Richard Johnson Jr." and a street address on Dartmouth in the student ghetto. I laughed out loud. Even if Richie never came back for his VW, I now knew where he lived. Which put me way ahead of William J. Pool, whose fancy computers hadn't turned up the address.

I wrote the address in a little notebook I carry in my hip pocket. Then I got out of the Volkswagen, back out into the snatching wind, to hightail it around the warehouse to the safety of my truck.

I was grinning broadly, even though the cold made my teeth hurt. Things couldn't possibly be going better. Then I heard the boom-boom of thudding speakers as a car pulled up out front. Mayhem had to be right around the corner.

EIGHTEEN

What to do when your world suddenly crashes down around you? If you're my mama, you cling to your faith. If you're Felicia, you snarl and bitch your way through the problem. In this case, I decided to take a page from Dub's book and haul ass.

The music stopped out front. Car doors slammed. I trotted down to the open end of the alley, trying to be as quiet as possible, and peeked around the corner of the warehouse. A sleek black Buick had pulled into the mouth of the other alley, by the street, and skinheads spilled out of it. Oh shit.

Even from this distance, I recognized Mayhem as the one who climbed out from behind the wheel. A cigar was clamped in his gnarly teeth and the question-mark scar stood out on his head. He was looking right at me.

I turned and ran back the other way, past the Volkswagen to the door I'd used to exit the warehouse a few minutes earlier. If I could get inside before they did, there were plenty of ways to escape. I turned the knob of the back door and nothing happened. I remembered that it had stuck before, so I yanked and jerked, but it wouldn't budge. I put one foot against the wall by the door and pulled with all my might. Nothing.

My breathing was labored, and I sounded like Donald Duck as terror closed my throat. I couldn't be in a worse place. Stuck behind this abandoned building with the skinheads coming my way. There was no climbing the fence, not with that razor wire strung along the top. I'd be mincemeat by the time I reached the other side.

I turned and sprinted back the way I'd come, toward the alley full of skinheads. Maybe Mayhem hadn't really spotted me, maybe they would all go inside and I could slip past and make it to the truck.

No such luck. When I rounded the corner, I found five skinheads headed my way, led by Mayhem. Richie Johnson wasn't among them, but I recognized the little smartass and a couple of others from Pandemonium. Two of them had picked up stray pieces of lumber and, as I watched, the littlest one found a nice brick that would make a deadly dent in my melon.

"Hi, guys," I called. "Just the fellows I was looking for."

The skinheads marched toward me, oozing menace. Mayhem tossed his cigar aside and doubled his knobby hands into fists.

"I, uh—"

I tried to think of something that might distract them from their promise to do me damage. But for once my mouth was out of order.

They closed the distance. I only had a few seconds to think of something, to do something, or I'd be on my way to the morgue. They had the alley thoroughly blocked, spread out in a flying wedge behind Mayhem. Nowhere to run, nowhere to hide.

I had surprise on my side, if only I was brave enough to use it. They expected me to run, but I'd be cornered in the back alley if I did. They expected me to whine, to cower.

Despite all my inclinations to do just that, I saw only one course of action that might save my skin. I ran right at them, howling like a Bolshevik.

The skinheads froze in their tracks, maybe expecting me to whip out my pistol again. I would've loved to oblige, but since I was unarmed, I had no choice but to use my feet and my hands. Mayhem put up his dukes, ready to clobber me one, but I cut left and dodged him. His fist whistled past my head. I headed straight for the smallest of the skinheads and I threw out a straight-arm that would've made Gayle Sayers proud. The shrimp was raising his brick, but the quick shove in the chest took him off-guard and he tumbled backward. Then I was past them, running like I've never run before.

They were right behind me, snapping and snarling, and my neck tingled from the expected blows. But my feet kept moving.

The Buick blocked the mouth of the alley, and I didn't have time to skirt around it. I leaped as I reached the car and landed on the hood on all fours.

" 'Ey!" Mayhem shouted behind me. If he was mad at me before, he'd be enraged at the way my kneecaps dented the shiny hood. I scrambled to my feet and ran up the windshield and over the roof of the Buick. When I reached the short trunk, I launched myself and hit the ground running.

Going around the car slowed the skinheads a little, but they narrowed the distance between us as I reached the truck. I grabbed the door handle and yanked, and about pulled all my fingers out of their sockets. It was locked.

Dub sat in the passenger seat, staring straight ahead, unbothered by the noise and panic that filled the street. I pounded on the window.

"Dub! Open the door!"

He didn't even look my way. This was no time for his brain to slip into neutral. I needed to get inside, and I needed him to be quick about it.

I glanced over my shoulder. The skinheads were running

full blast toward us. I had maybe fifteen seconds before they swarmed all over me. I banged on the window again.

"DUB!"

He looked over at me, and his eyes were vacant. His body was in the truck, but his mind was somewhere far away, perhaps reliving his life on the road, a life filled with speed and blurring white lines.

"Open the door!"

No recognition in his eyes. Holy shit, Batman, this could be the end. I was worried before about Dub witnessing me getting trounced, but now I could see it wouldn't matter. He'd never see a thing.

"Dad!" I screamed.

I said I'd never call him that, but panic sends such pledges right out the window. And it worked. Dub suddenly snapped alive. He focused on me, and he saw the skinheads, who'd almost reached me. He launched himself across the seat and unlocked the door.

I couldn't have gotten inside my red truck any faster if I'd been a fireman sliding down a pole. I locked my door. The skinheads surrounded the truck. The keys were in the ignition where I'd left them, and the Ram roared to life.

I heard a loud crash behind me, and looked to my mirror to see a skinhead swinging a two-by-four like a baseball bat at the Ram's taillight. Another jerked at the handle of my door, trying to get at me. Mayhem had run past the others, and stood directly in front of the Ram, blocking me.

Dares sometimes bring out the best in me just as fear brings out the worst. I threw the Ram into gear and stomped on the gas, headed straight for Mayhem. He lunged out of the way at the last second, flying onto the sidewalk and rolling into a ball.

I wheeled the Ram around in a tire-smoking U-turn and drove straight through the pack of skinheads. Sticks and stones bounced off the truck as I barreled past them. Might play hell with the Ram's paint job, but it was nothing compared to what would've happened to me if I'd stuck around.

I watched in the mirror as the skinheads picked themselves up from the pavement. Mayhem, back on his feet, shook his fist at my departing truck.

I knew I'd see him again.

NINETEEN

I drove fast, making several random turns in case the skinheads decided to chase us in their car. Once I was sure we weren't being followed, I let the Ram slow while I caught my breath. I cast a surreptitious glance at Dub.

He had slipped back into his passenger mode, watching the world zip past, not a word to say about our close call. I wanted to rant and rage at him, but what good would that've done? Look at him, sitting over there oblivious, occasionally firing a stream of tobacco juice out the half-open window. Something was truly wrong with his brain.

The human brain is a mystery, that's for sure. We tell ourselves we know how it works. It's like a computer, we say, downloading and processing sensory information. The truth, I suspect, is something more magical. Our brain may be a computer, but it's our *mind* sitting at the keyboard, and we don't understand how the two work together any better than we know why the universe is expanding or why women go to the bathroom in pairs. And nothing proves this better than when something goes kerflooey.

"Dub?"

"What?"

"Dub, can you look at me?"

"Sure, boy, what do you want?"

I know eyes are supposed to be the windows into the soul or some shit like that, but I found they worked pretty well as peep-holes into Dub's addled brain. They had a spark in them now.

"You feeling okay?"

"Never better."

"You seem kind of far away."

"Just lost in my thoughts."

"What are you thinking about?"

"I was thinking you very nearly got the whale knocked out of you back there."

So he *had* registered what happened at the warehouse.

"It was a close one, all right. You, heh-heh, you could've been a little quicker opening that door."

"What door?"

"The door to the truck."

"This truck?"

The fog had returned to his brown eyes.

"Never mind. How about we go to my house for dinner?"

That snapped him back.

"You betcha. That wife of yours whippin' up another big feed?"

I shrugged. I hadn't talked to Felicia all day. Who knew what she had planned? I had lots to report when I got home. Tell her what the doctor said and how Dub faded in and out all day. Maybe Felicia would have a solution. I sure didn't. All I knew was I needed to find Richie Johnson, damned quick, and I was spending all my time worrying about my old man instead.

Then I thought about the graffiti, and how the skinheads knew my address and how they had ever more reason to come hunting me. I hit the accelerator harder and whipped the truck through the last couple of turns before we reached my paint-scarred house.

Felicia's car was alone in the driveway, and I whewed in relief. Now I'd have some reinforcements in my ongoing reconnaissance of Dub's mental problems.

But first I had to inspect my big red truck. It wasn't as bad as it could've been. One tail light was bashed all to hell, its plastic shards like little red teeth around a busted bulb. The tailgate had a couple of dings from thrown bricks, and there was a nasty scrape on the right rear fender. The damage saddened me; I'd done a pretty good job of keeping the truck in good-as-new shape.

"Ain't too bad," Dub pronounced. "You can touch up that there scrape with some paint yourself."

I nodded, but my teeth were clamped tight against the anger that welled up inside me.

"At least," Dub said with a cackle, "they didn't get spray paint all over the truck."

I sighed deeply. "Let's go inside."

If I'd known what awaited us there, I might've jumped back in the truck and kept on driving.

A young woman dressed all in yellow sat at the kitchen table, her hands crossed on the tabletop and a bright smile on her face. I'd never seen her before, and I was a little taken aback at a stranger in the house. But Felicia's head poked around the corner from the kitchen, and she was grinning.

The stranger was pretty and wholesome and healthy. She could've been Miss Wisconsin. She had auburn hair that fell straight to her shoulders and a complexion like fresh milk and full lips painted a bright pink. Her nose was a button and her smile was perky as a daisy.

"Hi, hon," Felicia called. "I brought Meg home for dinner."

So this was Felicia's intern. I shook her soft hand, and she chirped about how nice it was to meet me. Then, muttering,

I introduced her to Dub, whose eyes lit right up.

"Ain't you just pretty as a pitcher!" he proclaimed, and I felt like stuffing my hand in his mouth. "You a college girl, huh? I love college girls. They're so smart! Pretty, too. What are you, about twenty-two? That's the perfect age for a woman. All growed up, but still round and firmly packed."

God, why couldn't he give it a rest? Meg Albright, to her credit, didn't let the old fool's overtures embarrass her. She smiled brightly, her head cocked to one side like a poodle being shown a squeak toy.

"Aren't you sweet!" she yipped. "I swear, I just love Albuquerque! Everybody here is so nice!"

"I ain't from around here," Dub corrected her. "I'm from Mississippi, born and bred. But the road is really my home."

I rolled my eyes, but Meg wasn't receiving any messages from me. She had the high beams on, smiling at Dub as if he were an emcee, rather than the unshaven, rumpled reprobate he appeared to be.

" 'The road!' That sounds adventuresome!"

"You betcha, sweetheart," Dub said as he pulled a chair close to hers. "The stories I could tell you!"

Aw, Christ, here we go. If I had to hear any more of Dub's highway heroics, I would ralph. At least it gave me a chance to get Felicia alone. I crept away from the two at the table, where Dub was telling Meg about blowing all his tires on a steep mountainside. I'd already heard this story at the doctor's office. If this tale was true, then I'm taller than Wilt Chamberlain and richer than Bill Gates.

"Hon, talk to you for a moment?"

I jerked my head toward the living room. Felicia frowned down at the burgers that sizzled in a skillet.

"I'm kinda busy here—"

"It's important."

Felicia turned the heat down under the skillet and followed me into the other room, looking none too pleased at the interruption.

I spoke quickly and quietly, not wanting the others to hear and not wanting to delay Felicia any longer than necessary. Those burgers smelled great.

I told her about the visit to Dr. Jasper Graves and what he'd said about the tests. Felicia frowned at hearing that Dub had no insurance, but to her credit she didn't interrupt.

When I ran out of steam, she asked, "How has he been today?"

"In and out. He'll seem fine for a while, then it's suddenly like his brain has been abducted by aliens."

Felicia squinted at me.

"You watch too much TV."

"You know what I mean. He turns into a space case."

"Checks out?"

"Exactly. He's been in and out of the Hotel Crackers all day."

Felicia nodded.

"I got chased by those skinheads today," I said. "Dub was sitting in the truck, waiting for me. He just sat there, staring straight ahead, while I banged on the locked door. He finally came around, but it was damned close."

I told her this only to build a case, to show I couldn't do my job with Dub tagging along. Count on Felicia to cling to the wrong thing.

"Skinheads? You hunted them down?"

"Yeah, but it went sour on me. Five of them and only one of me, and I thought I was going to get beat to death before Dub could rejoin us here on this planet and let me in the truck."

"Why didn't you use your gun, like you did before?"

"Um. Didn't have it with me."

"What?"

"I left it at home because I was afraid Dub would—"

"After what those storm troopers did to our house? What, you think they're joking?"

"Most certainly not, but—"

148

"You could've been killed."

"Exactly, because Dub was all checked out—"

"Then where would that have left Dub? Out there stranded in your truck, probably no idea where he was. Surrounded by skinheads—"

"What about me? I'm the one who would've been dead." Felicia glowered.

"Sounds like you would've deserved it. Chasing down those skinheads unarmed—"

"Hey, come on, I didn't know I was gonna find them. I was just looking around."

Felicia shook her head in disgust. She does that so much, it's a wonder her head doesn't twist right off her neck.

"How did you track them down?" she asked.

I told her, from Mike Sterling's tip to my nifty escape at the warehouse. I tried not to make myself sound overly courageous. There was enough hot air in the house already, with Dub spewing his windy stories. Besides, Felicia always punctures me when I start to inflate my tales of adventure.

She seemed thoroughly unimpressed until I got to the part about Richie's phone bill.

"This is information Pool doesn't have?" she said, cutting to the chase as usual.

"He didn't have any idea where to find Richie as recently as lunchtime. If you can believe anything that weasel says."

"Guess you've got some more work to do."

"I can't take Dub with me on another stakeout. I was hoping you could look after him—"

"What about dinner?"

"Sure, I guess I can take a minute to eat before—"

"You're damned right you can. You're not leaving me alone with those two."

She jerked her head toward the kitchen, where Dub hawhawed at something Meg had exclaimed.

"What's she doing here anyway?" I asked in a whisper.

"She didn't have anyplace to go tonight. She doesn't know

anybody in Albuquerque, and she was whining about being all alone in her apartment—"

"She can whine?"

"In a perky sort of way."

"Ah."

"Anyhow, I guess I had a weak moment. I thought she could use a home-cooked meal."

Great. Dick Johnson's having problems with his son, I've got problems with my father, and now Felicia's adopted a daughter.

"Felicia!" Meg Albright called from the kitchen. "Your stove's smoking!"

"Shit." Felicia turned and sprinted into the kitchen, me right behind her.

Smoke poured up the air vent above the stove. Felicia snatched the pan off the burner and blew on it, trying to clear the smoke and to see how badly the contents were burned. The burgers looked like something a Doberman might've left on the lawn.

"Maybe I should call for a pizza." It was all I could think to say.

"Sounds good."

I watched Meg and Dub while I was on hold with Domino's. Dub had a couple of empties in front of him now, and his chair was even closer to the coed. Flirtation hung thick in the air. Meg probably didn't realize she was encouraging the old coot. She's the type, so happy and friendly, who always are surprised when stalkers start following them home.

I ordered the pizza, hung up the phone and turned back to Felicia, who was scraping the black gunk from the frying pan into the garbage disposal.

"You know, hon," I ventured, "maybe I should go on about my work. You guys can eat and—"

Felicia gave me the hard eye and flipped the switch on the disposal, setting off its primordial, counterrattling growl. I suspected she was visualizing some portion of my anatomy in there with the whirring blades.

As soon as she flipped the switch off, I said quickly, "Or maybe I should just stay here."

"Good idea."

TWENTY

Once the pizza arrived, we settled around the table, Felicia to my left and Dub to my right. Meg Albright didn't waste any time turning her attention to me. I thought she was trying to head off Dub before he launched into another epic, but she was going someplace else.

"Sorry to hear about your trouble, Bubba!"

I blinked for several seconds before answering astutely, "What trouble?"

"The graffiti! I couldn't help but notice it when Felicia drove me over here! She said someone was after you!"

"Not exactly, I think—"

"We saw those boys today," Dub offered. "They almost kicked Bubba's butt!"

"Now, that's not—"

"The same guys?" Meg tilted her head again. I resisted the urge to reach across the table and straighten it for her.

"Think so," Dub said. "They look like some bad old boys. Bubba had to put the pedal to the metal."

"We're assuming it was the same—"

"Sure it was!" he said. "Bubba's done got crossways with those boys. Good thing I'm looking out for him."

"Wait a minute." I was tired of being cut off. "If you'd unlocked that door—"

"Bubba," Felicia's voice was stern, "give it a rest."

"But—"

"I told Meg I didn't want her to get too curious about it," Felicia said, turning a chilly smile on her intern. "I don't want to see anything about my house in the newspaper."

"Now that's a funny position to take," I began, "considering—"

"I told Felicia I'd do whatever she said!" Meg's voice really was beginning to grate. "She's been wonderful since I got to Albuquerque! She's been just like a mother to me!"

I glanced warily at Felicia, fearing an explosion, but Felicia's cheeks were pink, and she couldn't keep the smile off her face. What was wrong with her? Felicia and I have been together so long, I think I know what to expect from her. It's not always pretty, but at least it's fairly predictable. But the last couple of days, she'd surprised me at every turn.

"How long are you at the *Gazette?*" I asked Meg, and it felt good to complete a sentence.

"Six weeks! I'll be working with Felicia the whole time!"

Felicia stared down into her plate.

"It's already been two weeks!" Meg exclaimed. "The time has flown past! I'm learning so much!"

"That's great," I said, and chomped into a slice of Supreme Thick Crust so somebody else would have to take up the conversational thread. Figured it would be Dub.

"Where you from, sugar pie?"

"I'm a small-town girl! Little town you've never heard of outside of Madison, Wisconsin!"

What do you know about that? I'd guessed Wisconsin, and hit it right on a fifty-to-one shot. I was so busy applauding myself, I nearly fell off my chair when Meg yapped, "That's why I'm so excited about your brush with a gang! We don't have anything like that where I come from! I wish you'd tell me more about it."

Felicia had put the kibosh on the topic. I wasn't about to cross Felicia, but I didn't want to be rude and not answer at all. Fortunately, Dub had his own agenda.

"You want excitement? I'll tell you what's excitin'. Try sliding sideways on a sheet of ice in a semi! I jackknifed this rig one time in Wyoming—"

I stopped listening. For a man with a perfect driving record, Dub sure had a lot of close calls to recount.

I kept my head low, shoveling in pizza. I was itching to go after Richie Johnson, and anything I could do to rush along the meal would help. I could deal with the consequences later. I keep a big jar of cherry-flavored Rolaids in the Ram.

"Wow! That does sound exciting!" Meg's yelp brought me back to the table. "That's why I want to be a reporter! Just to hear stories like those!"

If Meg fell that easily for a fabrication, she wouldn't be much of a journalist, I figured, no matter how persistent she might be. Maybe she was just being nice.

"You're so smart and pretty," Dub said, "why the hell you want to work for a newspaper? Why don't you go into TV?"

Meg blushed furiously, and couldn't bring herself to look over at Felicia.

Felicia's jaw twitched, but she didn't seem to be chewing. Her eyes had that hard glitter they get when I say something stupid. It wasn't me this time. Felicia worked at a newspaper and not TV, and Dub hadn't asked her the same question. Perceptive journalist that she is, Felicia had picked this up right away.

And so had Meg.

And so, surprisingly, had I.

But not Dub. He stared blankly at Meg, chewing with his mouth open.

I swallowed a very dry mouthful of pizza and said, "Meg

probably prefers newspapers for the same reason Felicia does. They're more thorough and informative and they have, you know, long stories in them. More detail, and—"

"In-depth." Felicia said out of the side of her mouth.

"Right. They're more in-depth and all. It's serious journalism."

"Exactly!" Meg chimed. "No show biz for me!"

She beamed.

"Not even beauty pageants?" I asked this only because I'd pictured her earlier as Miss Wisconsin, and I'd been right about the Wisconsin part. I was curious. But as soon as it was out of my mouth, I realized it dug us deeper into the who's-the-cuter-reporter morass and regretted it deeply.

"Beauty pageants! Me? Never!"

Meg Albright seemed to find this terribly amusing. I watched her snickering, though it was annoying as hell, because I was afraid to look over at Felicia.

"More money to be made in TV!" Dub shouted crazily.

It took a second before anybody answered, but then Meg stepped up to the plate.

"I don't care about money!"

I found that to be an amazing statement, one on a par with, "No sex for me!" But I didn't get a chance to say so.

Dub proclaimed: "The only people I ever met who didn't 'care about money' were ones who had a shitpile of it."

Meg blushed. Guess Dub had her button. He seemed to have unerring aim.

"It's true my family's wealthy," she said quietly. Then she looked up proudly. "But I intend to make it on my own!"

Felicia exhaled loudly, and it sounded like, "Sheesh!" She pushed away from the table and went to the fridge for more tea.

Dub seemed willing to keep Meg busy, so I ate faster, one eye on Felicia. She seemed fed up with the lot of us. A full day of Meg certainly could wear down a person. And Dub was no picnic. Felicia moved briskly in the kitchen, putting stuff away, shutting cabinet doors just a little hard.

Was she upset because Dub showered his attentions on the younger woman? Actually, it was more like a downpour, but why would that bother Felicia? Was she, my God, *jealous?*

"Daddy's a developer!" That perked my ears up. Another developer. Just like Dick Johnson. Meg seemed to have turned out quite different from young Richie.

"He named the streets in one of his subdivisions after my sisters and me!"

"Is that right?"

"Meg and Amy and Jo."

"No fourth sister?" Felicia asked drily as she returned to the table.

"Ha-ha! Everyone asks me that! No, there's no Beth. But Daddy did always call us his 'Little Women!'"

"God, that's cute," Felicia said, and her face looked like she'd eaten a tablespoon of Karo syrup.

"What the hell are you talking about?" Dub snarled. "I said something about Felicia being the 'little woman' and Bubba dern near snapped my head off!"

Glances were exchanged around the table, and then Felicia burst out laughing and Meg felt free to join in. Dub looked mystified. I looked at my wristwatch.

"Hate to break up the party," I said as I got to my feet. "But I really do have to take care of some business."

Felicia tried to go flinty on me, but I'd caught her when she was laughing, and she couldn't quite manage it.

"You'll be all right to drive Meg home and all?" I asked her.

"Sure, go ahead. We'll probably visit awhile longer without you."

I told Meg it was nice to meet her and I told Dub goodnight and I was halfway to the door before Felicia called behind me, "Do you have your pistol?"

I was headed to my office to get my gun before she mentioned it. Really. Why do women have to do that? I can't walk out the door without Felicia asking, "Got your keys? Got your wallet? Got your gun?"

"I got it," I shouted over my shoulder.

"A pistol!" Meg's voice trailed behind me. "That sounds exciting!"

TWENTY-ONE

The address I'd found in the Volkswagen was my only clue. I hadn't noted how old the phone bill was, so for all I knew Richie had moved three times since he paid it. But it was a lead, and it was an easy one to follow up.

I located the address, and parked on Dartmouth half a block away. The address was in one of those apartment complexes squeezed sideways onto a narrow lot intended for a single-family dwelling. The student ghetto has a lot of those wedged between regular little houses, and the fact that they're usually set back from the street a ways doesn't make them any less an eyesore.

I had plenty of time to consider neighborhood development and miscarriages of zoning while I waited for Richie Johnson to show up. The phone bill said he was in apartment Eight, which I'd determined was at the rear of the apartment complex on the ground floor. Nobody was home, so I waited in my warm truck. If Richie's Volkswagen pulled into the narrow asphalt strip that covered what should've been the lot's front lawn, I'd easily have a minute or two while he got out of the car and walked to the back of the building. Knowing this didn't make waiting any easier, and it was a long two hours before the Volkswagen bounced into the parking lot and shut off its headlights.

Richie's arrival caught me at a bad time. Nature calls when you're on surveillance, and you can't just go knocking on doors, requesting facilities. I used to keep a wide-mouth jar under the seat of my old Chevy Nova for such purposes, but Felicia bought me a fancy version after I got the shiny new Ram.

The gizmo was, in fact, intended for use by long-haul truckers like Dub. It's a plastic quart bottle with a hose attached to the neck. At the other end of the hose is a funnel-like device so you don't have to try to aim for the little hole in the end of a hose. The bottle even has a twist-on cap dangling from a cord, so you can remove the funnel and cap the whole thing off until you reach a handy place to pour it out.

I was using the device for its intended purpose when the Volkswagen arrived. I finished as quickly as I could and carefully set the half-full bottle on the floorboard.

I zipped up and put my pistol in my belt and my cellular phone in the pocket of my trusty old denim jacket. Then I trotted across the street to the apartment complex. The light spilling from Richie's apartment vanished when he closed the door, but I scurried up to the door and knocked.

The door swung open right away, and I was eye-to-eye with two hundred thousand dollars.

Richie didn't look so good. He seemed paler than ever, and his shaved head looked chalky. He had dark circles under his eyes, and his leather jacket hung loosely over scrawny shoulders. His blue jeans were stiffly new—probably purchased with some of my ransom money—but he otherwise looked just as scruffy and sick and sour as when I'd glimpsed him at the nightclub.

He tried to slam the door shut, but I caught it in time

without losing any fingers. I muscled it backward, figuring Richie Johnson didn't have the strength to stop me from coming in, even if he threw all his paltry weight into the job.

He didn't even try. He leaped backward, letting me fly stumbling into the room, and he turned and tried to run. Where he expected to go in a one-bedroom apartment, I don't know, but he never got the chance because I snagged the collar of his jacket and yanked him off his feet. I couldn't keep my own balance, however, and we both ended up sprawled on the ratty carpet, huffing for breath.

"You all right?" I asked, when I could see he wasn't going to run for it again.

"Who the fuck are you?"

"My name's Bubba."

"What do you want?"

"I'm working for your dad. We've been looking all over for you."

"Fuck him. And fuck you, too."

That raised my hackles a little. It always does. You don't grow up in Mississippi without learning to react violently to effrontery. Southern gentlemen know such an insult almost certainly will result in bloodshed. Folks in the rest of the country toss it off as if they were saying, "Have a nice day."

I didn't answer. I clambered to my feet and reached out a hand to help him up. He glared at me for a second, but what could he do but play along? He reached up and I pulled him to a standing position.

"There," I said. "You finished cussing now?"

Every sullen teenager I'd ever met lived behind Richie Johnson's dark eyes. Okay, the kid's had a rough time of it, with his heart condition and all, but he didn't need to take it out on me. Guess he realized that, too, because he nodded and looked at the floor.

"All right. I'll call your father now."

That snapped Richie's head up, and resentment fled his expression, leaving behind puppy-dog eyes filled with pleading.

"Don't do that," he said. "Please. I don't want him to find me."

His sudden change in demeanor took me off-guard.

"You've made that pretty clear," I said. "Finding you wasn't easy."

"He'll make me go back home. I can't do that."

"Why not?"

Richie turned away from me, and took a couple of steps. I couldn't tell whether he was upset or planning a lie. But I told myself whatever he said shouldn't matter. I had a job to do, one that promised a big payoff.

"I can't face it," he said. "I can't listen to him nag me anymore."

"Nag you about what?"

"The way I look, the way I dress, the things I like to do, you name it. He wants me to be just like him, but I have to live my own life."

The Teenager's Lament. Haven't we all heard that before? Haven't we all lived it?

"He's worried about you," I said. The Adult's Ready Answer.

"No, he's not. He wants me home so he can control me. He tell you about my heart?"

"Yes."

"He thinks that gives him a license to run my life. 'You can't do that, boy. It's not good for your heart.' "

The kid did a pretty fair imitation of Dick Johnson. It helped that he had even less hair than his old man.

"Maybe he's right."

"No, he's not. I'm not worried about my goddamn heart. Why should he? If I've got to tiptoe around my whole life, then maybe it's not worth it. I'd rather live a little and take my chances."

"Hanging out with the Oi Boys? That's living?"

That shut him up. He frowned, then wandered off around the scantily furnished room. Plastic milk crates served as end tables on either side of a sagging brown sofa. He'd built a bookcase out of boards and bricks, but didn't have much to put on the shelves—a couple of comic books, a miniature boom box, empty bottles with the dried-out stems of pilfered flowers arranged in them. Posters of bizarro rock stars were thumbtacked to the paneled walls and the whole place smelled like spilled beer. A typical student ghetto apartment.

The room might've been bare, but it was warm. Richie had the heat going full blast. He shucked his bomber jacket. He wore a black T-shirt underneath, and his skinny arms looked like pipe cleaners sticking out of the sleeves. His pale forearms bore long scratches, and I noticed other scabbed-over cuts on the backs of his hands.

"What happened to you?"

It took him a second to realize I was asking about the wounds.

"Spike scratched me when I was shaving him."

"Spike?"

At the sound of his name, a cat padded in from the hall that led to the bedroom. It was a normal, healthy looking cat in every way, except that its coat had been shaved all over, exposing pale skin with the blue tinge of a five o'clock shadow. The only fur left was right around its mouth, a few stray tufts on its ears, and its whiskers.

"Jesus."

"This is Spike," Richie said brightly, as if he was introducing me to a friend.

"Why the hell do you shave him like that?"

"Mayhem makes me do it. He don't like hair. Not on anything."

"He makes you shave your *cat?*"

"Let's say it was a firm suggestion."

Sounded like the kind of thing Dick Johnson would have said, but Richie wasn't imitating him now. He was staring

162

down at his shaved kitty, and he looked kind of sad.

"Mayhem's got some kind of scalp condition," he said. "It's called alopecia something-or-other. Made most of his hair fall out by itself. So it was easy for him to become a skinhead. Guy's got a full heada hair, it's a bit of a loss to shave it all off. Anyway, Mayhem's kinda weird about hair. First time he ever saw Spike, he said either the cat would have to go or I would. I'd just met up with the Oi Boys, and I was having a good time. But I didn't want to give up Spike. So we compromised."

"You agreed to keep the cat shaved?"

"I know it sounds weird. But I thought it was kinda funny and it wouldn't be any big deal. Spike don't like it much, though."

That explained the scratches all over Richie's arms. Shaving a cat would be even tougher than giving one a bath. Spike sniffed the air near my feet, didn't like what he found and trotted away, looking miffed and naked.

"You ought to try that stuff," I suggested, "that chemical that removes hair. My wife uses it on her legs. What do they call it? Nair."

Richie perked right up.

"Hey, that's a good idea. Maybe Spike wouldn't fight so hard if I just smeared that Nair on him."

"I imagine he still won't like it, but maybe he'll draw less of your blood."

"Yeah."

After this little icebreaker, Richie seemed warmer to me.

"Better yet," I said, "why don't you get away from Mayhem and those other assholes?"

Richie's smile disappeared.

"There's no getting away from them," he said. "You don't just drop out of the Oi Boys. You've got to be voted out."

"They won't let you leave town? How could they stop you?"

Richie shrugged.

"I don't know. I mean, I don't know that I really *want* to leave. Those guys can be real jerks sometimes, picking on me and stuff, making fun of my cat. But they don't try to stop me from doing whatever I want. They don't even know about my heart condition."

"You think they'd treat you different if they did?"

His narrow shoulders rose again. Shrugging seemed to come easy to Richie Johnson, as if he was accustomed to going without answers.

"Maybe so," he said. "But they wouldn't be as weird about it as Daddy is. He wants me to take care of myself and live forever, just so I can look after his fortune. But I don't care about his money or making sure that his good name lives on after he's dead."

"Maybe not, but he's still your father."

Where the hell had that come from? A few days ago, I never would've defended the father's position in such an arrangement. Hadn't my own father abandoned me so he could go off and live his life any way he pleased? He'd left me with no expectations to meet, the reverse of Richie's problem, but that was just as bad. Had Dub's reappearance changed my outlook? And, why was that, considering he'd been nothing but a whopping pain in the posterior ever since he arrived?

I talked faster, trying to chase that from my head.

"Besides, you don't seem totally opposed to his money. You walked off with two hundred thousand dollars of it."

Richie tried to look shocked and amazed, but he wasn't much good at it.

"We saw you pick up that ransom," I said. "We've even got it on videotape."

Richie knitted his brows. Against all that pale background, his dark eyebrows looked like two caterpillars on ice.

"So that's what this is all about," he said. "He wants the money back."

"No, he doesn't care about the money. He only wants to get you back home."

"So he can push me around for the rest of my life."

"I don't know about that, but he seems really worried, Richie. I think you underestimate how much he cares about you."

Richie sucked a tooth, shaking his head slightly. He wasn't buying it.

"No, it's the money. I'm sure of it. Money matters more than anything to him."

"No, it doesn't, and I'll prove it to you. There's this other private investigator, name of Pool, and your dad hired both of us to track you down. He told us that whoever found you first got to keep whatever's left of the ransom money."

"And you believed that?"

"He only wants to get you back. He's not sleeping or eating. He's fretting all the time."

Richie pondered that, but I could see he wasn't coming around. He came up with something else.

"The money," he said, "I'll give you some of it if you won't tell him how to find me."

I was already shaking my head when I said, "It means that much to you?"

"I can't go back home. That's all there is to it. You don't know what it's like, mister, having Dick Johnson breathing down your neck every day."

I could imagine it fairly well, actually, and it wasn't pretty. But I'd hired on to do a job, and I couldn't skate on it, even if the kid was willing to pay. Besides, why take only part of the money when I could call up Dick and claim the whole enchilada?

"You still have the money?" I asked him.

"Most of it," he replied, and the surliness had returned. "I've got it hidden."

"Where?"

Richie snorted.

"Doesn't matter," I said. "We'll get it. I need to call your father now."

I pulled the cellular phone out of my pocket and flipped it open. I dialed the Hilton and asked for Johnson's room.

While I was listened to it ring, Richie said, "It won't do you any good. I'll run off again, first chance I get. I can't live with him anymore."

"How can it be that bad? Your old man's rich. He'd probably buy you anything you want."

"There's only one thing that I want, and that's to stay away from him. Ever since my mom died, he's ridden me hard. He wants me to join the family business."

Now I could see how becoming a strip-mall developer maybe wasn't what Richie wanted to do for a living, but even that beat the hell out of devoting one's life to the skinhead cause. Wouldn't getting him back together with his father be the noblest thing to do? I know what it's like, being separated from your old man, and I wouldn't wish it on anybody, even somebody who wanted to break free. If Richie succeeded in getting away from Dick Johnson, he'd regret it someday. Maybe not right away, maybe not even when Dick cut him off from the family fortune. But one day, once it was too late to repair the damage, Richie would wish he'd kept that relationship intact.

"Please, mister, just think it over," Richie was saying. "Maybe there's some way we can work out a deal. I've got a right to live my own life, right? Wouldn't you hate it if somebody was always telling you what to do?"

Richie was coming dangerously close to describing my relationship with Felicia, and I didn't want to start thinking about that.

The phone rang a fifteenth time. Even if Dick Johnson was sound asleep, he'd had time to answer. It was approaching midnight, and I didn't know where Johnson might be, but I admit I was a little relieved not to reach him. If Dick came storming over, we'd be up the rest of the night, talking it over and restraining Richie and trying to recover the ransom. It would be an ugly night, even if it meant a big payoff at the end.

I closed up my phone and stowed it away.

"He's not there right now," I said. "But he'll be back eventually. How about we wait until morning?"

"Then what?"

"Then I'm calling your dad. You've got to face him."

Richie shook his bald head.

"Look, kid, it's like this: I keep calling every few minutes until I get him or I call him in the morning. Either way, I'm telling him where you are."

Richie licked his lips and glanced toward the door, but something ticked inside him and he gave it up.

"All right!" he said petulantly. "In the morning then. I probably ought to get some sleep before I have to listen to what a jackass I've been, running away."

"Good idea. Go on to bed. I'll just set up here in the living room. I'll be listening all night, so don't try to go out the window. Don't make any phone calls."

Richie nodded me off, and he looked to be fighting back a grin.

"House arrest, huh?"

"Something like that."

"That's cool. But if you're gonna be sitting in here awake all night, think over my offer. I'm sitting on two hundred thousand dollars. We ought to be able to work something out."

"Go to bed, Richie."

He shrugged again and trudged off toward his bedroom.

I shed my jacket, then followed. I hung around the hall outside his bedroom, listening long after he settled down and the bar of light disappeared at the bottom of the door. Finally, when I was pretty sure he'd gone to sleep and my feet were killing me, I returned to the living room and tried to get comfortable on the sofa.

Less than an hour passed before my cell phone rang. It was still in my jacket pocket and it took several seconds of groggy fumbling before I could find it and answer.

"Bubba, you've got to get back here."

"Felicia? What's the matter?"

"It's Dub. He's gone crackers."

"What's he doing?"

"He's waving his arms around and yelling. He wants Meg to dance with him, and she won't do it."

"She's still *there?*"

"He won't let me take her home. And I can't leave him home alone in this condition."

"How long's he been like that?"

"He made a phone call right after you left, and when he came back he had this crazy look in his eye."

"Who'd he call?"

"I don't know. I didn't—"

A crash and a shriek sounded in the background.

"Oh, shit," Felicia said. "He's got his gun. Get here right away."

The line went dead.

"Oh, shit," I said.

I tiptoed down the hall and opened Richie's door to see if the call had awakened him. Light from outside spilled between the ratty curtains, and I could see Richie curled up in his bed, looking very much like a bald, skinny fetus. Spike was a naked ball on the foot of the bed until he raised his head and looked me over. I held a finger to my lips and backed out.

That's two hundred thousand dollars sleeping in there, I thought, *and I'm about to walk away from it—at least briefly— because my father is doing his Mr. Hyde routine.* I stalked back into the living room and snatched up my jacket and threw it on.

I didn't know where Richie left his keys, but locking the door wouldn't have done me any good anyway. I quietly closed it behind me, making sure it didn't lock so I could get back inside later. Then I sprinted for my truck.

168

I put the Ram into gear and shot off down the street. Something went thump on the floorboard and it took me a second in the dark to realize that the long-forgotten pee bottle had turned over and was leaking into the Ram's fine carpet.

TWENTY-TWO

Why do stoplights work in the middle of the night? I think small towns have a better idea with their flashing yellows after midnight. I sat at one red light after another on the way home, pounding my fist on the steering wheel in frustration. It was after one o'clock in the morning on a weeknight. Most of the intersections were as empty of traffic as Antarctica.

Some people driving at this hour might just do a pause-and-go, what we call out here a California Rolling Stop, but not me. No matter how desperate the situation, I try to obey the traffic laws. The odds might be thousands to one that a cop lurked nearby. But I believe too strongly in my own bad luck.

The delays did give me time to throw a dirty towel from under the seat over the spill on the floor. I cleaned up the mess best I could, cracked the windows, and rocketed to the next stoplight.

When I finally got home, I leaped from the Ram and sprinted across the lawn and up the steps. The front door was locked, which pulled me up short. I'd already pocketed my keys. I fumbled with them in the dark, trying to hurry, afraid of what I might find on the other side of the door.

When the deadbolt finally clicked, I threw the door open wide.

The living room was empty and only half-lit. One of the ceramic lamps lay on the floor in a zillion pieces, swept into a neat pile by the sofa. The broom and the dustpan stood nearby, waiting to finish. I took a few hesitant steps into the room, past the shattered lamp, until I could see around the corner to the kitchen. Felicia, Dub, and Meg sat around the table, nursing cups of coffee. Dub looked a little winded, but otherwise all was calm, all was bright.

My thought: *What the hell am I doing here?*

"Hi, hon," Felicia called from the kitchen. "Come on in. You want a cup of coffee?"

"I thought there was an emergency."

Felicia glanced over at Dub, but she was smiling.

"It's been a little wild around here, but everything's fine now."

Dub grinned absently, looking from her to me and back again. Meg studied the tabletop.

"What happened?"

"Sure you don't want some coffee?"

"No, I want to know what's going on here. I left Richie Johnson unattended."

"You found him?"

That seemed to bring Dub back to earth. He looked at me sharply and his thick fingers gripped the edge of the table.

"Yes, I found him. I'm sitting on him until morning, then I'm handing him over to Dick."

"You left him alone?"

"You said it was an emergency."

"You should've said something—"

"I didn't get a chance. There was a crash and you hung up."

"Right. That was the lamp."

Dub shifted in his chair and spoke up.

"Hell, son, I'm sorry about that there lamp. Guess I got carried away."

"You said he had a gun," I said to Felicia.

"He got it down out of the cabinet while I was talking to you on the phone. I thought he was going to shoot somebody."

"Aw, hell," Dub said. "I wasn't gonna shoot nobody. I was just funnin' around."

Meg looked up at me, and I suppose she thought she could help.

"He wanted to dance some more!"

"What?"

"We were dancing! But it started getting late! And he didn't want to stop!"

"You danced with him?"

"She was being polite," Felicia said. "I think Dub had too many beers."

"You said something about a phone call?"

"Yeah. He got off the phone and wanted to dance right away. When we tried to leave, he started running around and blocking the door. He's pretty spry."

She grinned at Dub again, as if it had all been in good fun, as if I weren't in the wrong place to be making a fortune.

"Where's the gun now?" I demanded.

"He gave it back after I called you. I put it away. Everything's fine now."

"Sorry they had to call you, son," Dub moaned. "I didn't mean no harm."

"You might be costing me two hundred thousand dollars right now."

Dub grimaced and chewed on a thumbnail.

"Who was on the phone?" I asked him.

"What phone?"

"The call you made."

"I never made no call."

I stifled a growl and turned back to Felicia.

"What do you want me to do?"

"I want you to get back to that rich kid fast as you can," she said, which was finally the right answer.

"Right. You'll take Meg home?"

"Sure. Just take Dub with you."

"What?"

"We can't leave him alone right now," she said patiently. "I don't think Meg wants him riding with us. She's had a bit of a scare."

Meg made wide eyes to show it was true.

"I'll take her home," I said. "You stay here with Dub."

"She lives way on the north end of town," Felicia said. "Up near Corrales."

It would take me an hour to drive there and get back to Richie Johnson's apartment. I sighed heavily.

"Okay, Dub, let's go. You're coming with me."

Dub touched the bill of his cap in a quick salute and jumped to his feet. Guess getting chastised had made him co-operative. For a change.

"I'll get my coat."

He trotted off toward my office.

Felicia stood and came to within whispering range.

"Thanks, Bubba. He's really out of it. You should've seen him, jumping around and hooting and swinging that gun around. He was like a chimp loose in the house."

"I haven't seen him like that. Usually, he just sort of drifts away."

Felicia frowned.

"Maybe he's getting worse."

"Dr. Graves said this could happen. Alzheimer's patients sometimes get aggressive."

"Think that's what it is?"

"I don't know. I can't think about it now. I've got to get back to Richie."

"Right. What are you going to do with Dub?"

I shook my head.

"Sit with him in the truck, I guess. I can't take him in the apartment with Richie asleep in there. Dub's too loud."

"Especially if he has another fit."

I gave her a peck on the forehead.

"I've got to go. Richie's probably on his way out of the state by now."

"I hope not."

Dub emerged from my office wearing his filthy denim vest. He was up on his toes, ready to go. I sighed again.

"I'll bring him back here when I get a chance," I said. "We need to call the doctor and schedule those tests."

Felicia nodded.

I told Felicia and Meg good night and headed for the door. Dub waved to the women, chuckling.

"Bye, y'all. Thanks for being my dance partners!"

That made me pause. I looked over my shoulder at Felicia. *"You* danced with him, too?"

"I'll tell you all about it later," she said. "Just go."

I hooked Dub's arm and started through the door.

Felicia shouted from behind me, "Got your keys?"

I hustled Dub out to the truck and opened his door for him.

"Damnation! Smells like a stable in here!"

"Had a little accident," I said. "Roll your window down. It'll air out while we drive."

Dub grumbled, but he climbed inside, looking all around as if afraid he'd sit in something vile. I ran around to the driver's side, and he still wasn't settled by the time I got behind the wheel.

"Would you hurry?"

"Keep your britches on."

Once he was buckled up, I cranked the engine and we roared away. We hit the lights mostly green on the way back to Richie's place, and it didn't take long. Dub had little to say for himself on the way.

"What got into you back there?" I asked, when we were almost to Richie's.

"I didn't mean any harm. Just horsin' around."

"More like a stallion. What were you thinking, putting the moves on that college girl?"

"What girl?"

"Meg."

"Meg who?"

"Meg back at the house just now."

Dub shook his head blankly.

"Never mind. Let me ask you another question: How did you find that gun?"

"What gun?"

I exhaled through gritted teeth.

"Forget it."

My heart leaped with joy when I saw the Volkswagen still parked where it had been. Richie must've slept through the whole thing.

The quiet street's curbs were crowded with parked cars, but I found a spot not too far away from Richie's. I couldn't see his door from this vantage, but I had a good view of the Volkswagen and the back of the building. Richie's windows were dark.

"Why are we stoppin' here?"

"That's Richie's place. We're watching it until sunrise."

"Sitting here in the truck?"

"That's right. Welcome to my world."

Dub grouched some more about the smell in the truck, but I ordered him to sit tight.

I hurried to Richie's apartment and slipped inside. Everything looked the same. I tiptoed down the hall, opened the bedroom door a few inches, and peeked through the gap. Richie was right where I left him. This time, even Spike didn't wake up to glare at me. I closed the door again and sneaked back outdoors, making sure the front door didn't lock behind me. All was well.

When I got back to the Ram, Dub greeted me by saying, "We're just gonna sit here all night?"

"It's only a few hours. Soon as it gets light, I'll call Dick Johnson and get this done."

"Dick who?"

"Why don't you try to get some sleep, Dub? You've had a big night."

"I have?"

"Yes. Good night."

Dub blinked at me awhile, but he finally tipped his cap bill over his eyes and nestled into the corner of the cab. Within minutes, he was snoring loudly.

I sat awake a long time, thinking about Richie Johnson and whether I was doing the right thing handing him over to his dad. I tried to tell myself I wasn't letting the money make the decision for me. Richie was okay, despite his sass and his stubbornness and his bald rebellion. But Dick Johnson was my client, and I'd deliver Richie to him. I'd do my job, take the money, and if Richie went home and couldn't stand it, hell, he could run away again. It would no longer be my problem.

A bigger concern was Dub, who snorted and wheezed next to me. Any final doubts I'd had about his mental condition were gone. The man was not right. Even the most drunken, oblivious trucker eventually gets the message that the party's over. But not Dub. He'd gone right on, knocking over lamps and brandishing a gun and saying God-knows-what to Miss Wisconsin. And now he seemed to have no memory of it, just like after the Great 7-Eleven Holdup.

Dub needed those expensive tests if there was any hope of sorting out his problem. I got the sinking feeling that much of my ransom money would end up in the sterile pocket of Dr. Jasper Graves.

The last time I looked at my watch, it was four o'clock in the morning. The next thing I knew the sun was in my eyes and Dub was gone.

TWENTY-THREE

I looked all around the truck, but there was no Dub dancing in the bright March sunshine.

I creaked out of the truck. The air was cold, but the sky was a blue so sharp you could cut yourself on it. The only clouds draped over the shoulders of the Sandia Mountains like a white feather boa.

Still no sign of Dub. I imagined Felicia's reaction when I told her I'd let him wander off. It wouldn't be pretty.

Then he appeared around the back corner of a frame house that squatted in the shadows of Richie's apartment building. He ducked under the reaching arms of a spindly mulberry tree and walked quickly toward me, sort of hopping on one leg when he remembered to zip his pants.

I got back in the truck, which was marginally warmer than outside, and Dub joined me.

"I didn't know where you'd gone," I said in a voice thick with too little sleep.

"Had to take a leak," he said. "Guess I could've whizzed

in your truck. Couldn't smell any worse."

"Roll down your window."

Dub cranked the knob, then fished out his plug of tobacco and bit off a chaw, looking thoughtful.

"You found that boy, huh?"

"What?"

"That Richie? He's in there?"

"Yeah."

"You gonna get that big reward?"

"That's the plan." I sounded nervous in my own ears.

"Well, son," Dub said, and his voice went soft and kind of squishy, "I hope it works out for you."

He stared out the window, and I couldn't make out his expression. But he sounded genuine, at least for the moment, and it gave me something to cling to, a life raft in the tossing seas of my own indecision and worry.

"Thanks, Dub. I mean that."

He answered by spitting out the window.

"Sure as hell stinks in here, though, don't it?"

My teeth ground together.

"Maybe you can use that money to have your truck fumigated," he said. "And you still gotta get that paint off your house."

"I know."

"That gal of yours, she wants that paint off there."

"I know."

"You oughta do whatever you can to make sure she's happy. She's a keeper."

"I know that, too."

If this was what passed for fatherly advice, I could live without it. I don't mean to sound like Richie, but I'm fully capable of running my own life, including keeping Felicia happy. Most of the time, anyway. I didn't need Mister Dub-Come-Lately to remind me of my husbandly duties.

"I'd better call Dick Johnson."

I pulled the phone out of my pocket and dialed the Hilton's number from memory and listened to it ring. When the front desk answered, I asked for Johnson's room. It rang twice before he picked up.

"Yeah?"

I guess you abandon "hello" once you make enough money.

"Good morning, Mr. Johnson. This is Bubba Mabry. I've found your son."

"Well, it's about time. Where the hell is he?"

A fine how-de-do. If I'd had doubts about Johnson, if I'd wanted to believe everything Richie had said about him, maybe it was because the guy was such a barking asshole.

"He's at his apartment," I said. "I located him late last night, and he promised he'd stay put until you got here this morning to talk things over."

"Say what? Why didn't you bring him to me right away?"

A storm was building in Dick Johnson's voice, but I tried to respond with calm.

"I tried to call around midnight, but you weren't there."

"I'd gone looking for Richie at that nightclub you told me about. Christ, what a noisy shithole that is. Is Richie there with you now?"

"No, I'm calling from my truck, but I'm parked outside his place."

"You fuckin' idiot! You let him out of your sight?"

"He was sleeping soundly when I last saw him."

"He seems all right?"

How to answer?

"He's a little confused, and he's real thin. But I think he'll be fine."

"Where are you?"

I gave him the address.

"Don't do anything until I get there. I'll grab him up and march him back to Fort Worth."

"You might want to talk to him first."

"What?"

"From what he said last night, I think you two need to talk. He wants you to treat him like an adult."

"What are you, his shrink? And, who says he's an adult? He's a *boy*, for Chrissakes."

"Legally, he's an adult. Old enough to vote, old enough to enter into contracts, the works. Maybe you should remember that when you come to see him."

"Maybe you should shut the fuck up and do your job. I'll take care of raising my son."

It was hard to swallow that. I was trying to give the man sound advice. I'd been awake most of the night, thinking about how to play Dick Johnson's reunion with Richie. But he was having none of it. He still was a loud Texan who bulled his way through every situation. Maybe I'd been kidding myself, thinking he and Richie could work something out and stop shouting down each other's throats.

It was too late to back out now. I'd already told him where to find his son.

"We'll wait for you out front," I said, and I hung up.

I angrily stuffed the phone in the glove compartment.

"Who was that?" Dub demanded.

"Dick Johnson."

"Who?"

"You remember Mr. Johnson. We had lunch with him?"

Recognition dawned.

"He gonna buy us breakfast?"

"I don't think so. It's a business meeting."

"Dang."

It took fifteen minutes for Johnson to arrive. Dub fidgeted the whole time, but didn't have much to say, which was fine by me.

Pool's rented Cadillac screeched to a stop across the street, and he and Johnson unfolded from it in their suits and matching Stetsons. The cavalry had arrived.

"Wait here," I told Dub as I leaped from the truck.

I met Johnson and Pool on the sidewalk by Richie's car.

Pool was squinting into the Volkswagen's shabby interior.

I opened my mouth to say good morning, but Johnson cut me off. "Where is he?"

"Far end. Apartment Eight."

Johnson marched down the sidewalk, Pool and me trailing behind. He pounded on the door, loud enough to wake everybody in the building. It wasn't quite eight o'clock. Maybe Richie was still asleep.

"It's not locked," I said.

Johnson tried the knob, but it didn't budge.

"The hell it's not," he said.

He banged on the door some more.

Despite the cold, I was sweating like a racehorse. I pushed Johnson out of the way and pressed my ear to the door, hoping against hope that I'd hear Richie coming. Nothing. I tried the lock. I knocked on the door so hard it hurt my hand.

"Goddammit, Mabry, I knew this would happen." Johnson spat. "Why the hell didn't you call me last night when you had him in hand?"

"I tried—"

"He's run off again, I guaran-damn-tee it."

"His car's still here."

"Hell, boy, there're other cars in the world. Maybe he called a taxi. He's sure got the money to pay for one."

"He promised—"

"I told you he's not right in the head! You can't take the promise of somebody who'd run away from home and join up with the skinheads."

"Hold on a minute, Dick," Pool soothed. "Maybe the boy's inside. All this yelling isn't gonna make him want to open the door any quicker."

Pool reached inside his suit jacket and pulled out a small leather pouch.

"Excuse me, Bubba. Mind if I give that door a try?"

I didn't know what he meant at first, but I stepped out of the way. Then the big showoff unzipped the pouch and selected a lock pick from a collection he had there.

Now, damn it, I know how to pick a lock myself, though I'm not much good at it. Why hadn't I thought of that? I just stood there like a rube, and let Pool steal my thunder.

He had the door open in twenty seconds or so, better than I ever could've done, which made me spitting mad. And then Dub came strolling up from the parking lot, going at his gums with a toothpick and promising to make everything worse.

"What y'all doin'?" he shouted. I made shushing gestures at him, and looked all around to make sure no one else saw us breaking and entering.

Pool ignored Dub and me, keeping his attention on the Texan with the big bankroll. With his hand on the doorknob, he turned to Johnson and asked, "Ready?"

Johnson nodded once, and Pool turned the knob and swung the door open.

None of us, it's fair to say, expected what we found inside.

Richie sat in his underwear in a kitchen chair in the middle of the living room, his hands pinned behind his back, his head hanging forward limply. The carpet at his feet was spattered with blood. Someone had carved his bare scalp with a knife, and the crusted blood formed an *A* inside a circle, the same symbol spray painted all over my house, the sign for Anarchy.

TWENTY-FOUR

Dead folks make me squeamish, especially ones I'd witnessed walking and talking only hours before. It was no different seeing Richie Johnson's corpse, but this time I felt even worse. Because this time, I could've saved him and I'd blown it.

Dick Johnson was the first through the door, and he hugged Richie and tried to pull him out of the chair. I came second, and it took me only a moment to check Richie's neck for a pulse and find nothing. His skin was already cold.

I gingerly grasped Dick Johnson's arms and broke the lock they had around his son.

"We need to leave him alone," I said. "Evidence. I'll call the police."

Johnson's eyes were wide and wet and his face had turned bright red. His mouth gaped and closed, a fish out of water, but he didn't seem capable of forming words. Not yet, anyway. I was certain I'd get an earful soon as he was over the initial shock.

I wrapped my arms around him and walked him away from the body, turning him so he could look away from his dead son.

"Come on," I said. "Let's find the phone."

I'd left my cellular in the truck, but I knew Richie had a phone somewhere—that's how I'd hunted him down. I kept my arm around Johnson's shaking shoulders while I looked for the phone, finally locating it in the bedroom.

Spike the shaved cat was disturbed by all the people in his house, and he scampered past our feet to shoot out the bedroom door. Dick Johnson didn't notice, which says a lot about the depth of the man's grief.

"Sit right here on the bed," I told him, and he obeyed without a word. He pressed his hands to his face and surrendered to weeping.

I dialed 911, and asked if Lt. Steve Romero had arrived for work yet.

"Romero," he barked in greeting.

"Hi, Steve, it's Bubba Mabry."

"What do you want? More of your work you want me to do?"

"Not this time. I've got some work for you, though. Somebody killed my client's son."

"Aw, shit."

"My sentiments exactly."

I gave him the address, and he said he'd be right there.

Dick Johnson hadn't moved from his spot on the bed, and he still had his eyes covered with his hands. Tears dripped off the tips of his mustache.

"Mr. Johnson? You sit right here for a minute. The police are on their way."

I'd left Pool and Dub back in the living room, and I wanted to check on them, make sure they were smart enough not to get fingerprints everywhere. The minute Pool picked that lock, we'd been guilty of invading a crime scene.

Dub squatted before Richie's body, looking it over but not touching him.

Pool not only was touching stuff, he seemed to be going through the whole apartment, leaving his fingerprints everywhere. I found him in the kitchen, opening cabinet doors and slamming them, searching quickly through cereal boxes and anything else he could find inside.

"What the hell are you doing?"

He didn't even bother to look at me. He was too busy hurrying through his task.

"Looking for that money," he said. "You called the cops, right? We need to find that ransom before they get here."

"Why?"

"Because they'll confiscate it if they find it first. Then it'll be tied up forever."

"Not like you're getting any of that money anyway," I said, an edge in my voice.

Pool turned to me, and he had an expression on his face like a car salesman.

"You got me all wrong, Bubba. I'm not trying to find the money for myself. It's for our client. Dick doesn't need two hundred thousand dollars of his money stuck in some police evidence locker."

"But it *is* evidence. Don't you suppose whoever killed Richie did it for just that reason? And don't you think they probably took the money with them?"

Pool came toward me, which made me back up a step, and he glanced down the hall to make sure Johnson wouldn't hear him. The sound of Dick's sobbing was all he found.

"Did you even look at the body, Bubba?"

"Not much. I was busy with Mr. Johnson."

"Check it out. Look at the bruises on the boy's face, the cigarette burns on his arms. All those scratches. Somebody was trying to make him talk. Probably asking him about the money, right?"

"His cat made the scratches, but you could be right about the others."

"I don't think they got the money."

"Why not?"

"Richie's heart. I'll bet the autopsy will find he died of a heart attack brought on by the interrogation. Maybe he died before he told them anything."

I glanced over at Richie's body. It still sat up, held there by two sets of handcuffs that pinned his wrists to the back legs of the chair. The wounds Pool described were plainly visible, but he seemed to be leaving something out.

"What about that knife work on his head? Don't you think that might've been why he died?"

Pool squinted at me like I was a jackass that wouldn't follow his lead.

"Naw, Bubba. Hell, there ain't enough blood for that. That was done after he was already dead."

"Looks like plenty of blood to me." I'm not crazy about the sight of blood, either, and I'd tried not to look too closely.

"Haven't you ever had a scalp wound? They bleed like a sonabitch. I think his heart had already stopped pumping. What's there just sorta seeped out."

I understood what he was saying and could visualize it a little too clearly. My stomach did a somersault.

Pool bent over and opened the filthy oven to peer inside. It was all I could do not to boot him in the ass.

"Hey, Bubba," Dub called. He'd risen from his squat, but he was still looking at Richie. "The pattern on this boy's head? It's just like that graffiti on your house."

Thank you, Dub, for weighing in with that little tidbit. As if I hadn't already figured that out. I tried to ignore him, but he wasn't done.

"You see this cat? Little shit ain't got no hair!"

"Why don't you wait outside?" I said. "The cops'll be here any second."

"I ain't a'scared of no cops."

"That's not what I meant. I—"

Then the sunlight pouring through the still-open door was blocked by the bulky figure of Lt. Steve Romero.

"That was quick." It was all I could think to say.

"Sure, Bubba," Romero said as he stepped inside. "That's why we have those cars with the sirens and the flashing lights."

Romero walked up to Richie's body and slowly circled it. He's got eyes like a freaking hawk, especially when he's at a crime scene, and I felt certain he was seeing minute clues the rest of us wouldn't recognize if they wore neon signs that said EVIDENCE.

When he'd completed his circle, Romero said, "Somebody worked this boy over pretty good."

"Yeah. We just found him a few minutes ago."

"You called me right away?"

"Right."

Another cop, one of Romero's people, stood in the doorway, chewing on a toothpick and making sure nobody left the scene. He was a goggle-eyed guy, lean and tan with a cop mustache, and he peered at us all as if we were suspects.

Romero squatted down in front of Richie, right where Dub had been a minute earlier, and tilted his head to look Richie in the face. He was careful not to touch the corpse and I remembered checking for a pulse and my fingertips burned at the thought of the prints I'd probably left on Richie's neck.

"You touch the body?" Romero asked. I often get the sensation he's reading my mind, and it bugs me.

"Just his neck," I stammered. "No pulse."

"Who's that in the back?"

I was so busy watching the homicide lieutenant, I'd forgotten about Johnson sobbing in the bedroom. Romero doesn't miss anything, though.

"That's my client, the victim's father."

"He all right?"

"No."

Romero nodded, his lips clamped together tightly.

"Guess that was a stupid question," he admitted. "Who are these other gentlemen?"

"I'm William J. Pool, private investigator outta Dallas." Pool came out of the kitchen to offer Romero his hand. Romero ignored it. The lieutenant knows a loudmouth when he sees one.

I spoke up quickly, not giving Dub a chance to introduce himself.

"And, this is my, um, father, Dub Mabry."

Romero's big head swiveled around, and he gave Dub the once-over.

"Didn't know you had a father," Romero said. "He wasn't at the wedding."

"We've been what they call 'estranged,'" I said. "He showed up a couple of days ago. He doesn't have anything to do with all this. He just came along with me."

Dub nodded vigorously.

Romero got to his feet, looking from me to Pool and back again.

"And what are the rest of you doing here?"

That, of course, was the pertinent question. Count on Romero to cut to the chase every time.

Pool stepped in between Romero and me.

"Bubba and I were hired to locate young Richie here," Pool said. "When we arrived this morning, we had reason to believe he was inside, but he didn't answer the door."

"So you picked the lock," Romero said.

That gave Pool pause.

"Yes, sir, I did," he said. "I thought it might be an emergency situation."

"You scratched up the lock in the process," Romero said. "I noticed it soon as I arrived. What if the killer got in the same way? Guess we'll never know now."

For once, somebody had gotten ahead of Pool, and it was all I could do not to hoot, which would've been inappropriate, given the circumstances.

"Seemed like the right thing to do at the time," Pool back-pedaled. "We didn't know Richie had been murd—"

Dick Johnson walked into the room, dabbing at his face with a white handkerchief. He carried his hat in his hand and his bald head was red and shiny. His face still was twisted with grief, but he wasn't sobbing any longer.

"You're the father?" Romero said to him.

"Yeah." Johnson's voice sounded like he'd been gargling sand, but he still managed to be rude. "Who the hell are you?"

Romero flashed a badge from a leather folder in the pocket of his blue windbreaker.

"Lieutenant Romero. Homicide."

Johnson gulped down whatever he'd planned to say next.

"Sorry about your son, Mr. Johnson. Any idea who did this to him?"

"None at all." The bark was back in Johnson's voice. "But I know whose fault it is. This man here."

I turned to see what he could possibly mean, only to find him pointing at me.

"Now, wait a minute, Mr. Johnson—"

"Shut up, Bubba," Romero said cheerfully. "Mr. Johnson, could I ask you to step outside with Sergeant Smithers here? We'll need to get a statement from you."

Johnson shambled out the door, but not before shooting me a withering look.

"The rest of you," Romero said, "can talk to me. But first I need to make some phone calls. Go sit over there on that sofa like good little boys."

"Now, hold on, Steve, you don't believe—"

"Go sit down, Bubba. I'll be with you in a minute."

I sat between Pool and Dub on the gut-sprung sofa, chewing on my lips to keep from arguing with Romero.

"Phone's back here?" he said in his all-seeing way, then headed down the hall without waiting for an answer.

I turned to Pool and had my mouth open to ask how he'd managed to poison Dick Johnson against me at such a tragic moment, but Romero's square head popped around the corner from the hall and he said, "No talking among yourselves."

So we were left there, three monkeys ordered to speak no evil, with nothing else to do but stare at Richie Johnson's battered body. Nobody even whispered.

Romero reappeared a few minutes later, and he looked as if he was trying not to grin at the sight of us lined up on the couch for him.

"Coroner's on the way," he said.

Romero grabbed a chair from the kitchen table—one that matched the one where Richie sat dead—and hauled it over to us. He set it facing away from us, then straddled it so he could use the back of the chair for a desk.

"Okay," he said, looking down at his notepad. "Who wants to go first?"

Nobody volunteered. If we'd been standing, there would've been a race to see which of us could step backward fastest. But since we were sitting down, we could only scrunch deeper into the sofa's frayed cushions.

"All right," Romero said. "Mr., uh, Pool, was it?"

Pool winced and nodded.

"You seemed pretty eager to flap your lips a little while ago. Why don't you tell me all you know about the victim?"

I must've been smirking because Pool got singled out. Romero said, "You're next, Bubba." That'll kill a smirk every time.

Romero took a few notes, but mostly he watched us impassively as we told him about the kidnapping hoax, the missing ransom, Richie's involvement with the skinheads, and our competitive scrambling around town, trying to find him first.

It was a pretty foolish tale under any circumstances, but it was even harder to tell it with Richie sitting there dead.

When I got to the part about the emergency phone call from Felicia and running off to save her from Dub, Romero slowed me.

"And what time was this?" he asked.

"Around one," I said. "I had no way of knowing somebody else might be after Richie. Except Pool, of course, and I figured I was way ahead of him."

Romero nodded to show me I'd said enough.

"When did you and your father get back here?"

"Before two. I don't know for certain. I came inside, checked to make sure Richie was still asleep, and then waited in the truck with Dub."

"So the murderer came into the apartment after two and left sometime later."

"Right." I hadn't sorted it out that well before, but that had to be the case.

"You didn't see anybody else come into the apartment building later?"

"No, but we couldn't see the doors from where we were parked."

"Do you think somebody followed you here?"

I shrugged. It was possible, I guess. But I hadn't sensed anyone else around. Of course, I'd been pretty excited at finding Richie at all. Maybe I hadn't been paying attention. And I'd been distracted by Dub and that business with the pee bottle. I didn't mention that part to Romero.

"Why didn't you hand him over to his father right away?" Romero asked.

"I tried to call, but Johnson wasn't in his room. He was out looking for the kid. Besides, it was late and the kid didn't want to go back home. I wanted to think it over—"

"Why didn't he want to go home?"

"He was on the outs with his old man." There. If Johnson was going to point the finger at me, I could aim right back at him. "Guess his dad bosses him around. He said that's why he ran away. And it's why he wanted to take off with a briefcase full of his dad's dough."

"And because you chose to wait until morning to call again," Romero concluded, "the elder Johnson is now blaming you."

"Looks like it."

While we talked, the coroner's people arrived with a gurney and a body bag to haul Richie away. They had to use tin snips to cut the handcuffs and free him from his death chair. The *chink* of the snapping chains chilled me to the bone.

Dub seemed not the slightest bit upset to be part of a murder scene. He cradled Spike in his lap, stroking its stubble and cooing at it like a retard. Once Pool and I had talked ourselves out, Romero finally turned to him and asked if he had anything to add.

"That design cut into that boy's head?" he offered. "Those skinheads painted that same thing all over my son's house. He's supposed to get it cleaned off, but I don't think he's done anything about it yet. Gonna make that wife of his mad at him."

Romero tried not to grin. He's been around Felicia and me enough to know that would be nothing new.

"What about that, Bubba? They tagged your house?"

"Oh, yeah," I said off-handedly, trying to show I hadn't intentionally forgotten to mention the graffiti. "Felicia told me it's their gang symbol. It stands for Anarchy."

"That's right," came a deep growl from the doorway.

We turned to see Sgt. Horton Houghton filling the doorway as tightly as icing between the layers of a cake. He must've tossed a butt outside before he entered because smoke trailed from his nostrils. I'd hate to think he could do that just because he was mad.

"Looks like the skinheads took out one of their own," he rumbled.

Romero nodded as he got to his feet and walked over to Houghton. Even Romero looked small next to the giant gang specialist.

"Seems the victim had scammed his father out of a bunch of dough," Romero said. "Think his pals were making him tell where it was?"

Houghton was busy scowling at me, but he nodded at Romero.

"I had Smithers check the car, and I think these guys already have done a pretty thorough search of the apartment," Romero said, looking pointedly at Pool, who looked away. "No sign of the money."

Houghton closed his eyes and shook his huge head in frustration.

"So now Mayhem and his boys have a bundle of cash?" he said in summation.

"Looks that way," Romero said.

"Shit. How am I ever gonna catch those assholes now?" Romero nodded sympathetically.

"I don't think they're going anywhere. You'll get 'em."

Houghton glared some more to show it was our fault his job had gotten harder. A team of evidence technicians arrived, carrying tool chests full of their equipment, and he stepped out of the way to let them pass, never taking his eyes off me.

Romero returned to his chair and sat facing us.

"Let's go over it all again," he said. "Take it from the top, Bubba."

TWENTY-FIVE

*T*he television trucks had rolled off to bigger stories by the time Romero let us leave. Romero had cunningly kept Dick Johnson separated from the rest of us the whole time, and had ordered Smithers to keep him away from the news media as well. I could just imagine what Johnson might've said about me with the TV cameras rolling.

Of course, once the interrogation was over, I got to hear all of Johnson's opinions directly. He was waiting for us outside when we emerged from Richie's apartment. It was a perversely sunny day, and fairly warm, but Johnson had his arms wrapped around his torso. Probably trying to keep from coming unraveled.

He gave Pool and me the hard eye as we approached, and said hoarsely, "Let's go back to my suite."

That's about the last place I wanted to be right now.

"I really need to take my dad—"

"My suite. Now."

Johnson fell in step beside Pool, his shoulders slumped

under a heavy burden. I got the feeling he planned to unload on me, but he still was officially my client. What else could I do? I ordered Dub into the Ram and headed for the Hilton.

"Mr. Johnson sure seems upset," Dub said, after we'd traveled a few blocks.

"Not surprising, I guess. He loved that kid. All he wanted was for them to be together."

"Hard on a man when his children die off before he does."

I thought, *How would you know?* I'm Dub's only begotten son, as far as I know, and he'd never come sniffing around about my well-being during all those missing years. I could've been dead long ago—Lord knows I've come close a few times—and he would've been none the wiser.

"I knew an old boy back in Mississippi," Dub said, "both his kids died. Ran off down to the bayou and drowned themselves. Fool kids. The boy I knew, their daddy, he couldn't live with himself after that. He drove his car off in a lake."

"Kill him?"

"Unless he grew gills on the way down. That was a deep lake, what they call a blue hole. They never did recover that car."

"Too bad."

I wondered if this story was supposed to warn me of something. Would Dick Johnson try to take his own life? Nah. He probably would just take it out on me.

I deserved some of the blame, but I wasn't ready to say it was all my fault, the way Dick Johnson was. I didn't kill the boy. And I wasn't the father who ran him off with his heavy-handed ways. And, even the part I'd screwed up, I'd had help. If Dub hadn't taken a bender with the ladies, I would've been on Richie's sofa all night. Of course, then maybe I would've been killed, too.

Dub had returned to staring out the window, perhaps remembering his friend who'd taken the Big Swim. Maybe he was thinking about Richie, but I doubted it. The whole time we were at the apartment, he'd seemed more interested in the hairless cat than he had in the human life that had been snuffed out.

"Sure could use a beer," he said.

"To soothe your frayed nerves?"

"Hell, no. I'm just thirsty."

Though I'd lost them in traffic, we arrived at the Hilton right behind Pool and Johnson. Pool circled the hotel's too-small parking lot in his rented Cadillac. I didn't even try to find a space. I drove around behind the building and parked with the employees. I'd probably still beat them into the lobby, and Dub looked like he could use the exercise. I couldn't leave him in the truck again, though the temptation was strong. Maybe Johnson wouldn't be so hard on me with my old man in the room.

As we walked to the nearest entrance, Dub hoofing it quickly to keep up with my longer legs, he said, "Reckon that Mr. Johnson would spring for drinks?"

"I wouldn't ask if I were you. Bad timing."

"Guess that's right."

We met Pool and Johnson in the lobby and rode up quietly together in the elevator. Dub hitched at his britches and jangled his pocket change and cleared his throat repeatedly. I could've throttled him.

I didn't want Dub to further annoy Johnson. With his bald head glowing, Johnson already looked as if he could chew his way through the elevator doors.

Fortunately, the doors opened by themselves and we stepped out onto the fourteenth floor. I brought up the rear on the way down the hall, walking close behind Dub, ready to slap him silly if he did anything obnoxious.

Dub whistled when he got a load of Dick's suite. Pool, Johnson, and I took our traditional places at the armchairs in the center of the room. Dub spotted two crystal decanters and an ice bucket sitting on the dresser and made for them faster than a speeding coyote. I hung my head, embarrassed by Dub going for a drink without even asking and bracing for what I knew was to come from Dick Johnson.

Johnson cleared his throat several times. He still grasped a crumpled wad of white Kleenex in both hands.

"I guess you boys know you've made a pig's breakfast of this."

"It's a sad day, Dick," Pool whinnied.

Johnson turned his glare on Pool full-bore. The smarmy Texan clammed right up.

Dub surprised all of us by walking up to Johnson and handing him the drink he'd prepared. Johnson looked at the drink with his eyebrows raised, and his expression softened some when he said, "Thanks, partner."

Johnson turned up the glass and drained it.

Dub patted him on the shoulder, and said, "Let me get you another. I think I'll have a slug myself. You boys want one?"

Pool and I nodded eagerly.

"That all right with you, Mr. Johnson?"

"Sure."

Dub hustled back to the liquor and clanked around ice and glasses.

Johnson's expression grew stern again when he turned back to Pool and me, but it had lost some of the ferocity of before.

"Bubba, I cannot believe you were standing in the same room with Richie last night and yet this happened."

"It was a mistake."

"It damned sure was. That mistake cost my boy his life. And the person who killed him walked away with two hundred thousand dollars of my money."

Pool cleared his throat but couldn't summon up the courage to actually say anything. Snake.

"I'm not gonna stand for it," Johnson said. "Somebody's gonna pay."

I didn't like the sound of that. I had a pretty good idea which somebody he meant.

"That's why I want you boys to find the killer."

Dub nearly spilled drinks all over Pool and me. We took the glasses from him and shook splashed liquor off our hands.

"It's a police matter now, Dick," Pool said.

"Hell with that. Those cops ain't gonna find whoever killed Richie. They're too damned dumb."

"That Mexican seemed pretty sharp to me," Pool said. He pronounced the word *Mess-can* in that slurry Texas way, and it took me a second to realize he was talking about Steve Romero.

"That 'Mexican' comes from a family who's lived here four hundred years," I snapped. "When did your forefathers get off the boat, Pool?"

"No offense intended. I said he was pretty sharp."

"The one I talked to was dumber than a box of rocks," Johnson said. "Besides, they've got every murder in this city to investigate. How much time they gonna give Richie's case?"

"You could offer a reward," Pool said.

"Hell's bells, that's throwing good money after bad. No, I want you boys on the case. You owe me."

"That's true, Dick," Pool said. "But I can't put my whole organization on hold for this. A murder case can take a long time to solve."

"I'll make it worth your while. I'll keep paying your daily fee. Same rules as before. Find Richie's killer, get a conviction, keep the ransom if we get it back."

Pool and I took only a moment before we muttered agreement. There was no arguing with him, and the temptation of that bundle of money was too strong.

"But I'm telling you now, Dick, this could take weeks," Pool said.

Johnson stood up abruptly.

"Then you better get off your ever-widening ass and get to work."

The three of us gulped our drinks and hurried for the door.

"Call me," Johnson shouted after us. "Every day, whenever you need to. I want this handled and I want it done right."

He might've said more, I don't know. The heavy door swung shut behind us, and we were moving down the hall at a good clip.

We entered the elevator and stood facing forward in the conventional manner. The inside of the elevator was polished brass and we could see rippled reflections of ourselves. Pool tall and broad and manly in his Western suit. Dub short and rumpled under his CAT hat. Me looking like a deflated balloon.

Despite the day's tragedy, Pool couldn't seem to stop grinning. Dub clucked his tongue and muttered under his breath. I was busy with my own thoughts. I could redeem myself if I found Richie's killer and brought him in. Not just in Johnson's eyes or in Dub's. And not just because it would mean defeating William J. Pool. I needed it for myself, so I wouldn't feel so bad about screwing up.

TWENTY-SIX

I'd cranked up the Ram's engine, but hadn't yet shoved it into gear when Dub said beside me, "Son?"

I looked over at him. He was staring right at me, and his eyes looked sharp, and a deep furrow creased his brow.

"I think you ought to drop this mess."

"What mess?"

"This stuff with Johnson. Finding a killer. Pah! That ain't no job for a man like you."

"What do you mean 'a man like me'? You don't know me. You don't know anything about me. I don't run off when things go wrong. I'm no quitter."

Dub snapped his jaw shut so sharply it made his dewlap waggle.

"This ain't about how I run off and left your mama."

"I didn't say it was."

"I knew we'd have to dredge this ditch eventually. Go ahead. Have your say."

I sighed deeply and stared at the speedometer. We weren't

going anywhere. Dub pulled his tobacco plug from his shirt pocket. The pocket was stained with brown juice, which irritated me more.

It would've been easy to dump on him. I'd harbored a lot of resentment over the years, but getting to know him now was beginning to seem better than nothing. We were both grown-ups now, and a tantrum would've been childish. Plus he was sick in the head. How could I yell at him?

"Sometimes, I think you did me a favor by leaving."

He scowled and chomped a chaw off the plug and gnawed vigorously, as if it was my ass he were chewing.

"I've thought it over," I said calmly, "and it might've been for the best. You were on the road all the time anyway. I was mad at you for a lot of years, but I learned something that's done me good."

Dub rolled down the window and spat into the parking lot. "What was that?"

"That you have to be careful who you trust. You have to question things and size them up."

"That's what it taught you, huh?"

"Dub, you know as well as I do there's something wrong with Mama's side of the family. No sense beating around the bush about it. I mean, Mama really wanted to believe that was Jesus who came to the house. She still believes it. And remember what happened to her father?"

Dub cracked a smile, and a little tobacco juice leaked out of the corner of his mouth.

"That old fool was crazier'n a betsy bug."

"Maybe so, but the main thing is that he was gullible. Don't you see? He *wanted* to believe the Martians were invading when he heard 'War of the Worlds' on the radio. I mean, lots of people made the mistake and thought it was a real Martian landing. But they didn't all go flying out their hotel room window."

Dub nodded and grinned.

"He was leaning too far out the window, looking for those spaceships."

I frowned at him.

"That's always been the family version. How do we know he didn't jump?"

Dub paused in his chewing for a second, then shrugged.

"Whichever. What does this have to do with how you feel about me?"

"I'm getting to that. See, I've got this gullibility gene in me. I know it's there. Lord knows, it pops up often enough in my life. But sometimes I overcome it, and I think that's because of what happened with you."

Dub squinted and ruminated.

"So I taught you not to trust people, and that's a good thing?"

"Doesn't sound good, does it? But it's kept me out of a few jams."

"Then why don't you listen to that part of you right now?"

"What do you mean?"

"You oughta drop this Johnson business. You're gonna get yourself killed."

I threw the truck into gear and rolled out of the Hilton parking lot.

"You're not gonna listen to me, are you?"

"Man's gotta do what a man's gotta do."

"Now, that's horseshit. You ain't gotta do nothing you don't want. I'd think about it if I were you, son. You don't want to go after them skinheads."

I gave the Ram some extra gas, climbing a steep curve in University Boulevard.

"That's where you're wrong," I said. "That's exactly what I want to do. I'm going to find them and take them down and get that money back."

"Why? You don't feel you owe it to that Mr. Johnson, do you?"

"Maybe I owe it to his son."

Dub let that one sit there a minute before he said anything. "You're a noble bastard, ain't you?"

That startled me. I looked over at him, saw that his stare was past me somewhere, following after whatever mental condition kept leading him away.

"You're gonna go after them for the dead kid. Make everything right again. Let me tell you something, son. That kid don't know the difference no more."

"Maybe not. But I'm going after them. Right now. And you're coming with me."

That shut him right up.

The warehouse was the solution to this mess. Tracking the skinheads down individually and proving they did it would take too long. This demanded a bold approach, one that Pool, for all his experience and whizbang technology, would never take. Of course, I was trusting that Pool hadn't guessed that the skinheads might return to their old party spot to count their loot.

Mike Sterling came to mind, with his busted leg and his warnings about the skinheads, as I turned onto the dead-end street. I was scared shitless, but I wouldn't let Dub see that.

"You always bite your fingernails like that?"

I snatched my hand away from my mouth. "Hangnail."

"What are you planning on doing now that we're here?"

"I'm not sure yet. Let me think."

I parked in the same spot as before. A couple of cars were in the alley, including the one Mayhem had been driving. I winced at the dents my heels had left in his trunk. He definitely wouldn't be happy to see me.

Still, boldness was the answer. I reached under the seat for my pistol, checked the cylinder and stuck it in the pocket of my old denim jacket. The butt hung out in clear view.

"What you plannin' to do with that?"

"Bluff 'em. Cut one out of the herd and make him talk. We both know these boys are the ones who killed Richie. I think Mr. Smith & Wesson can persuade them to speak up."

"Why are you talkin' like John Wayne?"

"Never mind. I'm going in before they scatter."

"Let's call the cops first."

Why hadn't I thought of that?

"Good idea. Give me the phone out of the glove compartment."

Dub fumbled with the latch, then fished out the tiny phone and handed it over. I opened it up, pushed some buttons, held it up to my ear. Nothing. I pushed some more buttons. Nothing.

"You know how to work that thing?"

"Yeah, yeah. I'm just not getting—"

I finally snapped to the battery light.

"This thing's deader than a bag of dirt."

"What?"

I pointed at the battery indicator to show him.

"You must've left it on too long."

"No kidding."

"Where's your spare battery?"

"My what?"

"Let's go find a pay phone."

"No, screw it. I've got them here right now. I'm going in."

"I'm going with you."

"I don't think so."

"I'm not staying out here in the truck by myself. We barely got away last time."

"If you woulda unlocked the door—"

"What door?"

"Never mind. I think you'd be—"

"Don't tell me what to do, son. I'm going in. Wish I had my pistol, but that wife of yours took it away from me. You got a tire iron?"

"Behind the seat."

"That'll do. I need an equalizer. I'm not as young as I used to be. Why, I'm nearly eighty!"

"You're sixty-four."

"That's what I meant."

Then we were out of the truck and crossing the street to the alley beside the warehouse and the only thought in my head was: *I must be insane.* Walking into this warehouse with only this addled coot as my backup had to rank with the absolute dumbest stuff I'd ever done. And it might just get me killed. But I was committed now, and there was no backing out. I reached the side door, pulled my gun, and looked to Dub to make sure he was ready. His eyes glittered, and he brandished the L-shaped tire iron like a tomahawk. Then his face softened, and his mouth arched into a little grin. I rolled my eyes at him, then grinned back. What the hell, we might not be around to annoy each other much longer.

I took a deep breath and flung open the door.

The skinheads seemed pitched into that drunken surliness you see in working-class taverns. I counted eight of them scattered around the big room, beers dangling in their hands, some sprawled on the floor, others just standing there like bald-headed mopes. One was whanging away on one of the ancient machines with a rusty monkey wrench. Another fiddled with the dials of a boom box that was, blessedly, silent.

They all stood stock still when they saw my pistol pointing at them, and it looked like a bad exhibit at a wax museum. Hall of Hairless Terrors.

"Hands up, boys!" I shouted, and I managed to sound almost cheerful about it.

Most of them shot their hands into the air, but Mayhem crossed his thick, pale arms over his chest. He sat on the floor, his back against a crate, and that position was the only thing that kept him from springing at me. I kept my gun pointed at his chest. If any of these knuckleheads was a killer, it was probably him.

I moved through the door a couple of steps, and felt Dub crowding in behind me. I hoped he didn't get excited and brain me with that tire iron by mistake.

"Let's everybody walk backward to the nearest wall," I

decided. "Except you, Mayhem, old chap. You stay right where you are."

They obediently started backing up. One or two stumbled against boxes on their way, but they all made it to the walls. I couldn't keep them all covered that way, but the distance was such that I could wheel around and fire if they tried anything.

"Dub, come over here with me."

I walked slowly over to where Mayhem sat, and Dub followed, backing up to keep me covered and to keep an eye on the door. I stopped in front of Mayhem, and Dub almost stopped in time and he only bumped into me lightly.

"Dub, you keep an eye on the ones over there. I'm going to have a little talk with Baldy here."

"I got 'em."

Mayhem glowered, his hairless brow deeply furrowed beneath the question-mark scar. His lips pulled back to show his crooked teeth, like a freaking Rottweiler, but he didn't move his hands. I took a deep breath and began.

"Why'd you kill Richie?"

His eyes widened briefly before he caught himself and scowled some more. And in that instant, I was filled with doubt. I had no proof these punks killed the kid. Nothing but the Anarchy symbol carved into the crown of his head. Anybody could've done that. That flash in Mayhem's eyes said he didn't know Richie was dead. It took the wind right out of me.

"Fook you, mate."

"Thank you very much."

I suddenly felt very tired. If I was wrong about Mayhem being the killer, then what the hell was I doing here?

Dub was getting restless behind me.

"Ask him about the money," he prompted.

"Where's the money?'

"What fookin' money?"

"The money you took from Richie after you killed him."

"You're fookin' barmy. I don't know nothin' about any money."

Barmy?

I noticed movement beyond Mayhem and I swiveled the pistol up to point at the littlest skinhead, the dipshit with the swastika on his neck. He'd eased away from the wall, and was looking toward the open door.

"Uh-uh-uhn. Back to the wall."

He spat to show his contempt, but he got his ass up against that wall.

Mayhem hadn't made a move, but I could tell he was thinking about it. He was mad as hell at me for dinging up his car and mouthing off at him and making him look stupid in front of his gang. But what the hell, I had plenty to be angry about myself. They'd damaged my truck, tagged my house, attempted to whip the crap out of me. We'd finally reached a showdown. I tried to work up some rage, but I had the feeling now that I'd blundered by coming here and it took all the salt out of me.

"You didn't know Richie Johnson is dead?" I sounded weary in my own ears. "You didn't kill him and carve an *A* into his head?"

I glanced around the room in time to see a couple of the skinheads flinch. Others had their mouths hanging open. They seemed truly surprised.

Dub hadn't snapped to it yet, and he nudged his way past me and said, "Let me give it a try, boy."

Mayhem almost smiled at the sight of the old fart standing over him, waving the tire iron.

"Listen here, you little bullshitter, you'll talk now or I'll put a knot on your head the size of a road apple."

Mayhem loosed a nasty bark of a laugh. Dub got red in the face, and I thought for a second he'd conk the Brit. But then I saw he wasn't even looking at Mayhem anymore. He was gaping past me, over to my left, and he shouted, "Look out!"

I turned, but not quickly enough. I got just a glimpse of the skinhead who'd come through the side door behind me. I'd never seen him before. But I was plenty familiar with two-by-four pine boards and one was swinging toward my head.

TWENTY-SEVEN

I knew I was still alive when I awoke because I hurt too much to be in heaven. And it was too cold to be hell.

The skinheads had stripped off my jacket, leaving me with only a thin cotton shirt. The cold from the concrete floor seeped up through my jeans. My butt was freezing.

My head hurt very much. And my knees. And the fingers of my right hand. And, oh yes, my ribs. Something could be broken there. It didn't help that I had ropes tied tightly around my chest. My wrists were bound in front of me, and something that smelled bad was lashed to my back.

It was Dub.

"Son? Can you hear me? Are you all right?"

His voice sounded strong, so maybe they hadn't worked him over, too.

I shivered against him. I needed to open my eyes, but I could hear the skinheads milling around, and I knew Mayhem would be standing over me, sneering around his thin cigar.

I opened my eyes. It was just as I'd pictured it, except

Mayhem also pointed my own gun at me.

" 'Ow much money?" he snarled.

"Wha?" My mouth hurt when I spoke, and I felt around with my tongue, seeing if all my teeth were still in place.

" 'Ow much? The money Richie 'ad?"

All my teeth were present and accounted for, though one molar seemed a little loose. My tongue was fat and sore, as if I'd bitten it, but there was no blood in my mouth or on what I could see of my shirt. Guess it wasn't much fun to kick me around after I was knocked cold. Maybe they'd just been waiting for me to wake up.

I tried to storm at him, but the words came out partly cloudy.

"Like you don't know it was two hundred thousand dollars."

"Two 'undred large? And it's missin'?"

"That's right," Dub said from behind me. "We thought y'all killed him and took it."

"We wouldn't kill another Oi Boy, you simple sod."

"How the hell are we supposed to know that?"

I could see Dub's point, but I wished to Jesus he would shut up.

"It's all a misunderstanding," he said. "Now why don't you boys untie us, and we'll go away peaceably."

Nice try, Dub.

"Right," Mayhem mocked. It sounded like "roit."

"I think I need a doctor," I ventured through chattering teeth, and I knew it was true. The left side of my head felt as if it was in a large vise that some ogre was squeezing tighter. Probably a concussion, some swelling of the brain that eventually would make my head explode like a puffball. I hated to see a doctor for any condition, but exploding heads definitely require medical attention.

"You're gonna need a fookin' coroner. Idn't he, boys?"

Mayhem wagged my pistol at me. Oh, please, don't shoot me while I'm tied to my old man. The way we were bound together, the bullets would get two for the price of one.

"Don't shoot."

"Shoot? I'm not gonna shoot."

I whewed in relief, which made my ribs stab with pain.

"I'm not gonna waste good bullets on the likes of you."

Uh-oh.

"You're gonna tell me where that money is."

"I don't know." It was getting harder to talk. I don't know if it was brain damage or the swollen tongue or just pants-filling fear, but the words came slow and thick. "We thod you had it."

"I 'aven't got a bloody thing. But I will get it. Faster'n you can say, 'Bob's your uncle.' "

He sounded very determined and, in my weakened state, I had no doubt that he'd succeed. But what was he going to do with us? And who was Bob?

"Just let us go," Dub pleaded.

"Like 'ell. Billy, come 'ere."

The littlest skinhead hurried over. So his name was Billy. Little Billy. Little Billy goat. Little . . .

Whoops. Slipped away there for a second. Probably delirium. Head trauma hysteria.

"Take my lighter," Mayhem said, as he handed Little Billy a Zippo. "Pile up some of those papers and shit and torch 'em."

"Hey now, wait a minute," Dub objected.

"Shut up, old man. You two should never 'ave come 'ere, crossing us again. I 'ate to lose me 'angout, but I'll be 'appy as 'ell to see you go."

I didn't track that. Why didn't the idiot speak English?

Little Billy set fire to a pile of debris off to my right. One of the bigger skinheads broke up an orange crate and threw the slats onto the pile, and they caught right up. Mayhem tossed in his smelly cigar butt.

"Dammit, come on, you can't do this!" I cried, but what came out of my mouth was, "Dabbib, cub oh, doo da do dis!"

A skinhead came through the alley door, a gas can dangling from one hand. I thought he was the one who'd brained me with the lumber, but I couldn't be sure. Hell, they all looked alike, except for Mayhem, and the only things that set him apart were that scar on his head and his snaggletooth choppers. Next to him, the rest looked like the children of dentists.

The fire burst higher with the gasoline, and the skinheads jumped back, laughing and dancing around. I didn't know they were capable of this much fun. Too bad I was the piñata at their party.

Mayhem leaned down into my face, his breath of cigar smoke and dental rot registering in my nose despite my pains. Up close, I could see his eyes were a strange light brown, like those of a gorilla.

"Last chance, mate. You gonna tell me where I can find that money?"

This would be a good time to lie. Buy a little time. Maybe get Mayhem to untie me and let me take him to the "money." But my head was like a bowlful of oatmeal. I barely could register what sensory input made its way through my blurry eyes and buzzing ears, much less come up with fresh thoughts of my own. I put all my effort into controlling my shivering and forming three coherent words.

"I don't know."

"Too bloody bad for you, mate. I'll find that money on me own."

He paused, waiting me out. The fire crackled and popped beyond him. It was catching on nicely. So many pretty colors . . .

I forced my focus back on Mayhem, whose eyebrows were furling again into his favorite Billy Idol scowl. He was through waiting.

"Bollocks."

He put one thumb up to his nose and blew hard to empty a nostril, the way football players do, and I distinctly felt a missile hit my shirt, but I didn't look down to see. I remember thinking this would've been the final indignity in the long string I'd suffered at the hands of Mayhem and the Oi Boys. Except the final indignity would be burning up in a warehouse fire, and that seemed to be coming soon.

"Mayhem," Little Billy called. "Let's get out of here."

The fire was roaring now. It slithered along a rivulet of gasoline to the back wall of the warehouse and the wall smoked and blackened and would burst into flame any second. The old clapboards on the wall were dry and gray and enthusiastic.

Mayhem straightened above me. He puffed up for his gang, who were huddled at the side door. I thought maybe he had more nasal ballistics to do, but he glanced over at the leaping flames and decided it was time to go.

I wanted to call after him, try to talk him out of it, come up with some canard that would persuade Mayhem to get us out of this burning building. But that vise still squeezed my head and things seemed to be shorting out under the pressure and I couldn't put together the words.

Mayhem paused in the doorway as he trailed the others out. He smiled at the fire and glowered at me, then slammed the door shut against the roiling smoke.

The back wall was blazing now. Fire rippled along the wall in orange waves. Little tongues of flame licked around the broken windows, drinking up air.

A thought pulled itself together in my head, a glimmer of how my brain used to work. Half the windows in this place are broken. The smoke will go out them. If we could keep low, on the floor, we might not die of smoke inhalation before the firemen come. Or, before the roof catches fire and falls in on us. Either way, the windows would buy us a few minutes.

I tried to act on this thought. All I had to do was fall over. But I caught on the ropes as Dub struggled against me.

"Son, what the hell are you doin'?"

I tried to form a word—"down" came to mind—but my

mouth didn't seem to be operational.

"Be still. I'm tryin' to get my penknife outta my pocket."

He writhed against me, a dead weight on his back.

"Lean over to the left, son."

I did it.

"Your other left."

Oh. I leaned the other way, as far as the ropes would allow. That way, I saw, Dub could cock his bound wrists around to the side, trying to get into the pocket of his jeans, and plant his bony elbow in my aching ribs. I gasped quietly.

"I can't get it," Dub shouted over the roaring blaze. "Lean over. Lie down on the floor, and I'll try it that way."

This agreed perfectly with my unspoken plan, and I think I was grinning happily as we toppled over onto the concrete floor.

The floor still was cool to the touch, but I wasn't shivering anymore. The bonfire had warmed things up nicely.

Dub wriggled behind me, still trying for the knife. I coughed against the smoke, which made my damaged ribs stab me, and watched the fire slink along the seam where the back wall joined the roof. The roof looked tinder dry, too. We didn't have long.

It seemed I should say something to Dub, though I hated to interrupt his determined squirming. Some final farewell seemed in order. Our reunion hadn't exactly been a "Kodak Moment." I'd been too gruff and grumpy and distracted. Dub had been crazy. It wasn't the best of circumstances (and it certainly didn't seem to be getting any better), but I could do my part. I could say something profound and forgiving by way of good-bye.

"Dub?" The word came out nice and clear, though since that whack on the head everything I said sort of sounded like "dub." "Howzit goin'?"

"I'm working on it, son. I got my fingers around the knife, but this gut of mine makes that pocket awful tight. My hand's kinda stuck."

He shifted against me again, trying for leverage.

"Dub?"

"Yeah?"

"I was glad to see you." That seemed simple and appropriate. Unfortunately, the words came out, "I buzz gwad to zee ya."

"You just hang on. I'm working—"

A shaft of light pierced the smoke, making me think of nightclub spotlights and torch singers. Here we are, enjoying ourselves in the smoky recesses of Chez Hell.

The side door had been flung open. A man in a dark suit burst through the door and hurried over to us. I immediately recognized him, even though he had a white handkerchief tied around his face like a bandit.

William J. Pool.

Pool reached inside his jacket and pulled out a fancy chrome butterfly knife. He opened the knife with a flick of the wrist and leaned down over me. The blade glowed orange, reflecting the flames all around.

Holy shit. Pool's here for his final revenge. He couldn't wait any longer to finally finish me off. Apparently, he couldn't even wait for the fire. But that didn't make sense, did it? Did anything anymore? As I wondered whether the crack to the head meant my brain now functioned like Dub's, Pool reached down and sawed through the ropes at my chest.

Dub scrambled to his feet, his hands bound in front of him.

"He took a lick on the head!" he shouted to Pool. "Help me get him up."

Pool waved Dub toward the door.

"I've got him!"

Pool bent over me, hooked my arms back over his shoulder and hoisted me into the air like a sack of manure. My weight rested on his shoulder, which pressed hard against my ribs. A beeping like a car alarm competed with the roar of the fire, and I realized it was me, breathing.

And then we were out in the fresh, cold, sunny air and Pool was setting me on the hood of a car and sirens were nearing.

And I was alive. Saved by Pool.

Damn.

TWENTY-EIGHT

I held my elbows tightly against my ribs as I coughed. It helped some, but I still felt like the heavy bag in Mike Tyson's gym.

The crisp air cleared my head a little, though. Enough that I could hear the sirens whooping to silence around me, could hear the fire crackling and Dub hacking nearby.

Pool's face appeared over mine, which was a clue that I was laid out flat on my back. The hood ornament between my knees was a clue that I was sprawled on his Cadillac. A strand of hair had blown free from Pool's smooth coif and dangled over a forehead smudged with smoke. He looked like Errol Flynn. I wished for unconsciousness.

"You all right, partner?"

"Um."

Pool sliced through the ropes that bound my wrists.

"One of those boys whacked him on the noggin," Dub said between coughs. "I think he's stove up pretty bad."

"An ambulance is on the way."

I didn't want an ambulance. I shook my head, which caused my brains to slosh around. Ooh, that hurt. Better to hold my head still.

"That's it!" Dub shouted, and I wondered what tangent he'd hit upon now. "That's all for me! I ain't riskin' my life like this."

It seemed an odd time for Dub to start hollering at me. I'm clearly injured here. I almost died, and now I've suffered the low humiliation of being rescued by an enemy who will become a headline hero.

"We had the drop on those boys!" Dub shouted, and I thought, *I know that. I was there.* But then it dawned that he was talking to Pool, not me. "One of 'em brained Bubba and the rest of them jumped on me like a bunch of mad dogs. They tied us up and tried to roast us!"

"I know," Pool said smugly. "I saw the whole thing. I followed you here from the hotel."

"You saw it? Then why the hell did you wait so long to come get us?"

"Too many of them. I had to wait till they drove off."

God, why don't they just shut up? I need medical attention over here.

"We nearly croaked in there!" Dub yelled.

"I got there in time."

"I don't give a red rat's ass! I'm through. I don't care how much it's worth to you."

What the hell was he talking about? I raised up on an elbow and looked over at them. Dub was standing about four inches from Pool's chest, shouting up into his handsome face.

Pool made a shushing expression, but there was no stopping Dub.

"You said this was a no-risk proposition! It's been nothing but risk from the get-go!"

"We don't need to talk about this now, Dub."

Pool jerked his head toward me.

"I don't give a good goddamn! You promised me easy

money, and there ain't been nothing easy about it!"

"Excuse me?" I held up a finger to get their attention, and Dub froze with his mouth open and they both looked over at me. "What are you talking about?"

Dub and Pool didn't know where to look. They tried their shoes and the sky and the flashing red lights and the rubber-coated firemen who scrambled to get their hoses into place, but they ended up coming back to me.

Dub swallowed and frowned and hitched at his britches.

"I was gonna tell you all about it, son. I've made a terrible mistake. I've been working with this boy here."

Working? Something was wrong here, but I couldn't get my aching brain around it.

"I know this looks bad, Bubba, but I've been havin' some troubles," Dub said. "The balloon payment's coming up on my truck loan, and I'm dead-ass broke. Then Pool here called me outta the blue and offered me five thousand dollars to look you up and pretend to be crazy."

Pain stabbed me in the temple and I felt dizzy for a second, but I fought against it and pulled myself to a sitting position, letting my feet dangle off the fender of Pool's car.

"But you didn't look me up," I said slowly. "I found you. A man named Ralph Upshaw called—"

"That was me," Pool said.

"You?"

Pool tried a grin, as if he thought I'd suddenly see the fun in all of this.

"One of my undercover voices. It was just a little game, Bubba. Something to keep it interesting."

"You wanted that ransom."

"Sure. Soon as Dick set up that competition, I ran the computer on you and turned up your long-lost pappy. One call to his employer, and, boom, it turns out the two of you are right here in the same city. I couldn't let an opportunity like that pass by."

"You fucking snake."

"Easy now, Bubba. You got back together with your old man. What did it hurt?"

"Hurt?" Dub screamed. "Look at him. He's hurt. I 'bout died here. I reckon this has hurt plenty."

I slid slowly off the fender, letting my feet touch the ground and testing whether my legs would hold me up. A little dizziness, but the pain in my head had been obliterated by a fuzzy red rage.

"You pay up," Dub demanded. "I'm shat of all this. Give me my money now."

"I don't have that on me—"

"Then write me a check, goddammit. I never want to see you again."

Pool kept glancing at me, as if still worried what I might hear. It was too late for that. Even as bunged up as I was, the situation had become devastatingly clear.

"I don't have the money now, Dub," Pool hedged. "I was counting on the reward—"

"Hell with that! We made a deal, and you'll pay off."

I couldn't stand it any longer. My legs seemed to be holding me up, and I willed them to move and I walked directly toward Pool. Dub stepped out of the way, watching me like he expected me to fall. Then, seemingly without any command from me, my fist came up and popped Pool squarely in the honker. His head snapped back and he stumbled backward with his hands to his face. Red oozed between his fingers, and he lifted his hands away and looked down at the blood and then looked at me.

Uh-oh. I was no physical match for Pool on a good day. I didn't know where the punch came from, and I doubted seriously whether I could throw another one.

But then Pool grinned and nodded and wiped gently at the blood leaking out of his nose.

"All right," he said. "I guess I had that comin'. It was a dirty trick, I guess, though I didn't mean it that way. Now we're even."

"We won't ever be even, Pool. Nothing could balance off what you did."

I turned toward my truck and took a step, faltered, then picked my way through the hoses crisscrossed on the ground.

"Son? Wait. You shouldn't be driving. You should be in an ambulance."

I kept walking.

"Bubba? Let me drive you then."

I wasn't stopping for Dub, not again. Besides, if I stopped walking, who knew whether I could resume?

He scrabbled up behind me. I shrugged his hand off my shoulder when it landed there.

"You can't just leave, son. We need to talk to the cops."

"They know where to find me."

I tried to turn away, but his hand was on my arm.

"Look, Bubba, I'm sorry. I didn't know about you and Pool. Your rivalry and all. I wasn't tryin' to hurt you. I thought it would interestin' to get to know you, and pick up a little spare change at the same time. I didn't expect things to turn out this way."

It was all I could do not to pop him, too. Guess he could see it in my eyes because he let go of my arm and moved back a step.

"You through?"

He dropped his head and nodded. I turned to walk away.

"Bubba? At least wait for me. You're my ride."

"Why don't you ride with your good friend Mr. Pool?"

"Aw, now come on, Bubba—"

"Come on yourself. Why don't you adopt Pool while you're at it? Get a son who'll appreciate your lies."

I stalked away to my pickup. This time he didn't try to stop me.

TWENTY-NINE

*D*ub's betrayal unscrambled my brains. I was so seething mad that I drove myself to the neighborhood clinic and walked right in and got seen without an appointment, and it was as if I didn't have brain damage after all.

The young female doctor was all business and I didn't even care that I was sitting on a hard table in my underwear. She and a nurse fluttered around me, sticking bandages to anything that moved.

The ribs weren't broken, only bruised. My knuckles were scraped enough to rate a Band-Aid on each finger. I got gauze around my wrists for rope burns I didn't know I had.

The doctor was most concerned about the goose egg above my left ear. She took X rays and said it looked as if my skull was intact, but she recommended that I go to the hospital and get a CAT scan to make sure. The mention of the test reminded me of how I'd worried over Dub's sanity. I brusquely thanked the doctor and paid up and picked up a prescription for Tylenol with codeine on my way home.

I hadn't been home ten minutes when the phone rang. I tried to ignore it, but Sgt. Horton Houghton's voice rumbled from the answering machine and I picked up the receiver.

"I'm here," I said. I felt a little woozy from the sudden movement, and slumped onto the sofa.

"You left the scene of a crime."

"I needed medical attention. I'm okay now, though I might drift away a little."

"No drifting. Just tell me what happened at that warehouse."

So I told him, though I left out the part about Dub's shenanigans with Pool. He didn't seem particularly interested in my observations on how Mayhem and the Oi Boys appeared to be unaware of Richie's fortune. He was hot on their trail. Torching the warehouse had moved the Oi Boys to the top of Houghton's list. They had no idea how much trouble was headed their way.

After Houghton hung up, I stumbled to the kitchen for a beer to wash down the Tylenol. I sat back down on the sofa, and the phone on the end table rang again. I thought it might be Felicia. She often calls late in the afternoon to tell me when to expect her home. Sometimes, I even have some sort of heat-and-eat supper ready when she arrives.

It wasn't Felicia on the phone, but it was the *Albuquerque Gazette*.

"Hello! Mr. Mabry? This is Meg Albright! We met last night at dinner?"

I was too tired and upset and foggy to listen to Miss Wisconsin. She talked faster than an auctioneer, and I was processing all incoming information slower than the U.S. Postal Service.

"Meg."

"You remember me?"

"Yes."

"You don't seem yourself, Mr. Mabry!"

"I took a whack on the head today."

"So I heard! I'm working the police beat today! I'm doing a story about the fire over on Memphis Street!"

It wasn't bad enough I had Felicia hounding me for stories all the livelong day. Now Miss Meg wanted in on the action. I could just imagine how it would go if I gave away one of Felicia's "exclusives." It would be awfully chilly around my house.

"Shouldn't I be talking to Felicia?"

"She's busy with something else! I can tell her you're all right?"

"Sure." If you want to lie to her . . .

"Okay! So tell me what happened!"

I told her a little of it. Not much. Certainly not enough to get Felicia riled. I didn't tell her anything about Dick Johnson or Pool or Richie or Dub. She asked about the fire. I told her about the fire. I said I'd gone there looking for the Oi Boys because of "certain confidential evidence." In my blithering state, I thought that was a pretty good way to put it. Of course, it probably would get Felicia shagging it home to pump me so she could bump Meg off the front page, but that was okay. I needed some company.

"Okay!" Meg said when I stopped talking. "You left out a few things, right? Is this connected to that gang graffiti on your house? And what about this Mr. Pool who saved you?"

"You've talked to Pool."

"Oh, yes! He made it all seem terribly exciting!"

"I'll bet he did. Listen, if you've got Pool, you don't need me. I'm not feeling so great. I've got to go now."

I hung up the phone before she could object. She'd probably call right back, yapping like a cocker spaniel, but she'd only get a busy signal.

I dialed the Hilton.

"Yeah?"

"Mr. Johnson, it's Bubba Mabry."

"Mabry. Where the hell are you?"

"Home."

"Pool said you almost burned up in a fire. Are you all right?"

"I'm fine. Pool's there?"

"He's standing right here. Sounds like you had a close call."

Pool must've gone to see Johnson right away, probably wanting to deliver his version of the facts first. I'm sure he hadn't made himself sound any more heroic than, oh, say, Odysseus.

"You know what made it so close?" My voice had risen a little. My pronunciation was improving, too. Outrage apparently will do that for you.

"What?"

"I almost burned up in that warehouse because of Pool!"

"What are you talking about?"

"I went in there with only my father as backup. Turns out he's been working for Pool all along."

"That right?"

He didn't sound surprised enough. Had Pool already put the spin on that bit of villainy? Probably told Johnson that I'd been knocked crazy, or that it was a big misunderstanding. Or maybe he told the truth, figuring a businessman like Johnson would be ruthless enough to appreciate the joke. I suddenly didn't feel like talking to Johnson anymore.

"Look," Johnson said, "I don't really care about this horseshit between you and Pool. Those boys who torched the warehouse, are they the ones who killed Richie?"

Ouch. Guess Pool hadn't told him everything.

"I don't think so."

"No?"

"No. After they had Dub and me trussed up like a couple of Cornish game hens, Mayhem was asking me questions about the money and where it could be. He didn't seem to know anything about it before."

"But they know about it now?"

Gulp. "Yessir."

Johnson was silent for so long, I almost drifted away there on the sofa.

"Maybe I ought to offer them the reward," he said finally. "They'd probably have a better chance of catching the killer than you and Pool."

"I thought they were the ones who—"

"I don't want to hear excuses, boy. I want results."

The steel had returned to Johnson's raspy voice, and I didn't feel up to arguing.

"Yessir."

"All right, then. You call me as soon as you know anything."

"Yessir."

Johnson's voice broke as he said, "You find whoever killed Richie. And you call me."

I hung up quickly. It's hard for me to listen to people grieve, though I seem to get more than my share of it.

That's the way a father should feel about a lost son, I supposed. What could be more painful than seeing snuffed out the life you'd so carefully nurtured all those years?

My father, on the other hand, was good-for-nothing trailer trash, who'd sold out his own son. And to William J. Pool, no less. He couldn't have betrayed me worse.

I didn't for a second allow myself to believe Dub felt bad about it now. When he'd agreed to help Pool skunk me, he didn't even know me. But even after we'd gotten reacquainted, he'd gone along with Pool's plan. He'd probably been telling the Texan my every move.

That got my head hurting again, and I stretched out on the sofa with a soft pillow under my head and my dirty sneakers hanging over the arm. I needed to pull my brains together and sort out who might've killed Richie, so I could still beat Pool. But exhaustion took over, and I was asleep when Felicia found me.

She stood at the end of the sofa, bent over me, so she was looking down into my face. I blinked open my eyes to find

Felicia's face before me, upside down.

"Aaah!"

She jumped back and I could see the ceiling right where it belonged. Maybe my vision hadn't scrambled while my eyes were closed. I turned my head to find the rest of the room in its usual place, and I took a deep breath and calmed down.

"What's the matter with you?"

"I've got a concussion."

She slid between the sofa and the coffee table, and I moved over so she could perch on the edge of the cushion by my hip. She studied my eyes carefully, just as the doctor had, and didn't seem to like what she found there.

"Does it hurt?"

"Now that you mention it."

The headache actually seemed to be a little better than before my nap—I guess the Tylenol had kicked in—but I'd take any available sympathy.

"Doctor give you Percodan?" she asked, still studying me.

"Tylenol three."

"Too bad. Of course, if you were loaded full of Percodan, you wouldn't be in any shape to tell me exactly what happened. So, good thing that's not the case, huh?"

"What happened . . ."

"Today at the warehouse. I hear you talked Meg Albright's ear full."

Oh, shit.

"I did not." I tried to sound indignant. "All my cases are confidential, as you know. I just told her about the fire. You know more about the case than she does."

"Tell it to that idiot Whitworth. He won't let me write it."

Whitworth was the city editor at the *Gazette* and Felicia's archnemesis. He seemed a miserable little fellow.

"He won't?"

"No, we fought that battle again today. Every time you're involved in a story, he yanks me off because of conflict of interest."

"It *would* seem to be a conflict—"

"Not you, too. I could cover my own mother and write it right down the middle. My biases never show."

This, in fact, was true. Every time I figured in a story under Felicia's byline, I always appeared just as much a hopeless buffoon as when I talked to other reporters. She plays everything completely straight. She just gets carried away sometimes.

"Yes, dear."

She frowned at me. She hates it when I say that. She likes the "yes" part, but she doesn't like my weary William Powell tone.

"Anyway, you talked to Meg. We've got the story, right?"

"Part of it anyway."

"Which parts did you leave out?"

I struggled to sit up, which made her get up and out of my face and rearrange on the sofa. She sat beside me and put her feet up on the coffee table, acting casual, as if she didn't want to jump down my throat and yank out all the facts. I sat with my feet on the floor, staring at them. My sneakers were gray and smeared with black soot. I'd tracked it around pretty good, too.

"Dub's a fake," I said.

"What?"

"Pool planted him in my camp."

"He's not your real father?"

"Worse. He is."

"And he was working with Pool?"

"That whole nutzo business was bogus."

"Get outta here."

"We thought he was an addled old hound dog, but he turned out to be a fox."

"Thank you for that homespun imagery."

"You're welcome. But you get the picture. He tricked us."

"He was working for Pool?"

"Exactly."

She thought that over for a second, and her cheeks glowed bright red.

"He sure had me fooled."

A noble admission.

"Me, too. I thought I'd taken it pretty well, him showing up again and all. But when that came out, I kind of went crazy."

"What happened?"

"Did I mention I have a concussion?"

"What did you do?"

"I punched Pool in the nose."

"Really?"

"Yeah. Probably hurt my hand more than it did him."

"Have the cops talked to you yet?"

"Yeah. Houghton. Brr."

"And Pool's pressing charges?"

That hadn't even occurred to me. I wouldn't put it past Pool to try to get me thrown in jail and out of the race for that ransom.

"Guess not. Houghton didn't say anything about it. And he'd be only too happy to serve an arrest warrant on me if there was one."

"Doesn't like you?"

"I bring that out in some people."

"I know."

"I don't understand it."

"We've talked about this before."

"Anyway I left Dub there. He was apologizing, but I was too mad to talk to him."

"Lucky you didn't punch him, too."

"It crossed my mind."

"I figured."

I stared at the floor some more. I shifted my foot and saw a smear of black grind into the rug.

Felicia saw it, too.

"You stink," she said.

"Excuse me?"

"You smell like smoke from the fire. The whole room smells like it."

"Sorry."

"You can't smell that?"

"I thought I just sorta had smoke up my nose."

"It's all over you. Why don't you get in the shower?"

"That means standing up."

"You can do it."

"I don't want to do it."

"You really stink."

"I don't want a shower right now."

"I'll fix you something to eat while you shower."

"I'm not hungry."

"You might as well get in the shower. You need to go to the bathroom anyway."

"I don't."

"Sure you do. You had a little nap. You had a beer."

"So?"

"So, you need to pee."

I paused at the sudden insistence of a silent urging.

"That's a dirty trick."

"See? You need to pee. Get going. Throw your clothes out in the hallway and I'll burn 'em."

"You're not gonna burn these clothes. They just need washing."

"Damn. I've been wanting to burn that shirt for months."

"What's wrong with this shirt?"

She rolled her eyes at me. We'd had that conversation before, too.

"I think my old jacket burned up in the fire."

That perked her up.

"That denim jacket with bleach all over the shoulder?"

"I didn't get home with it."

"Good."

I frowned at her.

230

"Go to the bathroom. Your bladder's bursting."

"Leave me alone."

I grumbled off down the hall. Felicia stayed behind on the sofa, laughing at me.

The hot shower soothed my tired muscles, though it didn't feel so great when it bounced off the knot on my head. I fingered the bump, examining its dimensions, making it hurt worse.

The skinheads had tagged my house and damaged my truck and roughed me up and injured my pride. But they hadn't killed Richie Johnson. The *A* carved into Richie's scalp had been something to throw the cops off the trail. And from the way Houghton sounded on the phone, it worked pretty well. He was a powder keg after seeing Richie's mutilated corpse. The arson at the warehouse lit his fuse. The skinheads didn't stand a chance.

But if they hadn't whacked Richie, then who had? And where was the money?

I opened my mouth and let the shower run onto my tongue. There was smoke in there, too.

The money had to be the reason Richie was killed. And there were damned few people who knew about that money.

Dick Johnson had insisted it was all very secret. No cops. No media. I knew. Pool knew. Maybe a few of Pool's "people" he was always talking about but you never saw.

I'd like to believe Pool got to Richie after I did, and killed him while trying to get him to reveal where he left the money. Pool certainly was quick with his theory about Richie's heart giving out during torture. Almost as if he'd been there. He'd gotten his fingerprints all over Richie's apartment while we were waiting for the cops. Was he covering up having been there before? Didn't seem possible. Besides, if he'd been there before, he would've somehow persuaded Richie to tell him where the money was hidden. He was oily that way. And why would he have been searching Richie's place so frantically after we found him dead?

Pool hadn't done it. I'd love to be able to pin it on him. But it didn't fit. He was too busy scheming with Dub to have found Richie on his own. And Dub hadn't known where I went when I headed over to Richie's apartment. He'd probably called Pool, who told him to act crazy and make Felicia get me back there. But he couldn't have told him Richie's address. He didn't know.

I shifted my thoughts to Johnson, but only for a second. He was too shocked, too deeply mourning the loss of his son. I couldn't consider that he might've tortured Richie to death. Besides, he'd said he'd been at Pandemonium when I tried to call and that would be easy enough for the cops to check out. I imagine Dick Johnson caused quite the stir at the nightclub in his Stetson and his suit.

That left who? Nobody. If Johnson was to be believed, nobody else knew about Richie's kidnapping hoax.

I held my aching head under the spray, turning it so that my goose egg was out of the line of fire.

Who knew about the money?

And then it came to me.

THIRTY

I didn't want to take Felicia with me, but she insisted. There's no arguing with her. I made it clear she was about as welcome as a clock in a saloon, but she ignored my protests and climbed up into the truck beside me.

At least I had a gun. Mayhem had kept my trusty Smith & Wesson, but Dub's big hogleg still was hidden away in our house. Felicia had fetched it on our way to the truck, and now I paused to check its cylinder. All loaded and ready.

"You'll wait in the truck," I told her, trying to sound firm.

"Sure, I'll wait in the truck," she said brightly. "I'll keep your phone handy in case there's trouble."

"Uh-oh."

"What?"

"The phone's dead. We tried to call the cops from the warehouse, and it didn't work."

Felicia sighed and opened the glove box to get the phone. She checked it over, and pronounced: "The battery's dead."

"I know that."

"You must've left it on."

"I know that, too."

I wanted to bang my fists on the steering wheel but I was too weary. I threw the Ram into gear and took off toward the Northeast Heights.

"Or maybe somebody left it on for you," she said.

"What do you mean?"

"Maybe Dub fiddled with it."

"He was in the truck by himself a lot."

"He's been acting crazy."

"You still don't get it, do you? That was an *act*. There's nothing wrong with his brain."

"I don't know," she said. "To agree to cheat your own son, that's not sane."

"It's just vile."

"He's really got you worked up, doesn't he?"

"Of course not. I thought the whole thing was fishy from the start, us getting a call about him like that. Turns out I was right."

"Just because you were suspicious doesn't mean you were right."

"Does too."

"Does not."

"Does too. We've got to learn to trust my suspicions. Sometimes that's all I've got."

She tried not to smile.

"So now you believe in going with your gut?"

"That's what we're doing now. I don't have any way of knowing whether Mike Sterling had anything to do with Richie's murder. He's got his foot in a cast, for God's sake. But I ruled out everyone else, and he's all I had left."

"Process of elimination."

"That's right. Richie was killed for that money. Only a few people knew he had it."

"Sounds like detective work. Maybe you're getting better at this."

She was just trying to tweak me, so I said flatly, "Thanks."

Felicia punched me in the shoulder—which hurt—and said, "Come on, Bubba, get excited. You're gonna go catch the bad guy."

"I've got no proof—"

"You'll figure something out."

Felicia rarely expresses any confidence in my abilities, so I basked in the moment and said nothing more. Then I started working on figuring something out. Sterling wouldn't confess everything if I burst in and confronted him. He was a pro, too wily to give anything away unless I was especially cagey.

Unfortunately, in my battered condition, nothing came to mind. Just driving and finding Sterling's house took all my energy. Then we were there, and it was time for Bubba Mabry to spring into action and show his princess how tough he was and how good he is at detecting.

I resorted to window peeking.

Hell, that's detective work, too, isn't it? I mean, it's part of the job just like interrogation and the process of elimination and the deductive leap. I've spent probably half my professional life hiding in shrubbery and peeping at people.

I parked down the street with the headlights off and tucked the long pistol into the back of my belt under my new coat. I slipped up to Mike Sterling's ranch-style house on foot, sticking to the shadows. If Felicia couldn't witness the tough-guy act, maybe she'd at least be impressed by my stealth.

I slowly circled the house, peering through gaps between curtains, until I found Sterling in his living room. He was sitting in an armchair with his big blue foot propped on an ottoman. A basketball game was playing on a TV across the room.

Sterling looked the same, robust and bemused, but he'd traded his Marlboros for a big cigar and his Bud for a tumbler of what looked like Scotch. He appeared to be a man who was celebrating something.

Hell, maybe he was just happy. I couldn't imagine sitting around by myself, smoking and drinking and watching basketball with a big smile on my face. I could imagine the first part. In fact, sitting in front of a TV with a drink sounded pretty good about now. And the being alone part sounded especially good after Dub's company. But I couldn't imagine such random smiling unless I'd recently come into some pretty great news. Or, two hundred thousand dollars.

I decided I should consult with Felicia before taking the next step. I slipped around the corner of the house and hurried across the small, elm-shadowed front lawn.

I figured Felicia was watching me now, had noticed me approaching across the dark lawn. I tried to look heroic or decisive or commanding, but I probably just came across as worried and pathetic. As usual.

Which made it all the worse when I stepped on the rake.

Now most people, they're finished with a rake, they'll put it away or at least lean it against a wall. Sterling's yard, though, was as messy as his house. He'd left a steel gardener's rake lying in the grass, tines pointed skyward, and I stepped right on it with my thick-soled sneaker.

The rake tipped up and the handle smacked me hard in the mouth.

"OW! Goddammit!"

I react to surprising pain like most people, dancing around and cursing. Of course, I was just outside Mike Serling's front door, so perhaps I should've restrained myself.

The light came on inside the Ram as Felicia opened the door. Naturally, she'd been watching the whole thing. Damn. She leaped down from the truck to hurry over to me.

Then another light came on. Sterling's porch light illuminated the whole yard, including the rake at my feet. His door banged open.

"Freeze!"

"Frozen!" I stood perfectly still.

Felicia ignored Sterling's command and ran right to me, looking up at my face to see how badly I was hurt. I tipped my hand away from my mouth to show her.

"A little blood," she said. "You'll be okay."

"I don't think so."

"I said, 'Freeze!' "

Felicia whirled on him.

"Why do you keep yelling?"

"You're on my property! Identify yourselves!"

Sterling sounded as if he'd practiced these commands before. I held up my hand to shade the porch light out of my eyes, and could see him leaning in the doorway, his weight off his broken foot and a revolver in his right hand.

"Mabry, is that you?"

"Yeah."

"What are you doing out there?"

"Wrestling a rake."

"Damn. You okay?"

"Yeah." My lips were swelling and explaining myself seemed like too much trouble. Hell no, I wasn't okay. I had a concussion and bruised ribs and I was sore all over and the last thing I needed was to get whammed in the chops with a rake handle.

"What were you doing out there?"

"I was coming to see you. Guess I shouldn't have cut across your yard."

Sterling's eyes narrowed and he glanced over at the Ram and back at me, and I could see he was thinking that I was on the wrong side of the door to have been coming from the truck. But he didn't say anything.

He did lower the gun, however, and that was a blessing.

"I thought those damned skinheads were coming after me again," Sterling said, and he grinned with relief. "I must've dozed off in my chair and had a dream."

He'd been wide awake when I saw him, but I wasn't about to quibble now. Not as long as he was holding that gun.

"Why don't you folks come on inside?"

"No," Felicia said, "we'd better be going. He's bleeding."

"I've got a first aid kit. Come on in."

He waved the gun toward us casually as he said it, and that somehow gave the suggestion more weight. We obeyed.

Sterling hobbled away from the door as we approached, giving us plenty of room, and we stepped inside.

"Shut that door," he said. "All the heat's getting out."

Felicia slammed the door a bit hard, in my opinion. We didn't want to tip Sterling off that we suspected him, not while he was holding that pistol. I believed he'd killed before to get that two hundred thousand dollars. What was to prevent him from doing it again?

He eyed my lip.

"That's not bad. Come on in. Sit down."

A battered sofa that had once had been beige sat against the wall near the door and he gestured us over there with the gun. Felicia was so busy watching the pistol that she nearly sat on my knee, but she made an adjustment at the last second and sat close beside me.

"Who are you, miss?"

"I'm Felicia Quattlebaum."

"Who?"

"His wife."

"You're Mrs. Bubba?"

She made a face similar to the ones she makes when she sees cockroaches in our yard.

"Just Felicia will be fine."

Sterling kept his distance, hobbling over to the dining table and perching over there, well out of reach. He set the gun on the table beside him. Dub's big pistol dug into my back, but I didn't see any way I could reach it before Sterling could snatch up his own and blast me to kingdom come.

"Bubba, you said you were coming to see me. About what?"

Everything was happening so fast, and my brain was reacting so slowly, I didn't have a ready answer.

"I was gonna warn you."

"What?"

"Those skinheads are on the rampage." This was coming easier now. "Yeah, they tried to burn me up in that warehouse today."

That got his interest.

"I saw that fire on the news. That was you?"

"Yeah. Mayhem and the Oi Boys tied me up and left me inside. Then they torched the place."

I held out my arms to show him the gauze on my wrists.

"Damn. How'd you get loose?"

I muttered something about Pool, and tried to change the subject.

"So I thought I ought to warn you, you know," I said. "That they know we're after them now, and, uh, that they were still using that warehouse, so you were right about that, and, oh yeah, Mayhem's got my gun now."

Sterling looked a little relieved that I couldn't come up with anything better.

"Thanks for the information," he said. "You know, I suspected as much from those skinheads. That's why I keep this gun handy."

He tilted his head toward the revolver on the table, as if we'd have any trouble tracking which gun he meant. The thing seemed to grow as it sat there. It looked bigger than Dub's gun now, well on its way to being a howitzer, pointed right at Felicia and me.

Sterling didn't have anything else to say, and I put my hands on my knees, ready to stand. Maybe he'd let us walk away. Just a friendly visit, after all. No accusations made, no offense taken. I'll come back at a more convenient time, like when I've got twenty cops with me.

Before I could stand, Felicia said, "Don't you have something else you wanted to say, Bubba?"

I stiffened.

"No. That was it. Guess we'd better get going—"

"Sure. You had some questions?"

What was the matter with her? Couldn't she see this had

gone badly? We're in this man's house, he's got a gun, he's most likely the one who tortured Richie Johnson with fists and cigarettes. What did she need, a freaking diagram? If he was willing to let us walk away, shouldn't we be walking as fast as we could?

"What about it, Bubba?" Sterling said slyly. "You got something else?"

"No, I—"

"Come on. What is it you want to say?"

He was taunting me now, I knew, and Felicia was watching me chicken out. But I've got nothing against poultry. I'd be a chicken if that's what it took to get out alive. Frozen as I was in a squat on the couch, I looked as if I could lay an egg any second.

"It's not important—"

"Come on. Out with it." He picked up the pistol and looked it over. It was the most nonchalant of gestures, but I loaded it with meaning.

"Some other time—"

"Oh, hell," Felicia said. "Ask him, Bubba."

She glared at me, impatient, but I had nothing to say. I could feel beads of sweat popping out on my forehead; I could almost hear them. She turned back to Sterling and I prayed for duct tape to magically appear in my hand so I could slap some over her mouth.

"Did you tell anybody about the ransom?" she asked him. "What?"

"Bubba's trying to figure out who killed the kid. Only a few people knew about the ransom money. We're trying to track it down that way."

Sterling looked relieved, but he kept the gun pointed our way.

"No, I haven't told anybody about it," he said. "I hardly ever leave the house."

He used the pistol to point down at the cast on his foot.

"Okay," I blurted, "guess that's all we need to know."

I went to stand again, but Felicia grabbed me by the wrist, which hurt my rope burns.

"See," she said, "Bubba thought the skinheads killed Richie to get that money, but they didn't know about it until he told them today at the fire."

"Is that right?" Sterling sat very still.

"Yeah, now they're looking for the money, too," Felicia said. "So whoever's got it could be in a lot of trouble."

"Only if they find him," Sterling said.

"They'll find him," she said confidently. "See, this person, whoever it is, he can't leave town."

Sterling cocked the eyebrow with the red scar above it.

"Why's that?"

"Because Bubba's going to tell the police the names of everyone who knew about the ransom, including you, of course. So if one of you bolts, it'll look suspicious to the cops. And, we're going to tell the skinheads the names, too. So whoever killed Richie, he's caught in the middle."

Sterling fidgeted in his chair, but he kept the pistol pointing our general direction. I saw what Felicia was doing here, and it was sly and manipulative. Just the sort of thing she's good at doing. I wished to Christ that she would shut up and let us get out of this house alive.

"Bubba," Sterling said, "have you mentioned me to the cops yet?"

"No, I wanted a chance to talk to you first."

A smile spread across his face, and I knew I'd said the wrong thing. Again.

"You think I did it, don't you?" he said. "That's the real reason you came here. You think I handcuffed Richie Johnson to a chair and roughed him up, trying to get him to tell where he hid the ransom."

My mouth went dry. Nobody had said anything about how Richie was killed. But Sterling knew, proving I was right about him. I wished the situation were different. I might enjoy being right for a change.

"Nobody told me the kid's heart was bad," Sterling said, and he was struggling to his feet now. "You should've mentioned that, Bubba. I would've taken it easier on him."

"You did do it!" Felicia sounded amazed, as if she'd never really believed me when I told her Sterling was the one. Not until it falls out of his own mouth does she think it's true.

"I didn't mean to," he said. "I was just trying to make him talk."

I clung to that.

"Then it was an accident. You should explain—"

"Shut up, Bubba."

I obliged.

"You carved that *A* into his head?"

He hadn't told Felicia to shut up, and she apparently thought it was all right to keep baiting a gunman, right up to the moment she got shot.

"That's right. After he died. I thought it'd throw the cops off the trail."

"It worked," I said quickly. "They're after the skinheads."

"Good. That's what I wanted. After the way those punks put me in the hospital, I thought they should get some police attention. Maybe somebody'll catch them now."

"They'll catch you, too." Fine, Felicia, get in the last word. And make it sound final. He only needed a little push to start shooting, and she gave it to him.

"Not once you two are out of the way."

He pointed the pistol at us and jerked the barrel up so we'd get on our feet.

This is it, I thought as I stood, this is the moment when I need to fast-draw Dub's overly long gun from my belt and open fire. I took a deep breath, flexed my arm—

And the doorbell rang.

THIRTY-ONE

*T*he doorbell startled Mike Sterling. It's a wonder he didn't jerk the trigger and kill somebody. He looked at the door like he'd never seen it before, and said, "What the hell?"

It was past the hour common courtesy dictates for surprise guests. But here we were, and somebody was at the door, and Sterling didn't look too pleased to suddenly have a houseful of people. Guess he wasn't crazy about the idea of killing us all, though that sure looked like the way things were headed.

He brandished the gun at Felicia and me and said, "Sit down. Don't make a sound."

We did as we were told, but my eyes kept darting to the door and Dub's pistol weighed heavily in my waistband. Wasn't this the time to do something, when Sterling was distracted?

"Probably just the neighbors," Sterling said. "I mean it. Not a peep out of you until I get rid of them, or it's gonna get real ugly around here real fast."

Felicia and I nodded carefully. She sat on the sofa close

by my right side, which meant she was in the way if I tried to go for Dub's gun behind me.

Mike Sterling hobbled over to the door and looked through a peephole. He shrugged, not recognizing whoever was on the other side, and he gave us one more stern look before he tucked his pistol into his belt under his loose shirt and reached for the doorknob.

Felicia and I leaned forward so we could see around the door jamb to who might be there. I wished for Romero, for Houghton, hell, even for Pool, anybody who might be wise to Sterling and would show up armed.

It was Dub.

Yes, it was my father standing there in the doorway, looking as if he'd just wandered over from Skid Row.

"Howdy," he said to Sterling.

I slapped myself on the forehead, drawing a quick glare from Sterling, but he didn't seem to understand that I'd recognized the old coot. I quickly fanned my hand at the air, as if slapping at a mosquito. In March.

Sterling looked Dub over but didn't seem to recognize him. Dub had stayed in the truck when we here before; maybe Sterling hadn't even noticed him out there. Or maybe he was preoccupied now with the dirty business he had planned for Felicia and me.

"I had a flat up the street," Dub shouted in his most neighborly tone. "Spare's flat, too. 'Course, I didn't know that until I got it on the ground."

Dub raised a tire iron as proof that his tale was true.

"Anyhow, I saw your light on and thought maybe I could use your phone."

"My phone?"

"Yessir, I figured I'd call my son and see if he'd come rescue me."

Dub glanced our way, twinkling, and I frowned at him. Don't get cute now, Dub. Let's just see if we can get out of this alive.

"Sorry," he brayed at Sterling. "Didn't know you had company. Hate to disturb you."

I slapped my hands on my thighs.

"That's okay," I said loudly. "We were just leaving."

Maybe we'd just get to our feet and mosey out of here. Sterling likely wouldn't shoot while he had a witness standing there, with the door open for all the world to hear the gunfire.

Sterling glared at me some more, but it didn't take. I had a plan now, my father was here to deliver me from evil, and I was following him out that door. I stood and reached for Felicia to get her on her feet, too. She looked from me to Sterling and back again, unsure whether to follow me or take her chances with the killer.

"No sense running off," Sterling said. "Not when we're right in the middle of something."

"That's all right," I said brightly. "It'll keep. It's getting late—"

"Sit down."

He let his hand drift to his waist, next to the hidden pistol, and I coughed and frowned and generally let him know I got the message. Then I sat.

"Sorry," Sterling said to Dub. "You caught me at a bad time."

"That's okay, friend. If I could just use your phone?"

"It's not really—"

"Just take a second."

"But I—"

"Looks like you bunged up your foot there."

"Yeah, but—"

"You kick something too hard?"

"No, I—"

"I had a cast on my foot one time. Got it caught in a trailer chain and chewed it up pretty good. It was hard gettin' around, but I drove like a bat outta hell for a while. Had it on my right foot and that's the one on the gas pedal—"

"Sorry, but you have to go," Sterling blurted, exasperation

reddening his face. I knew exactly how he felt. All my talks with Dub ended that way. "We can't be bothered right now."

Sterling tried to close the door, but Dub reached out and tapped it with the tire iron.

"Now just a second, young fella," he said. "I only need to make a phone call."

"I know, but—"

"Not very neighborly to turn somebody away in the dead of night."

Sterling was done talking. He grasped the edge of the door and swung it harder, and I could feel hope slipping way. Even if Dub understood our predicament and called the cops, it would be too late.

I goosed Felicia in the ribs.

"Run for it!"

Felicia leaped to her feet and hurtled over the coffee table and raced toward the back of the house. I jumped up and reached behind me for Dub's gun. Sterling whirled on me, one hand still on the door, the other going for his pistol.

Things slow down in times of emergency. Ever been in a car wreck? Remember how everything seemed to go in slow motion—the tires slipping, the metal crumpling, the strips of chrome flying like boomerangs through the air?

This was one of those times. Even in slow motion, I could see I wasn't fast enough to match Sterling. Not with a good five inches of chromed gun barrel to wedge out of my pants. Sterling's snub-nosed pistol came out of his belt and swung my way, and I still had Dub's gun behind me. I wondered briefly if his bullet would come flying out in slow motion, too, whether I'd be able to see it before it hit me.

Then Dub crashed against the half-open door and swung the tire iron down on Sterling's cranium. Sterling's head snapped back and he fell to the floor, lumpy and inert as a sack of peaches.

Dub spryly leaped over the fallen man, calling, "You all right?"

By this time, I had his gun in my hand and I was tempted to pull the trigger rather than admit Dub had just pulled my fat out of the fire.

"Yeah," was all I said.

I don't know where Felicia thought she was going, but she'd apparently run all the way to the far end of the house in search of an exit.

"Felicia! Hon? Come on back. It's okay."

I crouched beside Sterling and picked up the gun that had fallen from his hand. Then I backed away. Even unconscious, unarmed and with his foot in a cast, Mike Sterling scared me.

"That was a close one," I muttered.

"That's what I thought, son. Good thing I showed up when I did, huh?"

He was determined to take credit. I sighed.

Felicia peeked around a corner from the hallway and saw Sterling conked out on the floor. She sauntered into the room and said, "Want me to call the cops?"

I nodded.

She came into the living room on a beeline for the phone, and said as she passed, "Nice work, Dub."

"Thank you, sugar. Always happy to help."

Damn.

THIRTY-TWO

*S*terling regained consciousness before the first cops arrived, but he would say nothing about where he'd stashed the money. I pointed the pistols at him and tried to get him to talk, but my heart clearly wasn't in it, and it didn't work. The cops couldn't make him talk, either, and contented themselves with waiting for Lt. Steve Romero.

Romero took control of the crime scene when he arrived, and I briefed him on how I'd come to figure that Sterling killed Richie Johnson. Romero rolled his eyes when I revealed that I'd told Sterling about the money and the race to find Richie.

"He probably tailed you," Romero said, glancing over at Sterling. "Hard to miss you in that big red truck. You were the only one who'd discovered where Richie was hiding, right?"

"I thought so, but—"

"He probably followed you there, waited for you to leave, then pounced on the kid."

We both looked to Sterling, but he just glared at us, his

248

hands in cuffs and his lips shut tight as a confessional door.

Romero turned back to me.

"What happened to your mouth?"

"I stepped on a rake."

"Here?"

"Yeah. That's how Sterling nabbed us. I was too busy holding my mouth and squealing."

"And then your father showed up?"

I grudgingly told him how Dub had saved us from Sterling. Felicia and Dub stood to one side, grinning and elbowing each other.

"If it hadn't been for that rake, I would've caught Sterling myself," I concluded. "I'd spotted him inside here, looked like he was celebrating something. I figured he'd hit it big and was enjoying the idea the skinheads would catch the blame."

Dub and Felicia tried to control their snickering.

"I'll bet the money's somewhere in this house," Romero said. "Let's find it."

He turned to Sterling and said, "We don't have a warrant yet, but I feel we have probable cause to search your home. Any objections?"

Sterling sat mute, staring bullets at me.

"I'll take that as permission,'" Romero said. "Come with me, Bubba."

Romero walked straight back to the kitchen, as if the house were as familiar as his own. He opened the freezer, moved some icy stuff around and pulled out a big brown paper bag, folded closed neatly and glittering with frost.

"This would be it," he said.

He unfurled the top of the bag and looked inside.

"See?" he said, tipping the bag to show me the packs of money inside. "They never get any smarter. Every crook in the world puts the money in the freezer. If I was a burglar, that's where I'd always look first."

All I could do was grin at him stupidly.

"So we have our killer?" I asked.

"Looks that way, though he'll probably say somebody else put the money in his fridge, that you set him up, that he never left his home the day Richie was killed."

"But it won't do him any good?"

"Not if I have anything to say about it."

Romero tucked the paper sack under his arm and told the uniformed cops in the living room to stop standing around and take Sterling downtown to the police station. Then he turned to Felicia and Dub and me.

"All three of you will have to come down and give a statement," he said.

"Now?"

"It'll wait until morning. Long as I don't read it in the *Gazette* first."

He arched his eyebrows at Felicia, who must've had the same idea because she was looking at her watch.

"Too late now," she moaned. "The last deadline passed ten minutes ago."

"Fine," Romero said, grinning. "Then I'll see you all in my office in the morning."

Romero picked up the plastic bag where the cops had stowed the two pistols and carried it out with him to his car. We followed. The cops sealed off the door with yellow tape, and left Felicia and Dub and me standing in Sterling's yard.

Dub had kept quiet—for a change—while the cops were around, and he didn't seem ready to start crowing now that they were leaving. He trailed Felicia and me out into Sterling's yard as we walked to the truck, wringing his hands and muttering under his breath.

I turned to him when we reached the truck, ready to wave him away, but Felicia interrupted. "Don't you have something you want to say to your father?"

"What?"

"At least say, 'Thank you.' "

"For what?"

"For saving our tails." She smiled at Dub, and he grinned

raggedly. He looked like an old hound dog showing off a new trick.

"I guess that's right. Thanks, Dub."

Felicia made a face at me.

"That certainly sounded heartfelt."

I sighed, too tired to argue.

"Felicia, let's go home."

"I need to know something first. How did you happen onto us here?"

Dub hitched at his pants and chuckled quietly. I hadn't seen him this subdued before. It was a welcome change. Maybe he wasn't such a contrary old man when he wasn't pretending to be insane.

"I'll tell ya," he began, and it had the ring of one of his long-winded stories, "I was sitting outside your house there, trying to think of a way to apologize to Bubba for tricking him."

"You were?" I tried to sound skeptical, tough.

"Sure. I felt bad about it, and wanted to make amends."

"You should feel bad."

"Bubba—" Felicia had a warning in her voice.

"It's all right, sweet thing," Dub said. "He's absolutely right. I did a bad thing, even if my intentions weren't so bad. When I signed on with Pool, it was mostly because he told me I could meet my son. But it was also for the money, and I helped Pool when I should've been helping you. I was cussing myself over it, sitting there in the car, and trying to think of a way to make it right."

"You're in a car?" I hadn't bothered to think through how Dub had arrived here. I was too busy being thrilled and mortified over being rescued from Sterling.

"After we were finally done with the cops, I borrowed Pool's Cadillac. It's a rental, but he didn't pay me my money, so I took what I could get. I couldn't very well roam around your quiet neighborhood in my big rig. I told him I had to make it up to you, and I was going over to your house right away. But it took me awhile to find the place, and then I didn't know what to say. So I was just sitting there when you two ran out into the night and jumped into your truck."

"You figured something was up."

"Sure. Ever since I met you, something has been up. It's just one damned thing after another. I don't know how you survive one day to the next."

"It's not easy."

"No, it ain't. Not in any line of work. But you seem to have taken on more than your share. Anyhow, I reckoned that the way you lit out from there, you were up to something. So I followed you."

"And you recognized Sterling's house."

" 'Course I did. What am I, crazy?"

That presented us with some ground nobody wanted to cover again. Dub coughed into his fist.

"I saw you were just looking in the windows and maybe there wouldn't be any problem, but then you stepped on that rake and knocked yourself in the face."

Dub cackled, but caught himself and coughed some more. Felicia looked ready to burst out laughing. My face hurt from scowling. My lips still were achy and swollen, and I didn't see anything funny about it.

"When I saw the porch light come on," he resumed, "I figured it for trouble. Then I made out Sterling standing there with that gun in his hand, and I decided I better do something to help."

"You did a splendid job," Felicia said. "He never knew what hit him."

"I figured he wouldn't suspect an old cuss like me might be ready to cold-cock him."

Felicia and I nodded respectfully. It was a good plan. Even better, it had worked.

"So, son, I was hoping you'd find it in your heart to call us even," he concluded.

"What's that?"

"Even-steven. I mean, I know I wronged you by working for Pool, and I regret that now. But I thought maybe it evened us up, me coming here and helping you and all."

I stewed over that a long minute. Here was a man who'd driven me crazy my whole life, first by never being there and then by being here. But he *had* shown up at the right moment, hadn't he? No doubt Felicia and I would be wearing body bags by now if he hadn't rung that doorbell. I might've gone down shooting, but I'd still be dead.

"Sure, Dub," I said. "We're even. I've held a grudge against you my whole life, and it's time that ended. It's probably taking up space in my brain that I could put to better use."

Felicia and Dub laughed, though I hadn't intended to say anything funny.

"Really. I need to put all that to rest now. We ought to be able to part on good terms."

Dub sobered and nodded.

"I'm glad to hear you say that, son. Being separated from you all those years weighed on me, too. I often wondered where you were and how you turned out without me. Lotta guilt to chew on while I drove across the country."

I understood his regret, and I almost reached out to him. For what, I don't know. An embrace? A handshake? But nothing felt right, nothing could convey how strongly I felt the release inside me, all those years of resentment fluttering away.

"You know," I said, "this whole bitter business with Richie Johnson happened because he couldn't get along with his father. Now it's too late for them to ever get back together. And that's too bad. Maybe we ought to take a lesson from them: Fathers and sons need each other, no matter how much they get on each other's nerves."

"I'm glad to hear you say that, son. I didn't want to pull out of Albuquerque with you all swollen up, mad at me and all I've done. I want us to part friends."

"You're leaving town?" Felicia asked.

"Yup. After I talk to that police detective in the morning. I've got to get back on the road and earn some money."

I felt a strange mixture of elation and loss. Getting Dub out of town had been my goal since I met him and here he was, relatively sane after all, preparing to go. But now that we were reconciling, part of me didn't want him to leave.

"I thought you were about to lose your truck?" I said.

"I am. Repo men could get it at any time. But I'm tired of hiding from them, and I can't make any money with the truck sitting at the terminal. I'll take my chances, make a few quick runs, and get those payments caught up."

"You said there was a balloon payment."

"Coming right up, but don't you worry none about that, son. I'll figure out something. I always have before."

Felicia closed in on him and hugged him tightly.

"It's been great meeting you," she said as he broke the clinch. "I can see a lot of you in Bubba."

"That right?" He squinted at me. "I don't see it."

"Neither do I," I said.

Felicia laughed at us. I guess we must've been wearing similar expressions or something. I don't know. She laughs at me all the time. It's part of what keeps her happily married.

"The door's always open, Dub," she said. "Any time you're passing through New Mexico, stop in and see us."

I wouldn't have gone that far. Dub dropping in frequently could get damned inconvenient. I'm so distant from my relatives, I'd forgotten what it's like to have family obligations, to have guests sleeping in your office, guests you can't turn away. I wasn't sure I wanted to obligate myself that way, particularly with someone as loud and bothersome as Dub. But it beat the alternative, I guess. You can't go through life all alone. Dub tried it, and it never made him happy. You need friends and family and spouses and parents.

I can't imagine life now without Felicia, for instance, but there was a time not that long ago when we were ready to scratch each other's eyes out over some guy who was pretending to be the living Elvis. With time and enough exposure, I'd probably learn to love Dub, too. Forgiveness was a good first step.

What the hell. I stepped toward him and threw out my arms and we hugged each other tightly and awkwardly and long. And you know, it felt pretty good.

Once we disentangled, we didn't know quite what to say and both of us took a sudden interest in the ground at our feet.

Dub said, "I guess I'd better be going."

"Got to take that car back to Pool, huh?"

"Hell, no. I'm driving it straight over to my motel. He'll come hunting for it eventually."

"Serve him right."

"My feeling exactly."

We stared at each other for a while, and he looked a little misty, and then he waved and shambled off toward a dark Cadillac parked up the street.

Felicia came closer and slid an arm around my back.

"You did good," she said.

"It wasn't easy. He's a hard man to like."

"I don't know. I like him. He reminds me of you."

I think I winced.

"And that's a good thing?"

"Sure, and I can't get too much of a good thing."

We stood there a moment, arms around each other, watching Dub walk through the circle of light under a streetlamp. I hadn't seen him go for his chewing tobacco, but the light clearly picked up a glistening arc of spit before he disappeared back into darkness.

"Yuck," I opined.

Felicia laughed at me.

"He's got a few personal habits that take some getting used to," she said. "But he's a fine old man. Who knows? Maybe he'll make a good grandfather some day."

I gulped loudly, making Felicia laugh again.

"Get in the truck, Bubba. You've had enough scares for one night."

I did as I was told. As usual.

EPILOGUE

I wish I could say I brought the skinheads to justice, but that's not the way the world works. Sgt. Horton Houghton and his unit rounded up the gang a week later in a raid on Pandemonium. Houghton invited me along on the raid to identify Mayhem and friends as the ones who torched the warehouse and nearly reduced me and Dub to cinders.

The raid was fun for me. Much different from my own visit to Pandemonium: The doorman disappeared at the first sign of cops, so there was no cover charge. One of the gang unit members immediately pulled the plug on the loud music. Houghton's men sealed off the exits, and it was just a matter of sorting through punks until we found the right ones.

Mayhem, the dirty bastard, tried to hide in the men's room, so we found him last, crouching on the throne inside a stall. He tried that snarling and sneering bit on Houghton, who busted him one in the nose. That settled the Brit right down. After the way Mayhem had blown his nose on me at my worst moment, it felt pretty good to hand him a Kleenex for the blood.

The judicial system moves slowly, and I haven't testified against him yet, but I imagine that'll feel good, too. Houghton threw the book at the Oi Boys, charging them with arson and attempted murder and aggravated battery and resisting arrest and civil rights violations for their hate crimes, including tagging my house. I don't know if all the charges will stick, or whether my testimony will make any difference, but I figure it'll be awhile before Mayhem sees daylight again.

Mike Sterling's trial has come and gone. Murder apparently takes priority in court scheduling. The jury found him guilty of second-degree murder because they believed he didn't know about Richie's heart condition. First-degree murder requires premeditation, and Sterling swore he never intended to kill the kid. Still, he got sentenced to eighteen years in prison, and that seems about right to me.

Dick Johnson, naturally, reneged on his promise to give the two hundred thousand dollars to whomever found Richie's killer. I had nothing in writing—I'd counted on the man's word—and I couldn't press it. The cops kept the money as evidence until the trial ended anyway. Once the jury convicted Sterling, Johnson's conscience apparently got the better of him because I received a check in the mail for a hefty amount. Nothing like what he'd promised, but enough to get my truck fixed and the graffiti power-sprayed off my house, with a little left over.

Johnson knew Dub came to my rescue, I guess, because Dub told me he got a check for a similar amount and used it to pay up his truck loan. I don't know how Johnson even located Dub, since my father is always in motion. He probably hired a private eye.

Dub stays in touch these days, calling occasionally from the road and stopping by when he blows through Albuquerque. Our relationship is tenuous, and his chatter drives me crazy, but I've accepted that he's part of my life now.

He's become less of a loner. He has his cat, Spike, to ride with him on the nation's highways. Dub, I learned later, returned to Richie's apartment and rescued the shaved kitty after the police were gone. Last time I saw the cat, its fur was coming in nicely. Turns out it was a black cat with a long coat. Who knew?

More surprising is that Mama apparently has become part of Dub's life again. He told me he thought about her a lot after getting to know me. One day, while barreling along 1-10 through Mississippi, he turned off the freeway and drove to Nazareth and looked her up. He figured she might shoot him on sight, but she invited him in for coffee and her famous peach cobbler, and they spent hours together, just talking.

"She's still a fine woman," he said with conviction, prompting me to change the subject.

Those two have been separated so long, I can't imagine them in the same room. But stranger things have happened. Look at how Dub and I got back together. Maybe, once that spark of love is there, it's never entirely extinguished. I know I feel that way about Felicia, even on our worst days together.

Speaking of Felicia, I get an earful every night on the subject of perky Meg Albright. Felicia wasn't allowed to write the story about Sterling's capture—she had a conflict of interest—and Meg did such a bang-up job that the brass at the *Gazette* offered her a full-time position. She occupies the formerly vacant desk next to Felicia's, and her prattle is about to drive my sweetie nuts.

At least Meg's youthful enthusiasm has cooled any more talk of children. If this is what it's like to have a young person around all the time, Felicia says, count her out. I couldn't agree more.

Finally, there's William J. Pool. Last time I saw him, he was bleeding from the nose. But I keep an ear open for any news about him and his detective business. Seems Sterling was right on the money about Pool's financial situation. The Texan had banked everything on finding Richie Johnson. When he didn't get the ransom, Pool was forced to declare bankruptcy. I had a contact in Dallas send me a copy of the court file, and it was as I'd expected: Pool spent all his earnings on high living and high technology, trying to live the private eye myth. For all his bluster, he'd gone broke because the work didn't come in as fast as the money went out. The same sort of bind that constantly squeezes me.

I know I shouldn't gloat, but bankruptcy was the ultimate comeuppance for someone as slimy and grubbing as Pool and I'm proud I played a role in his downfall. I know that sounds petty, but revenge isn't a noble emotion. It's petty by its very nature.

And let me tell you something else: It's sweet.